M000317039

FOOL'S GOLD

MARO DOUKA

Fool's gold

Translation
RODERICK BEATON

THE GREEK EXPERIENCE
Books, Music, Videos, Art
www.GreeceInPrint.com
262 Rivervale Rd, River Vale N.J. 07675-6252, USA
Phone: 201-664-3494; Fax: 201-664-3402

KEDROS

The translation costs of this book have been covered
by the Greek Ministry of Culture.

Typeset and printed in Greece
by Kedros Publishers, S.A.
3, G. Gennadiou Str., Athens 106 78,
Tel. 210.38.09.712 – Fax 210.38.31.981
June 1991, 1st reprint May 2004

Title in Greek: Η Αρχαία Σκουριά
Cover design by
Kostas and Marina Bostantjoglou

© 1991 by Kedros Publishers, S.A.
Athens, Greece

ISBN 960-04-0481-X

For Nikos

1

NOT LONG AFTER CHRISTMAS, in 1974, a girl I used to know came up to me: did I want to join the political group she belonged to, and if so, would I please fill in a questionnaire. Her group didn't interest me at all, but I was curious. There was a certain fascination in trying to sort out all the hows and whys. What's more, I was used to it. Ever since I'd joined the Left, in the way of things at that time, I'd been constantly having to account for myself. To the point that even when nobody else bothered to cross-examine me I'd put myself in the dock, it had become second nature to me. There's truth in what they say: things hurt less if you talk about them, at least you don't feel so bad. I'd got into the habit of talking to myself constantly, like someone who's come to grief and can't accept the fact. So I keep on losing the thread, never quite get things right, and when I catch up with myself, by then it's too late. I'm hemmed in by the surface of a reality that's none of my making. I don't try to prove a point, I just ramble on. The point is that if *I* can't work out what it is that makes me tick, I can hardly expect anybody else to do it for me. The more I talk the more futile the sound of my own voice becomes to me; a delicious panic takes hold of me, my pulses race; just around the corner I'm going to make the discovery that will change everything. I feel I'm circling closer and closer to something fantastically important — a sort of fatal attraction — but I wouldn't care to go too close. I'm marking time, it's a heady, intoxicated feeling — a touch of impatience too. How long can I expect to keep it up, this taut, suspended state, something to weigh in the balance against the idea of my own death?

That's putting it rather grandly. The honest truth is that during these last months I've kept myself on a pretty loose rein, I've enjoyed myself turning over the pages of the past.

So, no newcomer to this sort of thing, I picked up the questionnaire without hesitation:

What is my name
My date and place of birth
Where do I live and with whom
What do my parents do
My resistance record (covert or other activities)
Trade union or similar affiliations
My family's politics
Why and how did I join the Left
Record of police harassment
My intended profession
Books I have read
Strengths and weaknesses (my own estimation)
What help do I expect from the group
My attitude to this particular group, and
reasons for wanting to join.

I chanted the questions aloud, trying to cram them into my brain. Their thoroughness intimidated me, but they also held a challenge. Try though I might I could never stick to them, as guide and compass. Gradually they curdled inside me and became a solid lump.

SEVEN YEARS AGO. I was mixed up with Paul, and that's how I put a date to the events of my life: Before Paul, After Paul. I don't exactly believe in watersheds, but that's the period I invariably look back to, when we were splitting up: a numbing, long-drawn-out business.

2

AS I SUNBATHED I was watching him tussle with his friends in the sea. They came ashore roaring with laughter, parked themselves nearby, and lit cigarettes. I eyed the water droplets on his body, reciting to myself, *Waves ebb and flow, a frothy reply in the ears of seashells.* Then I abandoned the poetry of Elytis, rolled over on my stomach, and pillowed my face in my arms. I could feel his eyes on me and felt irritated. I heard them getting up to play beach ball. I was waiting for the ball to come rolling up to my ribs, like yesterday. It did. He bent down to pick it up, and through the chinks between my arms I saw his eyes staring at me. He was pale-skinned, with curly brown hair; strong build, squint nose and drooping eyelids. From the first moment I'd set eyes on him I'd wanted him; I felt wild, and tensed all over like an animal caught in a trap. He mumbled something, ever so sorry, I raised my head and our eyes met. He said would I join their game, play the winner in the next round? He won, my name's Paul, and mine's Myrsini; we played and he won again. We all plunged into the sea together, I found myself swimming alongside him. He asked me about myself: Myrsini, what sort of a name's that? Doesn't it mean myrtle? His manner irked me: as though he'd read it up in a book on how to get an easy lay. And the hungry way he eyed my breasts, comparing them mentally, I'm sure, to some species of fruit. At one point he closed in, our heels seemed to touch and I panicked. Look down, I said to him, look at the bottom: if I had to drown, what a beautiful place for it. He gave a sly laugh and his eyes shrank to slits with a sort of complacency. It was obvious I was turned on, and it embarrassed me to feel my emotions written so plainly all over my face. He circled me once, then ducked me. It gave me a shock at first, then I went on down, his laugh still echoing in my ears, I watched the fish go by and slid through the water till I touched bottom. I squeezed the sand through my fingers and brought up a shell, remembering the woman in Ritsos' *Moonlight Sonata.* I'd read the poem only a month ago and couldn't get it out of my head — down there in the depths I felt mollified and let myself go with a pleasant sense of ripening, I'd grown up all at once in my longing for Paul. It was early days yet for the thought to occur to me that he was waiting for me supine on the foam, when he could have plunged down with me.

Next day was Monday and Paul and his friends left for Athens. We met again three weeks later. In those days we'd get into a lift to kiss and count how long we could hold our breath. I closed my eyes and entered a moist warm cavern. I opened them again to see myself mirrored in the pupils of his eyes. We'd meet and go on to the parts of town where his work took him. He wouldn't let me take his hand, when I tried he'd withdraw his discreetly, almost furtively. He realised I was upset by this and explained that we were there on serious business, people mustn't see us holding hands. I

wondered why he should apparently think so, but I
didn't like to press him. I thought he had an inhibition.
In everything else I looked up to him, everything he said
fascinated me, as though he was showing me the world
anew. And my part was to stand in awe. I don't know
how the idea came to be lodged in my mind, but it came
to seem a duty and obligation of love to go into ecstasies
over his every word. I followed him round in a daze, I
tried to walk exactly in step with his footfall on the
roadway. At his side I relived the loneliness of my
childhood, wandering and dreaming in my ignorance
about those great and wonderful things that weighed so
heavily on Paul's shoulders. And it moved me beyond
words to think that I was a helper to him.

Since I wasn't a virgin when we started, he made me
tell him how it had happened. I soon discovered that his
interest wasn't at all in learning about my previous
relationships. He liked to listen in, as it were, it seemed
to arouse him. I let myself go, too, to the extent that for
as long as I was talking I was untroubled by the
knowledge that most of it I was making up as I went
along. I found this exciting at first, then I got tired of it.
I couldn't understand what he saw in it. Always the
same, to the point of screaming boredom. And I longed
for the hours to pass so that we could go out again into
the street. I remembered that he shared this room with
a friend. Once we'd actually run into him in the
hallway. The type that smirks and smacks his lips, with
a girl twined limply round him.

There was a double bed with an orange coverlet and
next to it a bedside table. In the table drawer I'd found
various makes of contraceptives, aspirins, tissues. After
the first month I began noticing. Things like the spiders

on the walls, fluff on the floor, hairs not ours and yellow stains on the sheets. I'd shut my eyes, but that made it worse: the shrivelled spiders came to life. When I said what about cleaning it up his answer was always an indifferent, Why bother? We're fine like this. I felt sore at that — and it left its mark. I knew then that this room would always be a photographer's darkroom. A vain effort of the imagination to picture it with the window open, with the sheets hanging out to air.

I came to realise that if I moved at all it upset him, and tensed with panic in case I should put him off. This saddened me as well: the great and glorious love that had touched me with his wings a few short months before was gradually being whittled down to a mechanical arousal of the senses. I'd have had more pleasure from the scent of shampoo in his hair than from his odourless caresses. As there was no one I could talk to I went to a gynaecologist. He wanted all the details of my affair with Paul, but burst out angrily before I could finish. A brute, he called him, but it was my fault too for letting him. I hung my head in shame and confusion. Finally he turned pompous on me, telling me I was sexually incompatible with that coxcomb. He saw that stung me: Ah yes he knew the old refrain ... but you know, my dear girl, what the bottom line is? Harmonious sexual intercourse. We'd arranged to meet later that afternoon. I rehearsed how I was going to tell him, and broke out in a cold sweat as I walked, I was determined to get it out in the open. That afternoon every man I passed seemed threatening in the twilight, with a blind and suffocating magnetism. I suffered agonies as I waited for Paul but he never came. Later he phoned. He was sorry, he said, something extra had

15

come up and he hadn't been able to get out of it.

When we did meet two days later I seized an opportunity and asked him, did he love me? He evaded the question. I pretended not to mind and changed the subject. After a while, when we were making love he stopped suddenly and flung back at me: did I love him? Unthinkingly I answered yes, yes of course I do. He gave a nasty laugh, if we were talking about our little dog I'd say I loved it of course, wouldn't I? But we don't have a little dog, I cried, to extricate myself. Then we'll buy one. I began to cry and looked at the spiders. He glanced up. What's this? he asked in amazement. He held me close and kissed me, yes he did love me but there were so many things that came between us. What things? I wanted to know. Just about everything, he answered sorrowfully. What did he mean exactly, please tell me. Even then I'd still have gone through fire for him. What he meant was that all those months we'd been together, he'd had the feeling I was spying on him, why did I open my eyes like that? he broke out suddenly. Why did I keep opening my eyes with that great stare, as though I'd nothing better to do than watch him? I said that that's how it was, I didn't mean to, and if it upset him I wouldn't do it again. Then he complained that I was too quiet. Tears came to my eyes once more and he relented. He'd had the bright idea of giving me books to explain things to me, you see it isn't enough to feel that we're in love, we need to know how to liberate our feelings. He asked me then, for the first time, what I felt when we made love. I told him, untruthfully, that I felt good. This got him angry again: what was that supposed to mean, good? A walk in the country makes you feel good. I tried to explain, but I couldn't express it properly. It always upset him, the way I talked; I did my best to put it in a way that would get through to him. I thought that having got this far we would talk at last. But suddenly he turned on himself instead. It was getting late and what the hell, he'd work to do, how come he hadn't noticed the time? He was cross with himself and swore at random, finally he got dressed. As I looked at him I felt a wave of nausea engulf me. We fixed to meet again two days later.

That was all that happened; we saw each other regularly, either going to the cinema or to his bachelor pad. He no longer took me with him around town. And of course I was still at school, where the pressure was heavy, as though there was some kind of investment to be made out of my future. Sometimes my mind would disappear altogether into a bottomless pit full of English and German verbs. On the piano I'd made it into the 'competent' bracket, further progress was scarcely to be hoped for; dancing didn't seem to offer much of a future either. Resting squarely on my limitations I was cowed by the sense of mediocrity foisted upon me by the ceaseless demands of others. All I wanted was to be left in peace. Paul was profoundly uninterested in all this when I spoke of it once, and more or less bit my head off. He couldn't see what all the fuss was about. Was it so difficult for me to choose something I was good at? Or maybe I was the victim of my parents' pretensions, a jack of all trades with none to call my own? A point, I thought. But at the same time I was haunted by pretensions of my own, this was second nature to me. I'd grown up with the unshakeable conviction that sooner or later one of my talents would burst through the surface, like magic, and deliver me from all the dreary

17

trivia that dogged my footsteps and left me so discouraged. So I duly waited, patiently, for the fiery apocalypse as I imagined it that was going to burst within me.

Even my difficulties with Paul I treated with some detachment, though I really did feel I loved him or at least he always left me with the lure of something yet to be fulfilled. More from instinct I understood that Paul, as he appeared to me, was but the visible extension of the Paul who would remain forever unsharing and uncaring in the ordeal of human love. This sense of disillusion led me finally to a torpid state that afforded some comfort. With almost passive inactivity I learned to take the blows that came my way and repulse them, with mathematical precision, into the void. Now and then, perhaps, my need to keep him would revive, only to die down again at once. In this way I chalked up my first defeat, but it was a voluntary one. Regret and self-reproach came later, during the dictatorship — nor do I remember precisely how I first came to murmur to myself that I had been treated badly by Paul.

The last time that we met, on the eve of the coup d'état, he was taciturn. In the cinema he didn't lay a finger on me. Afterwards we went to the flat. He hurled himself on me, like someone intent only on his own pleasure. He hissed through his nostrils and pushed so hard that he hurt me. When it was over he let go of me and huddled up in a corner of the bed. I pulled up the sheet and turned to caress him. He muttered, let go, and pulled hard on his cigarette. Frozen, I drew back and stared at the ceiling. I felt as though I was eavesdropping on the revulsion that crept over me. He asked me to make him a cup of coffee. Reluctantly I got up and his eyes followed me with an appraising stare, crossing over with the intensity of his gaze. I said why was he looking at me like that, no answer, he merely pulled harder on his cigarette, mysteriously. Then he said something I found offensive. I put down his coffee on the bedside table and dressed, I had had enough. He pleaded with me to sit beside him, he seemed to be trying to revert to our earlier conversation. But the moment had passed and could not be recaptured. For me that matter was closed. He put it to me that couples split up because women are prudish, but love has no room for half measures, all's fair in love and so on. I lay down beside him tired out. I didn't know what to say, how could I make him see that he made me feel a whore? For a long time neither of us spoke. Then I heard him crying quietly, it was like someone weeping in the next room. I said what's the matter, what's wrong? The way he cried frightened me, as though the tears were going back down inside him. How could he explain? he said, I wouldn't understand. I said, tell me anyway, it'll make you feel better. When I pressed him, he confided that he'd been purged from the Youth Movement, just like Petroulas had been purged, only Petroulas hadn't been expelled so far — any day now they're going to expel me. And he fell silent. I couldn't tell if I was sorry. It's always the same when something upsets me, I can look in on myself being upset as though it were happening to someone else, like watching myself in a mirror, and can even be amused by the expression on my face. It becomes a game of grimaces, as I arrange the picture of myself in this way or that and endorse it or reject it, enjoying myself all the while. At the same time as I feel sorrow, I'll also be lucidly observing and annotating the feeling. I wanted to tell him how much I sympathised, but thought I should only be patronising him.

We parted coldly, without our usual kiss. He didn't even bring me to the outer door. With a defeated air he said, oh well, let's be in touch after Monday, then he waved with his hand, and turned to make his way clumsily back downstairs. For a moment I wondered if he were ill. But I let him go, and went crying in the other direction.

3

IT WAS A THURSDAY EVENING, which meant the house would be full of visitors. I tried to slip past them, I couldn't bring myself even to say hello, and shut myself in my room. I listened to their high spirits, which sounded tepid, their optimism about the coming general election. But Paul's crying wouldn't leave me. I thought I would never forget that valedictory wave of his hand, as though we were parting forever. I buried my face in the pillow and agonised over every minute detail of it, to draw out whatever meaning it perhaps concealed. Until it broke up into a million lighted dots flashing on and off. Paul was set aside on his pedestal, I saw wild ducks in slow flight and reed beds whispering; as I drifted towards sleep I surrendered to the perfect tranquillity I knew how to devise for myself. Ever since childhood I've known how to calm my emotions. In fact I always have found myself easy to deal with, even today, I'll hold forth and pontificate with the best of them, but there are other moments when I can wander in ecstasy and at perfect ease among past memories and revoke my words in tones at once provocative and neutral, as though at once in control of my voice and at the same time also a detached listener.

My father came knocking on the door, would I be so

good as to grace them with my presence? What's the matter, you're not asleep are you? I got up and saw in the mirror the lines of the pillow etched on my cheeks like weathered scars, my eyes were smarting and I said, all right, I'm coming. In confiding tones he told me the best thing to make me feel better was to come and listen to the composer talking about himself. My father's gentle tact could always disarm me. Two hours ago he'd seen me creep in like a thief, and pretended not to notice. He knew how to care about me discreetly, and also without worrying too much. I said OK, leave off now or we'll have mum up here. I'm on my way.

I found them in a generally rosy state. There was Anestis with his wife Zoe; he had been a friend of my dad's since after the war. And Vangelis, the bosom friend of the family. Most days, or to be more exact whenever my dad was at home, he'd drop in for just half a glass of whisky. Then there was Nancy, an old friend of my mother's that she'd known in Paris. Since then things had cooled between them, thanks to my father's extra-marital flings. But my dad was of such magnanimous temperament that she continued to be a regular, if not unreservedly welcome, member of their circle. Then there was my godmother, Victoria, first cousin to my dad. Said to have been a beauty in her younger days, and the cliché had haunted her ever since like a criminal record; perhaps that was why she created such a furore wherever she went. Lucy, a childhood friend of my mother's — I remember her at my elbow when we used to play board games. Xenia, next, was my father's mistress, though of course he used to say she wasn't. My mother kept harping on about it, as if she got a kick out of the idea or even wanted it to be the truth. New faces this evening were the young composer, who according to my dad when he'd been joking about him the other day was going through a crisis of megalomania; and Tonia a young writer of fiction.

Anestis was trying to bring Tonia out: what were her favourite writers? Tonia seemed to have very definite ideas. Apparently it was her turn to hold the floor. She was a protégée of Aunt Victoria, and already about to publish her first collection of short stories. My father was sitting next to Xenia and on Xenia's neck was a love bite. I greeted each of them and found a seat in a corner. Aunt Victoria came over and asked me what was the matter, were we down in the dumps? Dumps; it was her way of teasing me. But she saw how it was and left me in peace. Tonia was telling some anecdote about her Aunt Julia, who was something of a character in diplomatic circles. This Julia had one great weakness: she wanted to be a woman of culture. She had read her way furiously through *Eroica, The Schoolmistress with the Golden Eyes, Argo*, the classic Greek novels of the thirties, and in this way had cultivated an aesthetic sensibility. Until one day a friend of hers had initiated her into Russian literature, of the period known as tsarist. Soon after, Julia had found herself in a salon where the exclusive topic of conversation was books and writers. Where she delivered herself of the portentous utterance: Oh, Stratis Myrivilis is quite my favourite Greek tsarist!

Tonia's delivery went down well. Anestis was particularly impressed. He began some rigmarole about the social profile of the reading public, but was shouted down and had to stop. Lucy got up and took her seat at the piano. The young composer was asking Xenia meanwhile, had she read his latest interview in the press? Xenia shook her head. Nancy rested her palm on Vangelis' thigh. The composer began intoning aloud the content of his interview. The others listened with feigned interest. Xenia began to make faces and mimic him. Lucy left the piano, took up her glass and went towards the veranda, stepping as though she had little wings strapped to her ankles that lifted her up and prevented her from walking properly. My father asked in surprise why had she stopped playing? She went on past him without a word. Then Victoria broke out, we aren't in church you know, how demanding you are darling. Nancy laughed and allowed her palm to roam on Vangelis' thigh. Vangelis, it had been rumoured lately, was looking to start a family. The young composer conceded that the lady played very pleasantly. My mother chipped in that they had taken lessons together at the Conservatoire for ten years. Vangelis could hardly contain his excitement — you mean Natalie you play the piano? My mother gave a good-natured laugh — oh no, just the radiogram I'm afraid. My father detached himself from Xenia and went out to the veranda. He returned looking glum. He asked Xenia to tell us the one about the instructor in the Party. But Xenia wanted Lucy to be there, and what's she up to out there on the veranda? she asked, all innocence. Stargazing as usual, Aunt Victoria put in, and got up unsteadily to bring her inside. Calliope the maid heard this and came in unbidden to sit at Xenia's feet, as though to provide the accompaniment. Xenia launched into the joke. The love bite on her neck disturbed me.

I was watching my father in his impatience to laugh and felt sorry for him. It was extraordinary that he could take pleasure in so feeble a joke. But tonight when the punch line came, and even before Xenia had quite finished, Lucy burst out bitterly: Do you people really mean to say you find that funny? A deathly hush fell. I was secretly grateful for her outburst. As usual, only Victoria dared break the silence: It's all just propaganda, Lucy dear, that's all it is. Will you tell me what is the matter with you tonight? What ever happened to your sense of humour, my love? Lucy rising to storm pitch retorted that it was outrageous to make fun of a part of history that wasn't even any of their business. Anestis intervened: but what on earth do you mean, Lucy? Come off it now, you're not serious are you? You can talk, she flung back at him, but just take a long look into your own past my friend; and she flounced out into the corridor mouthing about Anti-Communism, Collaboration with the Enemy, Unyielding Struggle. Anestis ran after her, with Vangelis following. I stood up too, but changed my mind. I had had enough of her tantrums, and it wasn't as if I hadn't heard her often enough laughing till the tears ran down her cheeks at jokes of the same sort. Lucy was the family icon. Because Lucy had had a brother, Alexis, who had been killed fighting as a partisan in the mountains. Since then she had acquired an aura of sainthood and went around like Ava Gardner in her Citroen, while the rest of us bowed our heads in deference to her tragedy. A tragedy which gave her and those around her some leverage in left-wing circles. They used to make a fuss of her and took her seriously, since she knew foreign languages; at every big rally of the Left she'd be up there with the VIPs.

She extricated herself from Anestis and flung open the

door. Anestis let his arms fall by his sides, too taken aback to know what to do. But Vangelis made a grab at her handbag; galvanised into action he gave chase. He couldn't let her drive off in this state, she might take away a lamp-post. My father sat dumbfounded. Xenia looked him over with cold appraisal and malice, or so it seemed to me. Then she got up, said goodnight with a provocative air, as if now that she had done her duty there was no place for her here any longer. Tonia still stared open-mouthed, though she knew perfectly well that Lucy was unique. Nancy was at a loss for where to lay her restless palm. Anestis subsided again beside his wife Zoe, and Zoe rested her head against his shoulder. They stayed like that for a while, all of them exchanging uncomfortable glances. But their eyes registered something now, the bored look had left them. And little by little the chill began to thaw from the atmosphere. Anestis thought he could explain Lucy's outburst. They had something to get their teeth into now. Her brother, you see, had been an instructor in the Party. Hard-line and incisive, a Stalinist to the core — and who knows, maybe today was the anniversary of something, maybe she'd had a bad dream, something like that must have set her off, it was the only explanation. From the start of the evening she'd seemed moody, that was what it was, so of course she must have had something upsetting on her mind; that was why she'd been so affected, why she'd thrown such a fit. The composer was enjoying himself hugely, and kept tut-tutting to himself over and over again. My father, relieved, was quick to go along with this explanation. While Victoria's comment was that quite simply my dears we'd been treated to the most divine exhibition. Only my poor mother looked downcast, maybe because she was thinking of Alexis.

Victoria was regaling Anestis with the story of how she had sacked the three ringleaders in the strike. Anestis laughed and said good for you. Rising to the occasion, she developed her theme, she had strong feelings about the workers in her factory. What did they want, in God's name? Was it aspirins, paper hankies, women? They wanted her to shut up shop for good, that way they'd never have to do a hand's turn again. And there she was, come Christmas, come Easter, dishing out bonuses of twenty thousand drachmas, sometimes, to buy them presents for their little brats. Who else was going to treat them like that, she wanted to know. They even had Softex in the loos. What the hell did they want, in God's name? She asked us. My dad laughed indulgently: Victoria my love, they've found your soft spot, they're exploiting you. She turned to Anestis: D'you think they're Trots? Why surely, haven't we said so? Anestis returned. Thus bolstered, Victoria continued her tale of woe. See here now, some idle bugger grazes his little finger and the next thing is they're all out on strike? Do they expect me to give each one a partnership? Just imagine!

I was gazing in rapture at gigantic shells in a glass tank, hypnotised by a group of molluscs entwined in fatalist postures. Then the tank shattered and out they all poured across the floor. Legs and antennae, emboldened, came nearer; eyes gleamed monstrously and although the sight revolted me I took pleasure in it too. I allowed them to creep over my body, like sea grass in the vast depths. Then there was a bird that had a

27

damaged heart and I was this bird's nurse. I dressed it up in its wings, as carefully as I'd button a baby into his playsuit. The bird looked up at me timidly and I comforted it, you'll be flying again soon. I took it to a high point and said to it, on you go now, fly; but its wings wouldn't carry it and the bird huddled up in misery. And the more miserable it got the longer its neck became and the uglier it looked. By now I'd lost interest in the bird. It huddled abandoned in a corner of my room, when I saw my father naked in a tub, in the sitting room, with women soaping him; a hunting pack of women in riding hats, who tugged at his penis until it curled back like a mollusc and shrank from sight. But my father was laughing blissfully, at his ease in the water. Finally I was in the garden house at Kifisia. A gentle light was shining and I said, how beautiful it is! I bent to look in at the window; a young woman, her hair plaited into a crown around her head, was weaving and her mouth was opening and shutting, she might have been singing as her shuttle flew — I loved the idyllic picture. In the corner opposite I saw a small bookcase with books on it. So, I remember thinking, the weaver-girl has a taste for reading, and as I began to inspect them I was charmed to discover in the middle of the room a copper brazier, with a lemon-rind on charcoal giving off its odour. But to my surprise, just while my nostrils were tingling pleasantly with the fragrance of the lemon-rind, the young woman turned into my Grandmother Myrsini, a lady of breathtaking beauty, and ensconced on a gentleman's knee. I looked away in embarrassment — and so I awoke.

My father, thunderstruck, was demanding to know: but when? This is madness! Impossible. When at last he replaced the receiver in a grand Shakespearean manner — my father has it in the blood — he broke the news to us: Dictatorship. My mother cried out and collapsed in a heap on the sofa. Calliope the maid, as part of her duties, always manages to sense the moment for coffee at a wake, and set off in her ungainly waddle for the kitchen. My father repeated: Dictatorship, do you hear! I stared at him, shaking off sleep.

I had been hearing talk of dictatorship for years. Coups and juntas and clandestine organisations were things that people talked about, but on a purely theoretical basis. Rather like footnotes to a glorious past. That a good number of the military had in fact made careers for themselves in the Greek Parliament, that I did not know. If asked to name some, I would have had no idea; perhaps I might have hazarded Metaxas in the thirties as a dictator, although at my exclusive school we were taught about him only as the prime minister who answered Mussolini with the immortal *No* in 1940. None of this meant very much to me. I was for Democracy though, I'd no time for some of the prize young idiots at the tennis club who bragged about being fascists. I wasn't much drawn, either, to nightclubs, whisky, the twist and fast cars. With my girlfriends, Urania and Elvira, I used to read Cavafy. We fancied ourselves as intellectuals. I very much wanted to grow up like my father. I enrolled in the Centrist Youth Movement because I was starved for company. I stayed there until I met Paul on Mykonos. Then Paul brought me into the left-wing Lambrakis Youth.

I watched them in silence. My mother was staring

transfixed, as though at some terrible memory. But my father was holding forth and as he talked he began to regain his colour and his manner became more animated; these bums, he prophesied, whoever or whatever they might be, they'd have their noses rubbed in it, how long could they last? one month, two? Say until the autumn, no more, the buffoons. As I listened to him, I began to feel better. He was like a small child whose toy has been broken.

I was happy in the Lambrakis Youth. They struck me as well-educated, bright young people. My mother disapproved, I was becoming too involved, she said. My dad minded less; but had once put it to me that the sails I was spreading were set fair for the USSR and that personally he didn't like it. He explained to me about bureaucracies, totalitarianism, and things like that. I couldn't make head or tail of it, I knew only that my father was a bourgeois, therefore he talked like a bourgeois. Paul was a help to me here; he was a cadre in the Youth Movement and everyone looked up to him. Of my father he said: Don't listen to him, he employs the critique of the Right. But he supports Democracy, I protested. Yes, but he supports a bourgeois democracy, therefore he talks like a bourgeois. I wasn't exactly sure what bourgeois meant. But I never deigned to ask. That's the way I learned things. Like the sea, well that's what it is: the sea, and the same with the mountain.

My mother, from her place curled up on the sofa, watched dully as my father held forth and wagged his finger threateningly. Calliope had set her chin. The peroration was visibly getting on my mother's nerves, he was driving her insane, she complained, and in any case she failed to see why he had to vent his feelings quite so loudly. Calliope's chin began to tremble; I've often thought that she must be linked up to my father by some invisible mechanism, so that she reacts like a kind of extra hand or eyebrow. My father laughed savagely; savagely too laughed Calliope. He paraded in irregular circuits around the piano and ended up standing with his hands clasped together behind his back, facing my mother. For a moment I thought he was going to hit her; they'd taken to occasional fisticuffs, just lately. But abruptly he turned on his heel and banged the door of his room shut behind him. Performance over, I thought.

I was about to go back to bed when the telephone rang again. I got to it first and lifted the receiver. It was Vangelis, beside himself with panic: the area was being sealed off by tanks, an armoured column was heading for the telephone building, we might be cut off at any moment. Close to hysteria, he asked for my father. My dad appeared and snatched the phone. It made a real impression on me to hear Vangelis so jittery; I could never remember him being ruffled by anything. He told my father that the arrests had started, Anestis had been taken in. My mother began to cry for Anestis, Calliope started crossing herself. My father pressed his hands tightly against his temples. We sat down and he expatiated on the meaning of a coup d'état and dictatorship. He put the blame squarely on the king. It was a palace coup all right, it had been hatching for months and all the time we'd refused to believe a thing about it. Well, now it had come.

It occurred to me that if Anestis had been arrested, Paul must be in certain danger. I remembered how he had cried, but I was desperately tired. I couldn't feel

anything for him. Only the need to stretch out my legs
that had already gone to sleep.

Day broke to national folk-dance music and military
marches on the radio. My father said with an air of
bravado: I'll nip out to the newspaper office. My mother
had her problem with Liza. She asked my advice. They
were to meet today. The phone had been cut off and
what was my mother to do? Calliope, *in extremis*, urged
us to rush out to the grocers', the butchers' and the cake
shops. Buy in food, fill the larder. My mother rebuked
her sharply. What sort of a way was that to carry on? If
people heard her they'd think we had no finer feelings.
But Calliope was not one to care about appearances. Her
master had given her to understand that the situation
was serious. And she muttered something, paying no attention to my mother, she might have been cursing her
under her breath.

How many times had my mother asked him to put a
stop to Calliope's liberties, or at least to curb her
tongue? My father wouldn't hear of such a thing — a little understanding, Natalie, is all that's needed. But
understanding for what, when she could feel Calliope's
eye, like a Judas, always upon her? She remembered the
way she used to stand at the head of the stairway in the
great house, in the years when my father had first come
courting her. Even then he had had the habit of disap-
pearing for weeks together without explanation. My
mother would write him voluminous letters with dried
flowers folded inside them, jasmine was her favourite.
And Calliope would stand, like the mistress of the

house, at the head of the stairway, and turn those quiz-zical, insolent eyes upon her: What is the young lady's business with the gentleman, if you please? My mother would leave the letter, promising herself that if all went well, her revenge could come later. But although every-thing turned out perfectly, Calliope never lost her cheek. Hardly a day would pass without some such inci-dent, and it gave them one more thing to bicker over.

I felt braver now and said I'd go out and see what was happening. My mother shouted at me: you're not going anywhere, you're not going anywhere. I advised her to cut the hysterics, and went out.

My father had returned downcast, but was so worried to find me gone that it quite cheered him up. He became very talkative with my mother. I found them reconciled by worry, over glasses of spirits. Calliope made as if to tear my ear off. My father rose to his feet, fiery and pro-tective as a patriarch: Where on earth have you been? You gave us a bad turn, my love. He rested a hand on my shoulder as though I were an apple and he the tree.

I remembered those unbearable evenings, as cold as taffeta petticoats, wrapped in the velvet silence of ill-will. My mother fuming and filing away at her nails and my father maundering to himself quietly, philosophi-cally, Calliope drivelling from room to room, and me with my board game on the carpet. Then I'd pray to God to send clouds, lightning, thunderbolts, anything to give the world a shake-up. To make them raise their eyes at last and look at me. To make them look at one another. But God never listened to my prayers and I'd kick over my toys — just to see the shadow darken my father's eyes and make them beautiful.

It was the first time I'd seen them as anxious guardians of their treasure — meaning me. We sat as if in a family frame and Calliope served us. I told them all I'd seen and heard. But my father, like a dolphin on a sunny day, couldn't resist leaping up to shine with information of his own. There had been more arrests, people had been killed, and so forth. At this point my mother half-closed her eyes, weighing up how much to believe. She had a piece of news of her own, because it had been too much to bear, she'd gone out to visit Zoe. We ought to stand by the poor girl, she said sadly between mouthfuls. And went on to sing the praises of Anestis.

Once upon a time Anestis had been in love with Aunt Victoria. He'd married Zoe just two years ago. Until '58 he had been a political prisoner. During the Occupation he had been in the youth branch of the Resistance. And my mother used to extol him as an example of perseverance in adversity; in spite of everything he'd gone on to graduate from Law School, he'd never given up, after his release he'd had the staying power, to study in spite of all the years he'd lost, even when he was too old for it. I'd often heard him discoursing philosophically with my father on such matters as love and death. How much my father enjoyed a casual fling. The special affection he'd always felt for Nancy. One morning sitting in the Café Flore in Paris and as they talked their hands had chanced to touch. She began breathing heavily: let's go to that hotel over there, oh do come on. They went, and she wore him out. What an afternoon! It made him feel years younger just to think about it. But rather than talking about sex Anestis preferred to recite the errors of the communist party. My father didn't give a damn, as he put it, but for all that became wonderfully versed in all manner of error.

In a moment they would be Natalie and Telly once more, then the knives would come out and they'd be hard at it. Like last night all over again, after the party had broken up. My mother had forbidden him to bring that tart with her vulgar jokes to the house again. It had gone on and on last night, now for the big time I said to myself and sucked back tears until sleep took hold of me. Then I'd been awakened by my dad shouting into the telephone, demanding to know how the coup could have happened. Calliope set down the platter with the peeled fruit. She could hardly contain herself when my parents quarrelled, smirking to herself and pretending to pour oil on troubled water while actually egging them on.

Well then, my mother continued, since she'd popped out to Zoe's, she had thought she might as well go on and call on the General. He had been in a frightful lather, striding up and down the house in his pyjamas, and ranting against the evils of communism. But uncle, she'd protested, why involve the communists when it's the colonels that have taken over? His Majesty, he retorted, had not been apprised and therefore, of course, it could only be a communist plot.

My father asked irritably why on earth she'd gone to see the General. At that time my father and his uncle were about to go to law over the portions of their inheritance, there was a piece of land in Attica that the General coveted. My mother paid no heed and went on munching her fruit. The family frame became cloudy and faded. My dad asked Calliope to turn on the radio and make him a strong cup of coffee. As soon as she was out of the room, my mother burst out that she would not be insulted, and it was time he knew it. He pursed his lips. I left them to it and went to my room.

Of course he used to deny that Xenia was his mistress. Just one of Natalie's fantasies. How could he possibly have a mistress who was hardly older than me, his own daughter? But what could you do? he would sigh. Such things were not uncommon in Nataliology, a science to which he had applied himself since his first fateful meeting with my mother in Victoria's little green drawing room, a few days after the liberation of '44.

What could I do, but put up with them and pity them?

They decided to hold the wake for Democracy at Kifisia and I went along with them. There at least we would have the company of Victoria. I said let's call in at Lucy's and take her with us. My mother snapped back: she couldn't leave her mother, to say nothing of last night's fracas. A vein was beating in my father's forehead, but he held his peace. And when I suggested calling in at Zoe's I saw the two of them exchange glances: God forbid. It's one thing to stand by the poor woman, naturally, but let's not go looking for trouble. Even to drop in there this morning, my mother now conceded, had been an extraordinary thing to do, she hadn't fully taken in what had happened. We called for Vangelis. He was an architect, a good-hearted soul, and reputed to be gay. Always sorry for himself and full of how he was going to become a family man. Sometimes I even enjoy listening to him maundering on like an old shrew.

In the car we kept returning to Anestis: What rotten

luck, it's not fair. According to Vangelis all the political prisoners had been herded together in the racecourse. Poor, unlucky Anestis. It was years now since he'd done anything but mind his own business, and now for this to happen, just the same as if he'd been in the Party.

At Kifisia we found Victoria plastered in the company of two neighbours, harmless old boobies, who had once come under her spell. They used to sit up drinking till the small hours, bitching about the sex lives of their friends. They gave us a raucous welcome, and my father was rather put out. But we soon came to a compromise. They restrained their exuberant high spirits, and we in turn cast off something of our air of gloom. We mourned with moderation.

Calliope was staying with her sister in the garden house. I nipped out to our own house, next door, to fetch my dad's brandy. A shared garden wall separates the two houses, and in this wall is a communicating door. The place holds no memories for me. I was only four when Great-Grandmother Flora died. The house was left empty after that, or rather was exclusively haunted by my dad. But I often dream about it. Stepping lightly among the honeysuckle and ivy, and then I find myself in the little room with the young woman at her weaving. I catch my breath at the radiant beauty of my father's mother, and so I awake. Sometimes in fear, sometimes in embarrassment. Many things are said about my Grandmother Myrsini.

Around nine there came a knock at the door and we all froze. My father especially; his manner said, this is it, it's me they've come for. But it was only Franz, my German tutor. He explained that he'd been to our house and when we weren't there he'd begun to worry about us; he'd worked out that on this day of all days we were sure to be here and well, here he was. He spoke Greek rather charmingly, this classical scholar of the family. He was out to make an impression too. By now I had cottoned on to what he was doing here. He recounted his adventures on the way, a nightmare description of Athens under curfew. Victoria was blind drunk, overjoyed to be freed from strikes for evermore. The idle buggers had gone too far, you see. Her old dad when he was alive, now, had said: the worker's got to know his place. Give him an inch and he'll take a mile. Let a strike once take hold — you're finished. Of course you've got to see your worker fair, agreed. But he's got to behave himself, he's got to bloody well work. Not down tools at the drop of a hat. That old Papandreou had turned their heads, that was for sure. Know what I mean? They went swooning over Bithikotsis, songs of the Left. Know what I mean? With Papandreou this and heartthrob Bithikotsis that, just look at what it's brought us.

My father had had enough by this time and rounded on her. Control yourself I beg of you, you're sounding like a prize bitch. She grinned sardonically: birds of a feather, she said. She took me to the store-room. There she pulled some old curtains out of trunks. We brought them into the room and she lurched about putting them up over the windows. My father protested weakly. We'd made it just like the Occupation. Victoria and the old boobies clapped their hands: it's an air raid, we're a secret school hiding from the Turks! My mother kept thinking about Anestis and sighed. Franz sat next to me. Our hands somehow joined and I thought of him naked. My bosom swelled and cigarette smoke blinded my eyes.

The game was over; I sat huddled in a corner with no reserves of endurance any more with which to think of Paul. I had no tears.On Monday I would have seen him at the Youth Movement. I'd have got him on his own and we'd have talked it out. It's lies and evasions that make people split up, and a shame when they do. But according to Vangelis it was mayhem down in Piraeus Street. The police had burst in and smashed the place up. What price now the Youth Movement, and what price Paul? As midnight approached I became more and more irritable. It was as though coarse hairs were tickling against my skin. A burden had descended and I saw no way of shifting it.

For the last quarter of an hour my mother and the German had removed themselves to the dining room, and on my way through to the kitchen I caught sight of her sitting on his knee. Meanwhile my father continued his peroration and Vangelis glumly listened.

4

OUR UNCLE, the General, took a post in the military council. That settled my mother's doubts. But she found a more difficult dilemma in the Arab-Israeli war. She knew that the progressive thing was to side with the Arabs, but at the same time was deeply touched at the Israeli achievement and what about those wonderful Theodorakis songs about the concentration camps that she'd loved so much?

That summer was a difficult time. The tourists flocked to the smart pavement cafés in Constitution Square, and in the royal gardens nearby there was no lack of young army conscripts arm in arm with housemaids, listlessly seeking inspiration in the movements of the swans, a delight for any serious student of modern Greek society. I was working for my university entrance exams and nothing could please me.

Distant rumblings of resistance filtered through to us. Our friends still gathered in the evenings, the old set and others. They commented gravely on what was happening, chuckled over some anecdote and remembered to sniff my mother's flowers — jasmine was our weakness. Our veranda had a privileged position, with a marvellous view over Athens. And the famous Attic twilights came and made our veranda fragrant. We were shown handbills that read, Up with Democracy. My father had explained to me that the letters P.A.M. stood for the Patriotic Front against Dictatorship. Pam-pam, pam-pam, I used to murmur all the way home from evening classes — it sounded like a hornet's nest every time I went out with my girlfriends, Urania and Elvira.

My father had adjusted to the situation by taking refuge in the unconventionality for which he was well known, and now habitually sat lowering in his office. It's a notable fact that when he came back from his years in Paris my father had given up wearing a tie. The working class, you see, wears a tie so as to look like something better. A gentleman, on the other hand, is already quite aware of his superiority, and so has no need to prove it by wearing a tie. And so, you see, unconventionality is the hallmark of the gentleman, while the working class cannot help but conform!

And every morning my father no doubt remembered Cavafy's poem about the *gran rifiuto*. Every morning the same heavy lassitude, but he would always seem to get through his day without any signs of excessive exertion. Even his daily journey to the office and back — which was not more than a few streets away — seemed a wearisome effort to him. But he would also be charmed to watch the clockwork gait or the subtle body-language of passers-by, in the conviction that he had a fine sensitivity for such things. And truly it had happened to him, so he used proudly to declare, to have sometimes passed a sleepless night, thanks to the wizened face of an elderly man or the mournful eyes of a girl or a youth's bowed head — chance imprints upon his mind that returned to haunt him.

Every morning his greeting to the doorkeeper in the

entrance hall would be the same: Wotcher? And the doorkeeper would blush crimson to the tips of his ears to be addressed with such familiarity by Mr Aristotle; my father had this knack, of making you feel you'd known him all your life. If he was sometimes moody, it was rare for him to let the depth of his moodiness show, on such days he'd merely raise a hand in world-weary salute. And the doorkeeper would understand, and respond with a grateful smile. I'd often heard the doorkeeper telling someone: Say what you like, Mr Aristotle is a real gentleman. Not like some ...

And indeed my father comes of a family of gentlefolk. My grandfather, Agesilaos Panayotou, had been one of the best notaries in pre-war Athens, a supporter of the republican Liberal Party but careful also to maintain his firm links with the palace. In the photographs a gentle wrinkled face. He went for neither women, nor cards, nor kept bad company. And the one woman that he married, Myrsini, walked out on him. And she walked out on him to follow a painter to Paris. From then on his mother, who was called Flora, had begun to work on his misogynist leanings. He lived a bachelor life, all alone. And my dad, from the age of two, had been brought up under the eye of a French governess. We'd all heard the story of the children playing with the Frenchwoman's furbelows. And how later they used to peep through the keyhole to watch her taking off her petticoats. My dad used to recall his father as he sat hunched over his legal tomes. His heart would grow tender at the recollection — how his own whining was never absent from the rooms of the large house as he'd followed his father's every movement like a shadow. Anyone especially interested has only to glance at the psychological pretensions of the novels on which that class was brought up, to note the effect the absence of a mother's love can have in shaping the human character.

At school, at the American College, he'd begun to experience problems of a biological/sexual nature. Then he'd gone on to study Law at university, and taken a great interest in the restraining Christian overlay upon the unbridled Hellenic cult of beauty. He went overboard for the Paradoxographers, Paroemiographers, Apocryphologers. He was always going to visit the monasteries of Mount Athos. A great influence on his life at this time was the devout orthodoxy of Fotis Kondoglou. But instead he ended up marrying my mother, Natalia or Natalie, because he did not know, in Proust's phrase, that his character was other than he had supposed.

And naturally he didn't know, until forced by pressure of circumstances. He had been obliged to leave Greece in a hurry after the decree of June 1947 drafting students into the army. Because my father, upright patriot though he was, had not the least intention of being drafted to fight the left-wing partisans in the mountains. Moral patriotism is one thing, he used to argue, but it's quite another to go banging off at the enemy with every peasant Tom, Dick and Harry. So strings were pulled and wheels were oiled. A longstanding friend of the family, a retired diplomat with a distinguished career in the Middle East behind him, tried various backdoor channels to get him an exemption. But it was no good. In the end my grandfather had paid his weight in gold to a scientist who together with members of the government (themselves distinguished for playing the black market in ministerial posts under the Occupation) set up a top-grade escape network, a veritable gift to all those like my dad whose character precluded them from taking part in the bloodletting but who by happy coincidence were well enough provided for that they could choose to go into voluntary exile instead.

So my father had been left with no other option but to leave Greece. He would sit out the civil war in Paris. This being so, nothing would have suited him better than a clean break with my mother. He could have been content to relive in memory their happiest moments. With only his memories for company he could quite well have survived the suffocating Paris nights, a faint glimmer by the lights strung out along the banks of the Seine. Here I must explain, my father can be a terrible poseur, suavely eloquent on any subject under the sun, it's a compulsion with him. Since childhood I've listened to him eternally holding forth in injured fashion, it can make me quite ill, about some turning point in his life that he'll invariably describe as traumatic and even refer you to such and such a book, on such and such a page you'd find a case comparable to his.

This, then, was when he had begun to wonder. The day was fast approaching for him to leave, word would come at any moment, his books were all boxed up, he'd said his farewells to his closest friends, but to my mother not a word. And at dusk on one of those difficult days, while wandering aimlessly, he'd found himself all unawares in my mother's neighbourhood. And that he didn't regret it may be thanks to the saintly aspect of my Grandmother Merope as she came out at the head of the walnut staircase with an expression of amazed sweetness in the chiaroscuro of the crystal chandelier.

They were married there and then, and left simultaneously for Paris. He travelled under cover, she by normal channels. They were reunited in a hotel room with faded purple flowers on the wallpaper. The flowers in particular my mother would never forget.

Already by this time my father had begun to take an interest in worldly affairs, in a noticeable shift from the devout visions of Kondoglou. Indeed he numbered himself among those privileged Greeks who had seen Sartre at close quarters and even shaken him warmly by the hand. He began slowly to consolidate his circle of friends, and prospects for new departures began to emerge. He made excellent progress in his studies. And he began to make acquaintances among the Left. In those circles, as he later used to claim, apart from a few hard-core extremists, he had been lucky enough to consort with wonderful people, good friends, real intellectuals.

To those memories of his prime passed in voluntary exile, my father can add an affair with a blushing rose of the East. An Indian girl with a spot on her forehead. They were fellow-students at the Sorbonne. They went everywhere together, and got on so well that he even left my mother. But then without warning the Indian girl disappeared. He started to lose his hair, his health deteriorated and he got so thin that my mother became alarmed and made him go for X-rays; even he'd begun to think his days were numbered. Luckily it was nothing and soon passed. And one rainy afternoon, saved as though miraculously from the jaws of death, he had leant his head against my mother's shoulder and whispered: Natalie, companion of my life.

This story I have heard very many times and in different variants. My mother was never quiet about his wrongs to her; and often added that that was the moment when they should have gone their separate ways. The moment when she'd caught sight of him holding hands with another woman in the restaurant they'd used to go to together. The rest of that day she had wandered the streets in lonely desperation. With the sound of her father's voice in her ears, how he had planned otherwise for his only daughter. But she had refused to listen, too much thrilled with the idea of travelling to Paris. It had all turned out so badly. Hadn't she taken pity on him and looked after him, good heavens, all that time when he'd been lying there, white and ill. But in so doing she had signed herself a life sentence. Because you only had one chance, and if you threw it away, you never got another.

As for me, I was well and truly enmeshed by their stories; to the point that when I finally broke free I turned on them quite nastily.

When the civil war ended, the tale went on, they'd begun to work towards their return. As bad luck would have it, my mother was just then due to give birth to me. And this despite every precaution, because God forbid that they should have wanted to saddle themselves with children, how it had happened she would never be able to explain. She'd done everything punctiliously to the letter, but even so she woke up one morning and the vomiting and dizzy spells began. She couldn't bring herself to have an abortion, that would have been unthinkable she said. So, now that the Yankees had sorted things out in Greece, their sole concern was to go home. My father became incurably nostalgic: Dexameni

Square and the Zappion gardens, Grandmother Flora at Kifisia with her jars of preserve, the old puppet-master with his shadow-theatre, the horse-cab driver in the square, Victoria's little green drawing room, Lucy's pensive eyes. In the meantime Grandfather George had died and my mother was very cut up about it. Victoria had married an elderly diplomat, Grandfather Agesilaos was at death's door. Lucy, they learned, was engaged to a lawyer — this last seemed to upset my father.

So he'd embarked on a round of visits to the Embassy, putting out feelers. He found an old friend who worked in the chancellery, took him out to lunch and home to dinner; my mother who was fed up with Paris and had just given birth to me, laid on her smile. But while Plastiras was at the helm in Greece there was little chance that my father would escape service in the army. And my mother was still enough in love with him not to want to leave him in Paris by himself. They felt they had more than their share of worries. My own memories begin at this point, with a high-chair. I kick with my foot and cry in a panic with my rattle shaking by my ear. She's not there in the room and he tries to pacify me; then a horrid sensation expands through my body, pain and nausea together and I go quiet. Later I heard him telling how I had been bawling unbearably, his patience had been tried and he'd pinched me, and do you know? I'd shut up at once.

But just when everything looked bleakest, the Americans gave Plastiras the heave. Their man in Athens, Purefoy, placed Papagos in power. And my father managed to buy off his military service without difficulty, thanks to an official of the Papagos government who had once been a lover of my Grandmother

Myrsini. Grandmother Myrsini had just then died, and that was when it all came out. Only to be hushed up again of course. Grandfather made his confession to the priest, took communion and crossed his hands to die the lighter for his sins. My father, when a little later he had got over the shock, passed on my grandmother's name to me and so discharged his duty. It was a long time before I understood. All that about the painter and taking off to Paris — so much baloney. Because, if you please, my Grandmother Myrsini had been very beautiful but also very poor. A rags-to-riches romance that had ended in the madhouse. And all because one night my grandfather had caught her in flagrante. He went wild — he'd pulled her up out of the gutter — and he had every means at his disposal to have her locked up.

When I was a lot older, Victoria used to insist to me that there had always been something a bit odd about my grandmother. She could remember her father, she said, whenever his brother Agesilaos was talked of, always saying what a poor tormented soul he was, a real saint but stubborn of course, stubborn as a mule. Because one summer he'd come back from Lesvos with a peasant girl in tow. They'd done everything they could to persuade him to change his mind, but no, he'd had to have his way. And he'd paid for it too: his wife turned out to be an epileptic. That was what had happened, according to Victoria. And I wasn't to forget either that, although it was a terrible thing he had done to her, my grandfather had destroyed himself as well. He'd borne his cross until the end and never remarried or anything like that. He'd been like a mother to my father.

But however it had been, I couldn't quite take in anything so horrible.

Six months after our return my father began to gather the reins in his hand and to cast about with that cartesian mind of his that now came into its own, though he'd never had any head for figures before. Later he turned out to have a flair for the stock market. Perhaps, as he explains it himself, due to a special sixth sense. And it's true that he has his fingers so perfectly and coolly on the pulse that he often takes even his broker by surprise. In this way, when he buys and sells he never fails to invoke the subconscious.

It was at the same time that he realised a long cherished ambition to become a feature writer, and quickly established a reputation for himself. This he owed to some extent to his education and his family background, but above all, undoubtedly, to his own personality. These were the days when coca-cola was offered at parties as something exotic and the popular press was full of Queen Soraya. It was the time when *indigenous* Greeks thought of themselves as giants of western civilisation, while *theory* gave it out that communism is alien to the Hellenic character and to the gene pool of the race.

As time went by our all-party salon prospered. Famous names came and went and cast a glamour over the proceedings. This had its effect even on me, to the extent that my first experience was with the scenarist of a Greek film, at the age of fourteen. My father had the knack of spotting the talents that in due course would make for fame and fortune. But not everyone was equally pleased, and he soon acquired his band of detractors. These people had a lot to say about our family. They turned up skeletons in cupboards: where had the shares in the Mineral Mines come from? Rumour had it that

49

my Great-Grandmother Flora had had a lover; I was all
agog. The father of my great-grandmother's three sons
— my Grandfather Agesilaos, Joachim the General, and
Solon who owned the factory — was reputed to have
been a director of the Mines. Because my Great-
Grandfather Nestor, apart from being an admiral, had
been impotent. My father would smile good-humouredly
when all this was reported to him where he was holding
court at Apotsos' ouzeri. Nowadays of course all this is
water under the bridge. Which is not to say that
anything much has changed in this world of intrigue
and informers, but my father has long since learned to
cut his jib with the wind. But in those days, not long
after our return, a great feud had been declared between
Apotsos' where he used to go with his cronies, and
Floka's, the coffee shop frequented by his opponents. My
father had not only implacable enemies, he used to complain, he had implacable admirers too. Such was the
fate of remarkable men. So while he smiled his good-
natured smile, with an air of aloofness to the petty
foibles of others, his friends would bicker and pick quarrels on his behalf, pulling not just chestnuts out of the
fire but red-hot coals as well! Cold warriors clashed with
the peace movement, the thinkers took issue with ex-
istentialism. But it would be narrow of me to make too
much of the wretched triviality of my parents' lives.
That's the Greek middle class all over, that's sold out all
along the line, as we're told, to foreign interests,
anyhow we got rich without getting bored. And we certainly weren't waiting for Godot.

My parents went off to Skiathos for a holiday with Theodore, Victoria, Nancy and Vangelis. I thought of them lazing on the beach at Chrysi Ammos larded with sun oil, and cursed July. I'd go to the fridge and open the door for the sense of security I got from the colours inside; then to the veranda to stare across at the veranda opposite; I'd pluck some jasmine blooms and sniff them; drift back to my room to read two or three pages and then start over again on the circuit from kitchen to veranda. For me that summer was like a snake playing with its coils.

Only with Paul could I have discussed the prospects from now on. But we were out of touch, and what kept us apart as far as I could see was the dictatorship. I knew that he lived in the suburb of Kesariani, but exactly where he had never told me except vaguely, somewhere on the main street. Once he'd taken me with him to a 'cultural function' in the square. He'd recited *The Leader* by Varnalis and I'd watched in rapture from the crowd. His sister Dora had been with me.

He'd often talked to me about his sister. By hook or by crook, he said, she was studying to be a doctor. I was going to study medicine too, if I passed my entrance exams; Paul said he was going to be a surgeon and we planned how we'd set up a clinic together. Better that than have some smart ass sniffing round to marry me for my dowry — Paul was welcome to it all I said, and we both laughed. So Dora with the further qualification of her good looks married a famous pathologist. She did what she could for the rest of the family, and if Paul was then studying with the path laid smooth before him, that was why, he owed it to his sister. Their father had been a political prisoner in every prison in the land.

He'd been a *kapetanios* in the Resistance, with one foot on Mount Giona and the other on Parnassos. And their mother had ruined her health bringing up the children on her own. Paul's story moved me like a fairy tale.

I decided I would try to find him, no matter what the odds. When I asked, people answered me vaguely out of the sides of their mouths, but still I was going to find him. Urania told me that if he wanted to, he'd come and find me himself; he knew the house, and he knew where I went to evening classes. It annoyed me to realise that she was right, that it was all over with Paul, but she was so knowing and superior about it, I wouldn't have been more riled if she'd been prophesying my doom from coffee grounds.

In the words of Calliope, it never hurts to ask. I'd made a start already at the council offices in Kesariani. I'd been told the story of how the quislings would set up roadblocks in the area during the Occupation, you could still see the bullet scars on the walls. I plunged into the narrow side streets with a feeling of reverence, treading softly so as not to burden this hallowed earth. Pain and love combined to transport me back to an earlier time; I stood under the cypresses where so many patriots had been executed and felt something give way within me, as though it were the blood calling to me.

There was a story that my Grandfather George, my mother's father, had been a collaborator. He'd built up a business out of nothing, in olive oil. In the days of the Occupation he'd looked after his own, so much so that the very stones cried out racketeer. When I questioned my mother, she did her best to explain how it was a matter of chance whether you became one thing or another in such a time of crisis. My grandfather had been a devoted father. All that mattered to him had been to pay for my mother's education. And then when my mother left the Maraslian Academy, war had broken out. He sat tight, waiting for the liberation. Her father had framed her teaching certificate and hung it over the table with the business ledgers. That was the kind of man he was: he'd come to Athens from Tripolis with nothing but what he stood up in, and risen from grocer's boy to owning a shop of his own. Eventually he'd risen higher still and married my Grandmother Merope, with a good dowry; olive oil was getting to be big business. Anestis has a way of explaining these things, schooled as he is in the ways of the middle class that drop by drop nurtures the petty bourgeoisie beneath it. Naturally when they took off for Paris, my mother carrying a little bag stuffed full with earrings, bracelets, crucifixes, watches, the gold of Athens that had been given in exchange for two drops of olive oil from grandfather's barrels, my father saw nothing to complain of. They'd cashed it in together. By which he meant that nothing reprehensible attached to them any longer. That was the way in business.

Later I learned that her father had also denounced people to the Nazis. She denied it vehemently of course. She even suspected Lucy of having told me and began dropping hints about people's ingratitude and hypocrisy — I, my girl, am what I am and I'm not going to change. You won't ever find me changing my skin like a snake. I was greatly impressed by this outburst, especially her calling Lucy a snake. It was only then that I began to realise that Lucy really had in some way blighted my mother's life. And I wondered why they spent so much time together and claimed to be friends, when I saw how much damage they had done to one another.

I returned to the main road, and continued my progress. A little further up I saw a woman shaking flower-patterned sheets out of a ground floor window and asked her. Where could I find Paul's family? She muttered something and slammed the window shut. Not content with that she reached to draw the curtains as well, and I caught a look at once terrified and menacing, the look of an animal whose lair is threatened.

A little boy was staring up at me, he could have been following me for some time; he seemed ready enough to chat. We walked together for a bit in silence, then I relented and asked him his name, what class was he in at school, and so on. I bethought myself to ask him about Paul, all helpfulness he said let's go back where I asked first, that was where the guvnor lived.

It was the same woman who came to the door and looked me quizzically up and down; in a flash I was convinced that this was Paul's mother. He had just the same raking glance, from beneath half-closed lids, probing into me when he was angry. I faltered, then put my weight against the door and gave it a slight push. I wasn't going to be defeated now, be she never so formidable. She stood back for me to enter the hall, and shut the door with a sullen look. I said I was a friend of Paul's, I was worried about him. Her eyes flickered and she made a sour face — that's so, is it, and which of all his lady friends might I be then? She said it with an air of shaking out the words in the same way she'd shaken the flower-patterned sheets before, to get the dust out of them. She disappeared through a doorway and returned with a spoonful of sweet preserve on a tray. She invited me to sit down. And while munching her quince I held my eyes on the patterns of the floor tiles, following the lines inexorably until my eyes rested on the toes of her slippers. She asked my name and cackled unpleasantly. Pleased to meet you I'm sure, how come her Casanova of a son had never mentioned me? Her teeth were full of her last meal. I gulped and looked her straight in the eye, I don't know how I managed it, but it seemed to appease her a little. She became quite talkative. Not a day ever passed, she sighed, but they had terrible rows: his dad would tear him off, See here Paul, what d'you want with having so many women? Take Lenin, he was a good fighter he was, but he wasn't one for the skirts. Or Bukharin, that's what did for him, chasing a bit of tail. And Stalin nailed him for it didn't he? So what's the score?

As I listened the light seemed to drain away from the room. I didn't like this woman's face. She spoke with forked tongue and in her eyes smouldered a low cunning that fitted badly with the image of Paul's long-suffering mother as I had allowed it to form in my mind. It wasn't until then that I realised I was drenched in sweat, and not from the heat but from emotion. I made a move to go. She said stay put and get a grip on yourself, and stared at me appraisingly. She was all ears, why didn't I tell her about myself?

I told her my father was a cobbler and lived down by the docks. I enjoyed her look of chagrin and set myself to needle her further by painting my family's fortunes in the blackest of colours. When she asked what I did for a living I said I was a seamstress, and it made me feel good to see her change colour. I was starting to get the upper hand, because she was so obviously horrified at the idea of her darling hanging around with a seamstress, and her voice now chattered like a sewing machine as she went on to outline the fortunes of her own family. She told me about her wonderful son-in-law and her daughter's talent, to say nothing of all Paul's charms, he'd make a joke of it sometimes — mum, he'd say, it must be something I've got from you, the girls all chase me like a honey pot. Meantime I was taking in the fitments and fittings of the house, it was like a furniture shop window.

Just then the *kapetanios* came in, all out of scale, like a hulk run aground in the shallows. A frisson went through me at the sight of him. But the moment he opened his mouth I realised that this was a man whose spirit had been broken long ago. He dragged his feet tetchily, growled at his wife and went on in. I stood up and at the door, as my feet tripped over themselves in my hurry to leave, I heard her voice saying that Paul had gone into hiding right from the day of the coup, he'd made a run for it and got away, as the police burst in.

I went like a hunted thing; I wanted to cry out, to weep aloud and shock the people around me. But as I panted with emotion, I felt a sense of calm spread through me, giving me confidence that I had a long way yet before me. And forward I'd go, looking to left and right, voices began to sound in my ears like wind in the trees, I turned aside and measured my progress, following them by the clues they left me. If only I could avoid stepping on the land mines. But I didn't, I stepped on every one of them. I might as well have been doing it on purpose.

I kept going back to Paul's house. I maintained this vigil for almost the whole summer. Each time I'd ask his mother, how are things, is there anything I can do to help? Each time I'd leave a note telling him I loved him, and ask her to see he got it. I never had an answer. I told myself that it couldn't be easy for him to write, in hiding. I didn't want to be put off by Urania's promptings, or by the dislike I felt for his mother. I kept my patience and went on going to his house because I couldn't bring myself to think that I'd never see him again. It would be like uprooting a part of me — just when I'd come to realise that these things die away and vanish of their own accord, if you know that and expect no more, you don't need to make a fool of yourself.

His mother used to offer me sometimes quince and sometimes orange preserve, and I began to find her less objectionable. She always seemed pleased to see me, but on each visit there would come a moment when she frowned and froze, and while I still munched the preserve and asked her the same old questions she'd start moving about between hall and living room, pretending to dust, or make a sudden dash for the kitchen, oh good heavens, something almost burnt dry on the stove. I would take the hint but each time on leaving I felt more sure of myself, as though I'd won my point. I'd brought myself with a great effort of will almost to like this hard-bitten woman. With the hope perhaps of being able to ignore her and so to neutralise her influence. In any case I rendered her powerless to wound me any more; now I could contemplate with compassion the phlebitis in her feet.

It would have been November, about the beginning, I remember it was drizzling and I ran into him in Solonos Street. My knees buckled under me. I stared at him with rapture. His look said he was pleased to see me. I asked about my letters. That's all over now, he said sadly. I said can't we sit down somewhere and have a talk. No, he said, he was in a hurry.

Not long after the Law School sit-in in '73, I happened to meet a girl from the Youth Movement called Danae. We'd never been very close, but we had got on. We laughed like old friends. It was the times that brought us together, then. We sat down on a bench behind the National Library and started chatting. I knew that she had spent some months in prison, she'd been freed with the amnesty back in '68. But what I hadn't known was that she'd come before a military tribunal, charged with sheltering Paul in her home. This gave me a shock. She said she'd been Paul's girlfriend for years. Then when they'd been arrested, Paul had gone to pieces. Anything I cared to think of, I wouldn't be far out. He'd said yes to everything in exchange for a passport and a ticket to Denmark. She spoke about Paul with bitterness and passion. I didn't know what to say, I had forgotten even the features of his face, so much had happened since then, but I didn't like her manner. That Paul had turned stool-pigeon was too much for me to believe. He's left her in the lurch, I shrugged to myself, I suppose that's why; it can't be true. People were always being accused in those days of informing on their friends. Without any proof. It was sufficient for one of our circle to have suffered more lightly than ourselves at the hands of the Security Police — and that alone would be enough for us to bury him up to the neck in shit.

58

We parted, promising to meet again. But we never did. I'd said I would phone her, but I didn't in the end — I was put off by the easy way she'd cast aspersions on Paul. And I racked my brains to remember the times, at the offices of the Youth Movement, when we'd all been together. How had Paul managed it between me and Danae? It had never crossed my mind that he might have had another girlfriend at the same time. Perhaps this was why he never let me be intimate with him in front of others.

5

URANIA FAILED her university entrance in Medicine and
went off to Paris to study History of Art instead. We exchanged letters once or twice, then lost touch. At
University I'd got to know Fondas who was in his third
year and had a scholarship. I felt better for the interest
he took in me. We used to go to the cinema, we talked
politics, climbed Lycabettos, and sometimes found
ourselves behaving like lovers, then separated awk-
wardly. I still couldn't get Paul out of my mind, and
Fondas seemed not just hesitant, but actually intimidated. Whenever he looked at me tenderly his expression would change abruptly and I'd be disappointed.
I wasn't brave enough to try to unravel his secrets. If he
had made the first move it would have helped me,
because I was willing enough, but at the same time
hung back from getting involved. But all he did was
look at me. Then his political side took over; he often
scared me with his passion if I ever said anything out of
line. I suppose I could have been happy with Fondas, all
I had to do was to agree with him all the time.
Sometimes as I despaired of him, I'd make a mental promise not to contradict him, but I couldn't stand the way
he talked.

This was when I first began to run errands for P.A.M., which was at that time being taken apart by the Security Police. And found myself staring the dictatorship in the face. I collected cases of torture — waves broke within me and wires hummed; then oceans of pain expanded across a map with mountains and sea birds and University Street leading for all eternity into Omonia Square where the football fans hang about. As though they'd slunk out of the suburbs and were dazzled by the bright lights — they always reminded me of the mutilated bodies I'd read about in the Occupation, spewed up by the sewer that ran past the headquarters of the Gestapo and its local henchmen. But now a different set of people — the sewing woman engaged to Thomas who was in jail, Mrs. Paraskevi whose son Stelios had been deported to an island prison camp — all of them bound me to my country, and gradually I learned to divide people up into those who took an active part against the dictatorship and the rest who shrugged their shoulders, or not even that.

On the first day of the New Year my father lost six hundred thousand drachmas and it seemed his luck had turned against him. Because he always came out on top at cards, in love and play, luck had always favoured him equally. But this year everything seemed to be going into reverse. He had split up with Xenia, and from what I could see this hurt him a lot. Xenia was pregnant, by him it was whispered; he may have been upset too by the rumours that were flying around about him and Theodore, and now his luck had even turned at the poker table. So the New Year found him in the blackest depression.

I began to feel a growing need to leave home. They put

obstacles in my way, especially my mother. I got bored with her tears, though I would have liked to believe in them; I kept noticing her eyes — it's supposed to be the eyes that speak — and my mother's eyes, Calliope is quite right, are cold and blue, without expression. To make matters worse, our house became a venue for spiritualists. Every evening the teacup danced and the ladies oohed and aahed. And the odd thing was that my father, follower of Descartes that he was, offered no resistance. Night after night they'd summon up the spirit of Eleftherios Venizelos, the liberal statesman, and question him intently, how long would the dictatorship last?

And as if that wasn't enough there was also Theodore; Theodore the actor, Theodore the shooting star in my Aunt Victoria's arms. She'd installed him in Kifisia, ordered clothes to be made for him in London, bought him a car and presented him, on what was supposed to be his birthday, with three hundred thousand drachmas in shares in the Mineral Mines.

The first time she'd brought him to the house, he had impressed us with his groomed mane and the drawn gentleness of his eyes. Quite the Valentino, chuckled Calliope. But what charmed us most was his mellifluous, faultless diction: a perfect product of the National Theatre. He expatiated on freedom of the spirit and the bisexuality of sacred monsters. For myself I was merely irritated by the pompous way he had of vaunting his talent. He had a loud, braying laugh; and in a curious way his remarks often hit home, but he was also shallow and superficial.

He soon became a fixture in the house. He persuaded my parents to move the furniture around, he took down the pictures, some he directed to be hung in the bathroom, others in the kitchen. Above the piano he urged my mother to hang something fashionable and phallic. My mother swooned at his every compliment. It wasn't long before she was even asking his advice about her underwear. My father gave him a sympathetic hearing, apparently sorry for the man, and there really was something to be pitied about his appearance, an air of blitheness in adversity. He had the additional reputation of being an intellectual fascist, and it was his habit to declaim a stanza composed in the thirties about the dictator Metaxas: *Oh fiery light mayst thou make whole, Triumphantly the nation's soul* ... and so on; but now addressed to the dictator Papadopoulos.

He used to make advances to me and I enjoyed putting him down. I'd giggle for no reason, except to embarrass him as he stared at me open-mouthed. Then I'd feel sorry for him. But there were other times when I was repelled by the dimples that deepened round his lips and I was cross at the way he manhandled Victoria like someone squeezing out a mop. My aunt has something about her. It seems to be her lot, as Calliope puts it, to fall in with scoundrels. And in her cups she'll lament the fact. She's nothing but a wreck, she sighs, she's made a mess of her life. But how could she have been different? Too many memories, too many to forget, they haunted her, you couldn't keep track of them all. She could hate herself at times, everything was so disgusting. But for all that I have never once heard her, no matter how far gone in drink, ever question herself. Perhaps it was through fault of circumstance, she was led along by events.

In 1951 she'd gone overboard for an artist five years

her junior, called Andreas. She'd had no hesitation, as a trend-setter of the well-to-do class, in walking out on her husband, even though they'd only just celebrated their third wedding anniversary in some style. The strangest thing about it was that for Andreas' sake she gave up dyeing her hair, started to dress raffishly, in the way of artists, abandoned cosmetics and even, since Andreas belonged to the Left, set about systematically getting herself initiated into Marxist ideas. For a brief space she was even the darling of the society Left. And the Left, which has ever hailed an ideological victory in the conversion of a prominent member of the bourgeoisie, fell upon Victoria from the start, all but making her a cadre overnight and at every big rally giving her a place of honour on the platform. Victoria for her part revelled in the flattery, no one had ever taken her so seriously before. She reciprocated with blank cheques, as it were; enough anyway to cover the cultural needs of the Party.

During the trial of Beloyannis my godmother was indefatigable in lobbying all her contacts in high places, but to no avail. And during those years she found herself split two ways as she watched on the one hand the consolidation of American capital and the middle class making a hash of things in their so-called parliament, on the other the pathetic efforts of the Left to get its act together with anti-fascist slogans like *Peace and Liberty.* In those days Uncle Solon was still alive, so she had nothing to worry about either with the print works or the Mineral Mines. Those had been heady days, with nothing more to do than collect her rents for the office block in Piraeus on the first day of every month.

Then Andreas had got mixed up with a girl called

Helen. The ensuing bust-up led to scenes that were none too civilised, since my aunt since childhood has had a violent temper. She's supposed to have given him a hiding worthy of a fishwife. And when she'd run into Helen in the street, she'd slapped her face in full view. As these exploits were reported to her friends, many evenings in drawing rooms were taken up in commenting on them. But this plebeian streak of hers had them genuinely foxed. The kernel of fact became overlaid, but Victoria from that time had acquired a special mystique.

It came as no surprise after these goings-on that she began to distance herself from the Left. She'd gone back to her old ways — no time now for politics and all that bunk. Instead she acquired the hard-bitten integrity of a character in an American best seller. But she herself used to say that she had more in common with the world of Dostoyevsky's *Possessed.* Because her spirit yearned for a charged atmosphere and taut wires to perform its act. And here, it must be said, she was more convincing: fascinating so long as with perfect naturalness she was being swept along by any crazy fad, while the daily round reduced her to the level of any other woman past her best and wearing too much make-up. The time when we'd all been together at Kifisia on the day of the coup, her mind had gone back to the past and as she relived her days in the United Democratic Left, it had all come pouring out. What a chameleon she was, right wing, left wing, never mind, that was the one for her. What a load of shit. That was what she thought of Old Man Papandreou. Had we forgotten how the Centre Union began? It was the Right all over again. The Liberals that had once been the well-behaved tools of the British were just the same now with the Americans. Who was it put Batsis to death, that great scientist? And Beloyannis? Now there was nothing but Right and Right. Good God, who do you suppose it was backed Papandreou and Venizelos into a corner? The Americans of course. And why if you please? Because the United Democratic Left had won twenty-five per cent of the vote, that was why. They wanted a party that would be in their own pockets, so what did they do but sweep up all the remnants and stitch them together to make their own ticket so they could steal votes from the Left. And then just look at the Left, look at its policies. No, it's all a load of shit, that's what it is.

At least by this time, whatever literary camp my aunt belonged to, you couldn't say there was any false sentiment about her. She'd got her knife into the workers in her factory. And since Uncle Solon had died she'd become a worthy successor to him. All that her father had left her she was going to increase and go on increasing, and she proposed to enjoy doing it. Time for you men to stand aside and show off your liberal principles elsewhere, she'd no use for windbags like my father. Good grief what are you when it comes down to it, a socialist with shares in the Mineral Mines? Why don't you go and tie a stone about your neck and jump into the sea next time you hear of some miner buried alive down there? How can you call yourself a socialist? You can't and when all's said and done you haven't the right. You've got to defend your own class. The class you were born into. But no, that cousin of hers had never been able to see an inch beyond the end of his nose, even as a child he'd been like that. And just look at him, the man of principle, pretending he's superior to class

distinctions. Listen to him talking about progress, listen
to him talking about The People: what People? He's
pathetic really, and the awful thing is, he's made
himself believe all that about the People and all that
bullshit.

Then one day Nancy's foulmouthed bombshell burst
upon us: Theodore was having it off with my dad. My
mother took absolutely no notice. I don't know what was
going on in her mind, but her exterior betrayed no
change in its crevices and heavy make-up. It didn't matter at all to me the way somebody was made. But not my
father. I'd never set my parents on a pedestal as angelic,
sexless beings. From my earliest years I'd learned to
live with the way things were in our family, and was
used to lovers and mistresses being in the house. It
didn't worry me at all when some tender-hearted
scrounger latched on to my mum, or for that matter that
my father had his mistresses. Take Xenia for example,
I actually enjoyed that, because when she came to the
house she was always playing smart and getting under
their skin.
    But this was different. I wasn't a child to sit back and
let it happen. The worst thing for me was the sort of
man Theodore was, as Calliope put it, and she was up
in arms against this Beelzebub we'd taken into the
house — the very idea of him holding court in a smart
café in Kolonaki for instance and loudly declaring
himself an ace bugger, and a national socialist too. My
God, I thought, the more fool my father. I did wonder
about the truth of all this, and here it probably paid me
to heed Victoria. She was very touchy about Theodore at

this time, he'd only to glance at another woman and she'd wipe the floor with him. Nancy on the other hand had been left high and dry by Vangelis as yet another attempt of his to go straight had ended on the rocks. And now she was going round like a bitch on heat, spreading rumours so as to get her own back on the whole lot of us.

But I'd become an easy prey; it hurt me to see the looks people exchanged and their sadistic enjoyment. Even my father's colleagues, the old crows, didn't miss a trick with their hints and innuendoes. I conjured up a picture of Theodore's powerful body subjecting my father to medieval ordeals, that for a long time left me no peace. Then came all the lore about public lavatories. Parks and shady hotels, gay bars and squares, these were the limits to which my meagre imagination stretched. I was caught up in panic, my very existence seemed to be threatened. Of course I knew quite well that even if the stories had been true I was solely to blame for casting my father as the victim. This was what troubled me most of all, the idea of him being damned. By which I meant, I suppose, everything that I could neither accept nor explain. And as things fell out, it was also at this time that he broke off with Xenia.

She was pregnant and was pressurising him to get a divorce and marry her. He refused and suggested an abortion instead. All this Xenia told me one evening when she sought me out. And tried to sound me, did I love my father? If so it was my duty to persuade him to leave my mother. I listened thunderstruck and wondered how she could possibly have found the nerve. All right damn you, I said to myself, but not this way; at that moment I almost disliked her. She was quite convinced that my father was hiding something, that was the only explanation. Now listen to this, she said, pouting with malice, listen and tell me if I'm mistaken, but I've had my suspicions for a while. Did I remember an evening at our house when Lucy had made a scene? Everybody had pretended not to suspect anything, but she was no fool, she'd seen through it at once. Well see here now, wondered Xenia. Hadn't I noticed how Lucy kept changing poses like a tragic actress, did I remember that? It was all to make people look at her, the jealous old maid. When she saw your father couldn't take his eyes off yours truly, she went green with envy. That's the reason I'm not going on with the abortion, it isn't that I'm squeamish or anything. You're to tell him that, I'll get level with him, I'm not going to let him walk out on me. He'll always know that I'm the mother of his child, and that way he'll never get rid of me. At this she broke down and wept: she did love him a lot. She felt the same way about me because I was his daughter. What else could she do? She wouldn't forget how sweet he'd been to her once, how caring he'd been, everything he'd done for her. She owed him a lot, she knew that. If it hadn't been for him she couldn't have managed. And now with her whole future before her, she wasn't going to let him go. Of course every young woman, specially if she isn't married, gets driven to having an abortion, but that wasn't for her. She was keeping it and what the hell. She was an independent person, she'd no real ties. Her family was all over the place. She'd been brought up by a stepmother. There was only her brother and it's true, she didn't know how he'd take it. But what the hell, he'd just have to live with it.

This was when Anestis got back from his island prison, the shadow of his former self. When questioned about his experiences he would answer vaguely and gruffly, almost in riddles, and deny us the horrific details we were all, in our different ways, eager to hear. As though trying to curb the excrescences of our political and human curiosity; to help us to leave him alone.

Anestis was determined to put a face of calm resignation on his act of surrender — but deep down he bore the scars of the fighter who has given up. The exact opposite of the exaggerated and shallow sensitivity of my father, who went on as if the imposition of the dictatorship had been directed solely against himself. Having no notion or experience of active resistance, it cost him nothing to expostulate against the regime and give expression to his disappointment, most often after a bout with the ouzo bottle, on those occasions when Anestis had failed to fulfil the expectations of my dad's euphoric commitment.

It cost me nothing, either, to pucker my brows and reprove him that committed partisans should never surrender. I even dared to despise Anestis then, for all the sympathy I showed him for his experiences, with no sense of the liberty I was taking in trying to hold him to a cause that had already scarred him for life. With the same scars that in time would come to determine my own mythology.

The circle was complete again — the windbags. My father speechifying all over again, the well-worn tune of the Centre government's five hundred and twelve days

when the country breathed freely, and all about Papandreou's Unyielding Struggle, and sounding off until the
tears came into his eyes at the memory of the march
from Kastri to the palace. My earliest memories of
political debate at home are of the 1963 election. I've got
used since then to hearing my dad describe himself as
a social democrat. In my mind it all got mixed up with
Roland's *L'âme enchantée*: the Unyielding Struggle at
home, vote-rigging by the Right, Papandreou's triumph,
elections again, the apotheosis. From the winter of 1964
to the summer of 1965 we'd rejoiced to be living under
true democracy. Not that any of this made much impact
on my own life. Later I filled in the details — reform of
education, agricultural policy, that sort of thing — but
they meant nothing, by which I mean I'd no need of
them. And when after the street clashes of July '65, a
succession of hopefuls stepped in and out of the prime
ministerial limousine, our excitement knew no bounds
as we anticipated the advent of socialism. I even tried
to recruit Calliope to the cause, but she said the gospel
I preached only put people down. Men are equal in
heaven, not on earth, was her refrain. Because if all
men were equal here on earth, there'd be terrible
unemployment, dearie, and then who'd find work for the
unemployed? For Calliope, so intimately versed in the
hierarchies of the heavens, the idea of equality was
scarcely to be distinguished from degradation. Needless
to say I got very cross with her — it was my first failure
in the art of fitting practice to theory. Later I learned to
see Calliope's simple-minded clichés as merely the most
debased of all the guises in which the capitalist system
rears its head. And even my own stirrings in the direction of equality as nothing but the sickly blooms of

71

bourgeois morality sustained artificially in special hothouses. Like my exclusive school for instance, once my last illusions had gone.

Vangelis had an easy, sarcastic grin on his face; secrets of state, his expression seemed to say, hung clustered like bunches of grapes about his head for the casual plucking; he was so fully *au fait* that he could sit back and enjoy the discomfiture of the rest. He himself was untouched by it all, a detached observer, infinitely indulgent: hadn't he spent a lifetime listening to Telly chewing the fat?

Victoria and Theodore were resolving their most recent differences in the far corner of the room, and when all was said and done Victoria wasn't going to be naive, he'd got to be hers and no one else's. She'd paid good money for him, damn it, and wasn't going to share him. Not long before, she'd lost her temper and told her erring Don Juan to his face: who did he think he was? He was a failure and deep down she pitied him, he was a boorish lout. Then he'd gone, she'd moved heaven and earth to find him, and when she did she'd grovelled and pleaded with him to come back. And it was still going on. I caught a phrase, she wasn't going to stand by and share him with that tart so-and-so. Poor Victoria. She'd point the finger at her girlfriends for being easily hooked. And there wasn't a single one her own age that she hadn't branded a baby snatcher. But when it came to herself, oh no. And only last week Theodore had been holding court at Floka's. According to Elvira a whole clutch of middle-aged boozers had been buying him drinks and getting him oiled. He'd put capitalism in its place, he boasted — he'd buggered it!

I was reduced to listening in on Lucy's efforts to console Tonia. For Tonia had discovered the emptiness of her life and was suffering from depression — to be quite frank she'd even thought of suicide. It affected her writing too, you could tell. She became too vocal about her writing, and I put myself out of earshot. I approached Anestis and my dad, who'd just been left to themselves and were chatting quietly. They made room for me between them. I'd once had a dream in which my first lover had a look of Anestis, those eyes of indefinable colour, the same dark complexion and thoughtful expression, and me curled up like a foetus next to him. But later on I couldn't dream about him. And later still Paul had got me to tell him in every detail how the scenarist had got me on my back.

They clinked glasses the way I used to imagine soldiers did, fists clenched round their drinks in out-of-the-way dives. I was swept along by the comradeship of drink, only I wasn't drunk, I had to listen to them. Anestis got out between hiccups: who was he? What had he fought for, could someone tell him, what price now his youth and his dreams? He was brought up short by his hiccups, and his gulps became drawn-out, like the plucked necks of water birds riding on a swell of tears and sweat. My father began to participate in Anestis' sorrow, but he overdid it; for all his good intentions he was innocent of Anestis' suffering. It dawned on me then that there can be nothing more humiliating than to bare your soul before an ideological outsider. For now and then my father's eyes would betray a hint of pity, of superiority that *he* had never been taken in. And

Anestis would end up being shifty and defensive about the very things he had most right to be proud of.

He turned and put his arm round me; embarrassed, I buried my head in his shoulder. I'd nothing else I could give him at that moment but myself. But Paul's face came vividly into my mind, wearing a quizzical expression. A shadow slid by my feet and suddenly I was afraid. Like walking carelessly on the road when suddenly you trip or a car's horn makes you jump. An incautious moment when you're caught unawares and freeze as though surrounded. Then it passes and you heave a deep breath as though you'd stared panic in the face and got away with it. And you seek refuge in numbness to avoid the despair that lurks in the wake of your one and only effort at self-control.

I said goodnight and went to my room. I heard their voices droning on until sleep overtook me. Throughout the night a young boy with skinned kneecaps kept pointing somewhere I had to go, and I lay curled up in the roadway stuttering with fear as if the soul were being dragged out of me. Further on I heard Anestis weeping and his sobbing merged into Paul's. He held me close and kissed me. He'd opened the lid of a carved box and was offering me all Zoe's gold jewellery. But Zoe came up behind him and stood threateningly, I said to her you needn't worry, I'd never accept anything from Anestis. Then the sea became wild and we ran for safety. I was holding a plate of chips in my hand and turned back to watch the sea, I liked to see it in such a fury. Until I found myself in a dank cellar, shrouded with funeral wreaths that hung on mouldy walls crisscrossed with voracious plants and Paul like an embryo draining out my being; all that night I tossed and turned with the idea that I had to get out.

The days passed heavily; we wanted for no creature comfort. I was level-headed and appalled. Day would dawn, like the yolk of an egg breaking soft and warm, I'd start to yawn, the sky would go cold as the day began to heave like a ship at sea with the nausea of cold, dry egg against my cheeks. I said to myself, How are you Paul? See, I've forgotten all about you, and quailed at the prospect of running into him in the quad. Well, how are things? I'd say and go on into the labs without a backward glance. Or perhaps better: Paul, what a coincidence! I'd be cordial but not too warm, to let him see I'd stopped thinking about him. Or maybe I wouldn't? So what if I no longer loved him, it upset me that he didn't know. I kept saying to myself, time to forget about Paul, you've got to forget about him. I ground my teeth — much more of this and I'd be vomiting blood. Later when I thought it over carefully there was nothing to forget — I couldn't even remember his face exactly.

Calliope fussed over me and clucked tenderly, it was my wisdom teeth coming at last. There's hurts and hurts, she said philosophically. A pain isn't so bad so long as you know what it is; the worst thing's not knowing and then it's such a worry, life's full of aches and pains.... I let the torrent of her words pass over me, idly noticing her wrinkles under the deep layer of powder that covered them day and night. If ever I tried to warn her that she was making herself look ridiculous she'd compress her lips and toss back her head like an Amazon.

Calliope has always had a weakness for reflected grandeur. After all, our house was frequented by captains of industry, politicians, musicians, all sorts of grand folk who never failed to shake her by the hand and make a point of asking after her health, was she keeping well, oh yes quite well thank you. Not forgetting the time when Telly took you with him to the Zappion gardens and his friends mistook you for his mistress. It wasn't as though Calliope had a lot to reminisce about, or could ever forget for instance the skirt with flowers on it, the first thing she'd ever worn that had been cut and made to measure. When at the age of eight she'd been running about barefoot among the olives, her skin and bones covered by odds and ends of castoffs. When she'd been sold into service she'd begun to put flesh on her fingers, how soft and white her palms had become in just a couple of months.

But she wasn't always so long-suffering. Sometimes she'd launch into her grievances against my grandfather. It had been she who had closed his eyes, she that looked after him like a daughter when times were hard. But in his will not a mention of her. And that old vulture Flora deaf to every hint. Well now she too had been gathered up to the Lord, though she thought she'd live for ever. It had been Telly who brought Calliope in from the cold. He'd provided for her and more. Made her practically one of the family he had, with her own room, her wages paid in at the Bank. Had it not been for Natalie with her airs and graces, Calliope would have been without a complaint in the world. But bless her if Telly, when all these girls of good family had been after him for years, hadn't fallen for the olive-oil monger's girl from the wrong end of town. Who never did a hand's

76

turn but paint her nails all day: that was Natalie, the creeping poison in Calliope's life. And lie abed till past midday sometimes, too. Like a broody hen. And finally get up after ten o' clock and start to crow: haven't I laid a splendid egg today?

Calliope could remember my dad, what a fine figure of a man, he'd been still at the exclusive American College then, and a High Court judge's wife had fallen in love with him, what an affair that had been. Calliope had kept watch for them and heard the sounds of their passion through the wall, until vicariously for her too the world had become beautiful in the white heat of their lovemaking, her cheeks flamed like poppies. Next had been the actress, when he was up at varsity, she'd had a way with her, that girl. When the Occupation was on the whole Gestapo had been after the actress but she was in love with Telly, and so Calliope never went short for coffee. These women had been special, they'd had class. It had been all Victoria's fault he got mixed up with her gawky girlfriend and the women of charm and refinement had vanished from the scene.

Then when he'd absconded to Paris she had stayed behind to look after the old man. He'd bought her to skivvy for him in his wifeless state, from her father whom God rest though he didn't deserve it. When one child after another had turned out to be a girl he'd lined them up for distribution among the houses of the better off, and got cash for them. Her sisters had done better than she had, though. Look at Soula. That same year she'd been placed with Uncle Solon. It wasn't long before she got pregnant by the gardener and Uncle Solon, like the man of principle he was, said: You can make an honest woman of her or you can get out. So they got married and he let them have the little garden house, before he died he even passed them the title to it. And now there was Soula, bandy old shrew, with two hulking boys so big if you please, she seemed to get younger with every year that passed. While Calliope had remained forever a maid, half-weeping that the archangels in heaven could have it. Not that she hadn't had the chance. But when the right time came there was no one to take her out. She had had her hands full coping with the old man while he breathed his last.

Later, when we'd returned from Paris, with me a three-year-old delight, she'd taken to me and been devoted to me ever since. Grandfather died and my father had the old two-storey house with its twelve rooms demolished to make way for his very own apartment block. The capital came from his shares in the Mineral Mines. And hey presto, a brand new block of luxury flats arose, five floors high, on the site. That had been the most dangerous period for Calliope. Natalie had set her heart on bringing her mother in from the suburbs and installing her in the flat. And where were they to put her? They had a whole penthouse to themselves, but nowhere to put Calliope, after all she'd done for them. The only room going spare was the one Natalie had earmarked for her mother. But Telly had stood up for her. No, he'd put his foot down, Calliope is closer than a sister to me. Madam was sore as a boil but she couldn't do a thing about it. Her mother went into a two-room flat on the third floor instead. As luck would have it, she'd been the next to go to her Maker, Calliope was rid of her always poking her nose in. Because the daughter had set her mother to snoop after her, Calliope, while Madam was endlessly out visiting. And to add insult to injury they'd brought in a foreign governess, from France. A Catholic who wouldn't shave her legs, but at least she'd got a proper pair of them, not skinny shanks like Natalie's. Once more Calliope's position became precarious, there was talk of making her an outside help. They could be shot of her and when they were at it why not put her on the ground floor, in the bachelor flat? The very idea, that they could even think of burying her down there! But there, Telly was a good man but didn't know his own mind. He could walk off the end of the pier and not notice. Talk to him and he looks at you with that glazed expression, but you're wondering all the time, what's going on in there, is he listening to you or saying his prayers? Not that he'd be likely to say his prayers, mind you, with him not being a religious man and not even ashamed to say so. Thank goodness the French woman, bless her foreign heart, refused point blank to live in the same flat with them, and Calliope's bacon was saved again. But it had been a close thing, Natalie had talked him round, she might have got away with it that time. Snob that she was, she'd have loved being able to brag she had a governess sleeping through the wall from her little precious.

Her tirade was inexhaustible. When I was little she used to lull me to sleep with her grumbling. As I grew older I'd listen without attending to the words. It was like an innocuous, ageing bleating. That's my principal memory of her: indeterminately, profoundly, at once ageing and ageless.

Our dentist thought it nothing serious. The pain was due to the wisdom tooth coming through at an angle, it might be best to have it out. But no hurry, best give it a couple of days for the tooth to break through the gum. I'd fallen so much under the spell of his voice, I was beginning to feel I'd a plane tree growing out of my mouth. Elvira had been on the phone, how about going to a film, but even with painkillers I was in no mood for going out. The pain had induced a sort of hallucination. Image succeeded image with astonishing rapidity. As though one moment I was being catapulted through the air, and the next sunk in lethargy, until I'd jump up again with the aftertaste of a nightmare. My home was a castle with trees and birds, a river and elegant ladies playing Bach in the small hours.

I was whiling away the time as my mother's cronies prepared to call up some spirit. From my room I could hear their ecstatic whispers, Victoria urging them to ask for the spirit of Nikos Beloyannis. At first the others showed some reluctance, the leader of the group was particularly against the idea. But in the end they agreed. They were plunged into darkness and the martyr of the Left, no less, was about to appear in ectoplasmic form for the benefit of the ladies. The teacup was to move across the board to spell the letters: *Down with the dictatorship.* Then, when the ladies had dismissed the spirit and turned on the lights, they would all chuckle happily because Beloyannis had prophesied the end of the dictatorship. As it happened they were all on the same side; one had a boyfriend who was a disgraced royalist, another's husband was a right-winger discharged from his post, and so on.

When they'd gone, I began. A kind of hysteria held me

in its grip, I was so furious, I was ashamed to have her for a mother. Even while I was shouting I became frightened and wished I hadn't started, but it was too late to go back. She fell back in a faint, she came out of it, and Calliope when she'd finished reviving her started to scold me for being cruel. Then she bounced back, she hadn't been the one who'd said to call up the communist and what did she care anyway for the opinion of a communist? And besides she was my mother, I was to treat her with proper respect, even supposing I was in the right. Where had all this hatred come from? She began to cry again and wave her hand about to show me how deeply her feelings were hurt. All those years my God, all those years and all of them wasted.... She'd given up everything for my sake, she wrung her hands together. Oh my God what was that look on my face! Now she knew I hated her. She wasn't putting up with me any longer. She'd had enough of me.

Calliope tried to pull me out of the dining room and I screamed that the time had come. I pressed on, what had she ever given up for my sake? Would she please remind me exactly what it was she'd done for me? But I hated the torrent of abuse that came from my lips, it sounded like soap opera, I'd sunk so low. I was trembling on the brink of catastrophe. I even felt sorry for her, but this only fuelled my anger.

Right on cue in this terrible scene, in came my father. At first he was quite enlivened by the spectacle we made. But then I rounded on him too, and in a moment the miracle happened. Their differences vanished as if they had never been, as they leapt to one another's defence. Late that night with grand words and in tones of excommunication it was resolved that I would leave home. But of course I was still their daughter, in name at least and in the eyes of the world, so they would pay my rent and give me a monthly allowance for expenses. This would keep me from complete ruin. My father laid such stress on the word 'ruin', enunciating it with such an aura of respectability, that I felt ready to spit in his face.

There had been times in the past when I could have killed them for the sick disgust that their antics provoked in me. How could it be, I wondered, that this flaccid man could so influence me, keeping watch like a prophet over my most tender and vulnerable moments? With those narrow shoulders, trim thighs and high buttocks, my father resembled a stag with his almond eyes and sparse eyelashes that lent a tearful look to his face. And on the other side my mother, with her despairing flesh and fallen breasts, pearly blue like the dying fall of the wave at the water's edge, just where the shallows begin and the waves sink exhausted on the sand. I loved my parents like divinities, but the moment had come for them to become flesh inside their stinking hides, and the stench they gave off made my stomach turn — though I could ward it off by despising them, I still had to get clear if I was ever to feel whole again.

So I packed up my things and moved to Ambelokipi. That way I'd save on fares and the wear and tear of the buses. I took my meals in the student canteen. It was even fun to make little economies, to go short of things I needed, to want to buy shoes and not have enough money. I began to feel more relaxed. At least I no longer felt their presence as a threat.

6

WHEN FONDAS suggested to me I should get involved in the resistance — we'd spent a whole afternoon sitting at Piraeus by the Old Customs House, gazing wistfully at the ships flying the hammer and sickle — I was ready to agree at once. And so I found myself one of an underground cell with Angelos and Stefanos, those were the names they used for cover.

Angelos was in his fourth year at Law School. We'd no sooner met than he seemed to set himself up as judge and jury over me. I kept trying to please, but actually it was to please myself I did it. It delighted me to receive back, duly magnified, whatever satisfaction I managed to give to others. I was convinced he was always watching me, absorbing me with his eyes; it was as though he could see into my thoughts as they welled up inchoate, and discard them as useless into oblivion.

It was Angelos' job to write the texts of the leaflets we produced, and mine to type them on to cyclostyle sheets. Then we ran them off on an improvised duplicator. Had it not been for Stefanos, who was a deft craftsman, I doubt whether we could ever have got out a single legible page. I suffered more than anyone from an excess of zeal. I believed it diminished our effort and even harmed the cause if our leaflets failed in the least degree to match up to my expectations of them, with perfect syntax, spelling all correct, and boldly and clearly printed. Sometimes Stefanos would explode: Mother of God, he'd shout. When I should be caring about what was written on the paper and how we were going to get it to people's attention, all I could do was sit and fret about what the thing *looked* like. Did I suppose it was an easy matter to get hold of cyclostyle sheets and printer's ink, was I imagining we were going to send these leaflets to some university professor to be marked out of ten?

He was right of course. As time went on it became more difficult to get supplies. At the stationers' they'd often ask for ID and give us funny looks, you never knew if they were going to call the Security Police. I was the most jittery, and could feel the colour drain from my face beneath the rouge I plastered on so as to try and seem tarty for the shop assistants and divert their suspicions.

Stefanos was right, too, that I hadn't much interest in what the leaflets I typed actually said. I knew the gist of course, but it wasn't important, I never stopped to think about it. What counted for me was the process that transformed a crumpled cigarette paper into a leaflet, duly printed and distributed. Stefanos, on the other hand, would pore over the text, weigh up its words and often suggest to Angelos that so much of *Up with this, down with that* was just sounding off after the event. He thought we ought to make our meaning plainer. Angelos didn't demur, but he kept it from us that the texts as he wrote them were not his own, but were dictated to him. He explained there was no chance yet of the struggle against dictatorship getting past the

84

point of putting out slogans. *Up with this* and *Down with that* it had to be. He'd also often make the point, keeping all emotion out of his voice and trying in his vague distracted way not to implicate us in his personal, private opinion, that for what it was worth, as he saw it we oughtn't to deceive ourselves, what we were doing couldn't ever be a class struggle. Barely even an anti-imperialist one. Stefanos objected, and Angelos would laugh wearily: look what happened to the Liberation Front during the Occupation, a truly popular movement if ever there was one, when once the war was over. But Stefanos wouldn't accept this line of argument, there was nothing you could tell him about the Liberation Front, he said, his parents had been in the thick of it.

I was never sure to what extent Stefanos joined us in printing leaflets because he was committed to class struggle, while we were content to pit our energies against the dictatorship alone. What I do know is that the dictatorship for him wore the blank concrete face of the Fix Brewery. Stefanos must have felt something over and above what we did, and this surely made a difference, just like the sticking plasters all over his fingers from the cuts of broken beer bottles. One day he came to the flat where we were working with his whole hand swathed in bandages. And told us the story, eyes wide with mockery. It had been such a wide cut, he'd gone down on his hands and knees to find the bit of his hand that was missing, all his mates had joined in too, to look for the missing piece of his flesh.

That afternoon I felt cut down to size, no more than a dimple on the face of society. Later on that sense of inferiority became pathological. Even today I find it difficult to listen to workingmen talk about the conditions in which they work. Once a bakery worker from the north said to me: Have you any idea what it was like to work in a baker's in 1929? Ten drachmas a day, two hours' sleep at night, nowhere to lay your head but lice-ridden sacking, nothing to hope for but TB and the mercy of providence. Mixing and kneading dough, shaping loaves, it turned your brains to flour. I listened with impatience, as though he'd only told me all this on purpose so as to upset me. For a long time afterwards I couldn't chew a piece of bread without it setting my teeth on edge, as though I were lacerating his fingers.

But the really terrifying part was when we made the leaflets into bundles and began to distribute them to other cells. Without telling Angelos, Stefanos and I used to keep back a bundle to throw out in the streets ourselves. We knew it was dangerous and foolish; if we got caught the whole organisation would be in jeopardy, as many other cells depended on us for material. But despite the risk, we'd have a go from time to time in one of the poorer, outlying suburbs, once we even went as far as Piraeus and the geraniums in their tin cans fluttered in the breeze outside the low whitewashed houses — and all the rest of it. Each time I was terrified, but with Stefanos for company it was a baptism of fire. He cracked jokes and called me comrade and it was all I could do not to kiss the earth he trod on.

It was at times like these that I used to remember Paul. The year before we'd had our brusque encounter in Solonos Street. I'd been pleased to see him then, and he'd looked as though he felt the same. I'd stood still in front of him as if to bar his way. It was his eyebrows that held my attention, I'd even smoothed back one of them where it had begun to droop and darken his expression.

It had seemed for a moment as though all could go on as before, as if nothing had ever come between us. I'd said to him, let's go somewhere quiet where we can talk. He was sorry, but he'd a lot to do, he looked pale. Good for you, he added, getting into University, we're in the same racket now. The tears rose in my throat as I remembered the clinic we'd once planned to set up together. With an access of bravery I laid hold of his hand, but he gave no sign, his expression was remote. I asked what had become of our room? I'd gone and found the locks changed. One day he'd be able to tell me, he turned to go: Take care of yourself, Myrsini. I'd followed him at a distance, I tailed him through the steep back streets behind Lycabettos, I was out of breath by the time the pavement gave way to steps. He went into a two-storey house, I hung around for a little, then got bored. That was how I'd come to the end with Paul, back in November.

But each time I went out distributing leaflets with Stefanos the memory came back and cast its shadow. It had been with Paul that I had first set foot in these mean streets. And he had shaken my belief in love. I'm not sure now how much I did love him. Even in our happiest moments together I'd felt a secret communion with a love quite other. And perhaps, if we'd been allowed to go our separate ways like all the rest of the world, he wouldn't have become such a part of me. It had been the dictatorship that, right from that first evening, had taken all the petty problems and sexual wretchedness of our relationship and transformed them into devoted patience and longing. It was what came of reading too much romantic fiction, there had been moments when I saw myself as Paul's only lifeline, and had allowed myself to suppose that throughout those months he was in hiding he would have kept me similarly in his thoughts. I had to wait until I heard it from his own lips that it was all over between us.

In my spare time I used to get together with Elvira. That wasn't often, I was busy and she had her Dentistry and Fotis. Fotis was the most well-read communist I ever met. Elvira hadn't a clue, but nonetheless followed him in everything, she ticked me off for being a 'revisionist' because I admired the Soviets. I made a joke of it and found myself condemned to act the fool. At other times I really did see red. Couldn't they just mind their own business? It drove me wild when Fotis and his comrades got together and clucked like broody hens to hatch the true, the perfect communist party of the future.

According to Fotis the dictatorship was purely the concern of the bourgeoisie; it wasn't in the interests of the revolutionary avant-garde to dissipate its energies in combatting it. He used proudly to declare that he'd managed to bypass the Lambrakis Youth, he'd not been corrupted by those revisionists. That was Fotis all over, and that was the level of our arguments. Politics apart, he was conventional to a fault. From what Elvira used to tell me, he seemed a model student, we counted on him to do well in Law.

I didn't get on with him, I'd never known anyone so unbending or so touchy. I couldn't understand what Elvira saw in him. Blackheads covered his face, he had the eyes of an avenging angel. When he attacked the Lambrakis Youth, I tried to prove him wrong and he made me feel as though I were defending my holy of holies. According to him the United Democratic Left was in no position to safeguard the popular movement, it left its own supporters out in the cold. How *can* you raise the cultural horizons of ordinary people in a class society, except through class conflict? And he went on to denounce the United Democratic Left for not coming out and giving its full backing to strikes. By now I was seething: you narrow sectarian, petty bourgeois twirp! But I heard him out in enigmatic silence, and grinned as sarcastically as I could, to annoy him. I didn't know enough, not just to accept or refute the truth of Fotis' diatribes, but even to follow them properly.

At any rate his words fell like a blight on my ideological euphoria. Pitfalls gaped up beneath my feet, faster than I could cover them up. My Marxist thinking — half a dozen pamphlets put out by Themelio, the left-wing publisher — which up till then had been sailing on a tide of childish bliss, had taken a buffeting. Because of course when Fotis talked of the betrayal of socialism in the USSR, *he* wasn't flogging the jackboot of right-wing patriotism, nor did he exercise the critique of the Right, like my father, and of course he wasn't talking about nylon socks for sailors or detergents· for housewives. A consistent Stalinist, as he called himself, he was precise with facts and figures, an endless amount of them, and fluent in elucidating events both before and after 1956, as he juggled dazzlingly with the pronouncements of Lenin, Stalin and Mao — behold and your eyes will be opened, his gestures proclaimed, by which time my head was full of doves turning into rabbits and umbrellas into handkerchiefs.

Once a fortnight we'd go to a workingmen's taverna in

Kesariani and sip cheap wine. Our group included Thodoros. Thodoros showed us his bullet scars — he'd been a *kapetanios* in the urban division of the Popular Army, but since then had fallen on hard times, with a shrill wife and two daughters, by hook or by crook he was going to marry them off with decent dowries. He got maudlin, and brought a lump to our throats; we shared vicariously in a community of suffering, adrift among ineffable visions, we flung our arms round one another and gave ourselves up to all the great victories the Left might have won — we certainly wallowed in it. And to this same taverna years later, when Democracy had been restored to Greece, we would come to celebrate the wedding of Fotis and Elvira. And pin red carnations on our lapels. That was when they accused me of being like the romantic anarchists at the turn of the century. Perhaps they were right; for my part I was sustained by a warm glow of cynicism for all those great men of the Party sitting round a table in a workingmen's taverna in Kesariani. And beneath the cypresses the ice began to break. Behind Tsitsanis' place where they played old-time bouzouki, was the rifle range, site of so many war-time executions; we'd sing our hearts out with the old resistance songs of the Left. We could have been cut out of a TV picture, in the middle of an ad for coca-cola or cigarettes. Except for the red carnations, they made us different, but anyway we were still living under the Junta then, that's why in those days I was really frightened by Elvira's lack of discretion, whatever bits of gossip came her way she'd pass on to all and sundry. But always taking good care of number one. Even today if I'm in her house and she offers me coffee I need to think carefully before I answer, I know she's liable to grudge even a cup of coffee. Not that she'd ever refuse a favour, if you asked. On the contrary she'd be only too eager, but her eagerness would have a bad smell, you'd know you'd have to repay the debt four times over. She's always had that faintly scheming air, that's what I can't stand. Not the fact that she's mean, but that she always seems to have an ulterior motive. Never mind the way she'll let you pay for her ticket every time, and stand there behind you taking no notice. But if she's in front she'll only get her own. That apart though, Elvira's OK, she has her good side. And for all the times that she took advantage of me, she did stick by me while I was splitting up with Paul and when I left home. She can be so caring, she wins me over completely. Maybe she even liked things to go wrong for me, so that she could show off how kindhearted she is. She manages to make us all oblivious to her faults, I've even caught myself often enough thinking I've been unfair to her, that I'm the one that's tightfisted.

Be that as it may, she often scared me in those days, when I heard her prattling on. It all got mixed up too, did I remember So-and-So, well now he was working for such-and-such a resistance group, someone else we knew had made a statement to the emissary of Amnesty International, one by the name of Beckett, denouncing the tortures that were going on at Security Police Headquarters, and then had I heard the latest joke about bald Colonel Pattakos, or which of our circle had got into bed with whom, your mum's gone and bought a poodle and taken it to the vet to have its tail docked, and all of a sudden my father had gone off to London with Lucy.

I tried to warn her once, but she blew up in my face. I couldn't convince her that such talk was dangerous, that walls have ears. She wasn't taking that sort of garbage from me. Who did I think I was? I was the one that stuck out like a sore thumb, with all that hush-hush mumbo-jumbo I went in for, I was about as discreet as a red rag in the bullring. She rounded on me with everything she'd been saving up for months. I took it all meekly — she was the only friend I had then. But we only tolerated one another. I began to be bored by her and couldn't think of anything to say; I daresay she felt the same. We talked about clothes or the latest thing that had come into this or that boutique. I found it tedious to sit sunning ourselves in the square and affect to be superior about the ladies going by with their lap dogs. And be told the exact length of Fotis' organ.

Elvira's parents knew mine, they had friends in common and our mothers would often meet round somebody's bridge table. I got titbits of news through Elvira, the snippets that had escaped the watchful vigilance of Calliope, who used to come and tidy my room once a week. Calliope! In all my bleakest hours her face brought me hope and a degree of comfort. My mother, she now told me, had taken up with a gigolo. I'd no regrets about leaving home, but sometimes nostalgia would cast its shadow. It had been three months since I'd seen them, but I couldn't make up my mind to take the first step. Fondas said I should make it up with them — I could still keep my distance if I wanted to. I wouldn't have minded, had they but shown the slightest interest in seeing me. I was hurt that they didn't appear to care. Whenever Calliope tried to bring my name into the conversation, my father would hold up his hands in a gesture of finality. This I found monstrous of him. Deep down, though, I also felt vindicated. I'd long guessed that his love for me was a love born of necessity. A psychiatrist friend had once said jokingly that my father saw me as an adversary. Because I was a constant reminder to him, he went on, that he was a father, and therefore adult. Which was as much as to say that my father was afraid of growing old, i.e. of dying. No doubt when they probed back into my father's childhood they'd discover the catastrophic influence exercised over him by Victoria. He had vivid memories of her riding her horse at the gallop, when it was more than he could do to keep his place in the saddle without vertigo. Later on it had been she who had introduced him to my mother, and egged him on, dangling her before him like a lace collar, that maddens you to crumple it. The two cousins, my father and Victoria, had been so affronted by her starched virginity, they had laid a bet between them, and set to work to deflower her with despatch. At this time my father used to tease my mother, telling her she was like an onion, you could peel off layer after layer and never get anywhere. Afterwards, when he married her, he felt cheapened. Although Victoria has never reminded him of the bet, there are moments even today when he can detect a reproving irony in her glance. And to this day he has nightmares. And I, because I've a strong resemblance to my godmother, especially about the eyes, intimidate my dad especially. I make him feel a failure.

My mum had adopted an attitude of grieving motherhood. And let it be known that she was waiting for an apology. But I was never going to be a prima ballerina as once, when she had played a more tender role, she had dreamed, and tried to instil so many talents into me. From the moment when I knew that all my patient application to dance was doomed to failure, I'd learned to live with what I was. A good student, and though I knew my potential for disaster, I still felt profoundly elated. I lost my scholarship by a whisker at the end of my first year. But what I remember most is the high marks recorded in my course book. I suppose even then I was inwardly getting ready to shit on their universities.

The sun rode high in the sky; tourist coaches were parked in phalanxes outside the National Museum. Tourists were herded in and out in groups, the sight made me feel sick. Lumps of parboiled flesh with greasy hair, that was how they looked to us, they gave us a sense of the superiority of our race and made us feel like heroes. Stefanos thought it would be fun to take up squatter's rights on the steps and bar their way with a staff. Wouldn't it be great, I told him, living with all that gold in there, with the Mask of Agamemnon for company, how peaceful. But while we were chatting a shadow fell upon us. We were bitter about the people who'd turned our country into a glorified museum — more of a doss house really! Stefanos added.

While we were waiting for Angelos, we talked. Nothing seemed to be changing; our minds had gone blank. In a state of lethargy, while the split in the Party went on around us, we stuck by the Rigas Pherraios group, and Rigas Pherraios was at that time being hammered by the Security Police. We'd kept out of the split — who would have cared what we thought anyway? — and concentrated on our leaflets and the feverish excitement of the job. We were the good kids, the ones who stuck obediently to their posts. We talked of Vietnam, and our admiration for Guevara. Not long before I'd translated a poem of Che's dedicated to Castro before the start of the revolution: *fiery prophet of the dawn*, it began, something like that, and there were times when tears would come into our eyes as we repeated the English words, *We'll be there, hearts full of pride, swearing to win or die.* But we Greeks had Aris Velouchiotis from the civil war to call our own; he'd never been much in fashion, but he'd belonged to us from a long way back and we brought him to life in our dreams and thumbed through dictionaries to discover that Velouchi means a spring of water.

We'd had enough by this time, and began to talk about ourselves. Stefanos' real name was Dimitris. The more we talked, the more things began to slip out about our real lives, why not open up completely we thought, if we got to know one another properly it would only strengthen the bonds between us. We felt very strong, we weren't worried that one of us might break down under torture, if we were caught, and betray the other.

Dimitris was still haunted by the massed slogans for *constitutional rights* and the choking memory of tear gas from the troubles of July '65. On the day of the coup he'd gone straight into hiding. For three months he'd kept moving from one friend's house to another. By the time his friends had tired of sheltering him he was tired of keeping on the move himself: give it a go at home in broad daylight, he'd decided, and see what happens. The police had forgotten about him. They'd gone to the house the first time and smashed the place up, pulled his sister by the hair, slapped his mother across the face,

95

stolen a camera that belonged to him, and shipped his father, an old man of seventy, out to one of the prison islands. Next time they'd played it cool, nonchalantly flicking their worry-beads and dangling keys, they'd picked their noses with their little fingers to show how bored they were. They'd left him an ultimatum and gone. The third time they hadn't even come themselves but sent a doddering lackey with a written warning. After that they'd forgotten about him. There had been so many arrests, they'd run out of prison space for all of them.

So he'd come home and nobody bothered him. He'd gone to the machinist's where he worked and asked for his job back. The boss had been sarcastic: *Isn't* this a nice surprise, and what can we do for *you* sir? A machine shop ain't a free-for-all you know, unemployment was high, he said, off you go now, and showed him the door. Gave him a thousand drachmas out of the goodness of his heart, not a word about his leave allowance or Easter bonus. It had ended in a shouting match, on yer bike scum; the boss could have had him sent down for good. Dimitris was silenced; not that it mattered, just that in the troubles of July '65 his boss had been in there with the best of them, shouting centre-left slogans in the march from Kastri, the hypocrite.

He'd spent a year after that looking for a job. And ended up loafing outside the borough offices to earn a day's wage on a building site. Some days he'd be disjointing timber, others he'd be digging foundations with a pick. And all the time watching the small ads in the papers. He went to a factory where they'd advertised for an experienced machine operator — sorry, no vacancies, he was told curtly by the doorman. A week later the advert was still there, he went back — sorry, no vacancies, the doorman yawned at him. He offered him the cutting from the newspaper — can't tell you nothin', we ain't taken on no one these three months, came the answer. Then why do they advertise? Why pay to put it in the paper? None of my business, the doorman bristled. In the end Dimitris had lost heart and gone to work as an unskilled labourer in the Fix Brewery. An unskilled auxiliary.

There was a great moving strip, the conveyor belt. The conveyor belt never stopped, they worked in time to it. To one side sat the overseer, keeping an eye on the work force. The conveyor belt must never be left unfed. A labourer would bend and straighten, bend and straighten, as he lifted the crates of empties off the conveyor belt and stacked them alongside. The bottles went into the tub for washing. One by one they emerged again on the conveyor belt. That's the way the Fix beer bottles go, in their hundreds and thousands. The conveyor belt had always to be kept fed. And there was Dimitris, who from the age of twelve had gone from one machine shop to another five times to learn the art of lathe-turning — a good lad to do the donkey work, you don't think I'd teach him the craft and have him demanding a job on the payroll, do you? — there was Dimitris the lathe-turner, working as an unskilled auxiliary feeding the conveyor belt for the bottle cleansing department of Fix Beers. Eight hours a day bending and straightening, loading crates in time to the conveyor belt, ssomething had well and truly snapped inside him.

It gave me a thrill that he was a real worker. Like the textbook middle-class girl who renounces her class, and

97

adamantly believes that the pioneers of change will be the workers, I saw Dimitris as the personification of our cause. I think he realised the aura that he held for me. He went too far sometimes and tended to over-dramatise the difficulties of his life. And there were other times, when he'd patronise us in broken tones, the good samaritans, he called us, who'd been leading the workers up the garden path for years; students, he'd go on contemptuously, what a shower.

Angelos would trot out some Marxist dictum to confound him, usually to the effect that the petty bourgeoisie had always been the vanguard of the working class movement, it was a historical fact. The workers not being, unhappily, themselves in a position to comprehend their world historical role. All that guff about the workers, it's old hat now, so what do you mean going on about the working class? Angelos would end up. This would always get Dimitris on the raw, but it wasn't easy for him to argue his case. Angelos was far gone. His bossy, didactic manner annoyed me. Maybe he was in the right in his arguments with Dimitris, but I had the feeling he was patronising him, if not actually laughing at him.

Dimitris, his head swimming from the fumes of the ink he was spreading on the duplicator, would wipe the back of his hand across his eyes as though to mask tears. I knew he had a lot of respect for Angelos, and looked up to him, but I always had the sinking feeling on these occasions that he was ready to explode. I used to leap in provocatively to defend him, I wanted him to have pride of place in the defence of our cause. In the same way that I'd once been taught to feel compassion for the poor, from Marxism I had picked up that I ought to feel a similar compassion for the workers. And with Dimitris I tried to put this system of justice into effect. I believed the purpose of my existence was to serve the working class, nothing else mattered in my fervour to make myself useful. At night, I used to sink utterly exhausted into a kind of heroic ferment, it was like the effect of an ideological overdose, or resistance fever, that would disappear in the laboratories of the Biology Faculty only to grip me once again as I typed the texts of Angelos' leaflets.

One Sunday Dimitris asked me to his home. That was how I met his father. And it is to that veteran communist that I owe the thought, how different the face of Greece might have been, had it not been for the refugees from Asia Minor.

He'd been born in 1900, in Cappadocia. Orphaned early, he'd taken to the roads and ended up in Smyrna where he worked as practically a galley slave for a local Greek entrepreneur. He'd come of age in a carpentry workshop. And when the Asia Minor adventure began, he'd got carried away and joined up with the Greek army; any day now they'd take Constantinople and King Constantine would be crowned in the church of Saint Sophia. Then came defeat, and mass deportation. At the age of twenty-two he'd begun to make his way slowly down through Greece, learning trades as he went, until finally he'd wound up in Athens.

In '33 he'd joined the Party. Arrested in '35, he was tortured and sent to prison, first on Aegina, then on Corfu. He'd been released in '39. Then had come war against the Italians in Albania, and after that the Nazi Occupation, the great famine, months of hiding. In '42 he'd taken to the mountains, to Parnassos. And served in the Popular Army of the Resistance, second regiment. Wounded in the arm, he'd been lucky not to die of gangrene. In hospital he met Sister Olga, one of the nurses. By the time he was convalescent they'd been married by the revolutionary priest from the next village. Then they'd gone their separate ways: he to his regiment, she to her wounded. Came the liberation. Time to go down to Athens, to walk free again in Constitution Square. Through Lamia, Livadia, Thebes the second regiment of the Popular Army came down — and there spread out below them from the foot of Mount Parnes was Athens, the city already lost to them. On December 3rd in the rain and freezing cold they handed in their weapons. The next minute the British had been after them. Back to square one, on the run once more, it was enough to make the very stones weep. Then back into hiding; scapegoats once again and the shoddy truce of Varkiza like a millstone round their necks, how much more could the soul of man endure? In '47, with 'Napoleon the Great' in charge of public order, he'd been arrested again and brought before a military tribunal. Poor Olga spent all her time going backwards and forwards to the Averof prison, lining the lawyers' pockets with gold sovereigns — it had been at about this time that my father had crossed the palms of government officials and gone into voluntary exile in Paris. Dimitris' father was moved to the Itzedin prison on Crete. His sentence ended in '58. When he got home he found Dimitris, now rising fifteen, flogging from one machine shop to another, Irene in the fifth class at primary school, and his wife working as a char. Kindhearted neighbours would sometimes bring him odd jobs, could he repair a table or a chair? He'd resumed his Party activities. That was all he got in the way of recognition for his services. Every May Day he'd pin a carnation to his lapel, but the rest of the year he spent sitting idly by the stove and in summer beneath the mulberry tree outside their shack.

I found him with his friend from Epiros, drinking spirits. Olga muttered crossly, the doctor had forbidden him ouzo, salt food and cigarettes. After the latest ravages of prison on the island he'd gone downhill a lot. But comrade Gregory wasn't going to be held back. You know what it's like to remember and not be able to give it up? Nothing left to do, is there, but tell the same old stories, it helps to take the bitter taste out of them. No use saying I told you so, or trying to pin blame and paper over cracks, a waste of time. Now where could I have read that? And do you know why it is a man sleeps soundly in his bed when his duty's done? 'Cos next day he'll back at his post. Doing his duty all over again. The cause never ends, comrade. The cause is like the sea.

Olga came up and tried unobtrusively to whisk away the ouzo jug. The man from Epiros struck up with the tune: *Rifles crash on either hand, Aris is marching with his band*, but his voice failed him, he was racked with a fit of coughing — and then he began to intone, like a dirge: see here now, we could talk of self-respect and respecting others till the cows come home, but had we any idea what these things really meant? Our mothers

were to blame, they'd fed us on the milk of slavery.
Taught us to bow the knee to God, the king, the rich
neighbour, the priest, the schoolteacher, the policeman,
the justices' clerk. Anyone that stepped out of line, that
dared raise his head, he meant, got caught in the trap:
he'd be going against his mother. And for the rest of his
days, the shame of failure, he'd broken the unwritten
law, you see. And what good did that do? Just look and
your eyes will be opened. Blows raining down thick and
fast. And for why? Why d'you think, who was it made
you put on your Sunday best before you went on a demo?
There was no way out of the trap, you were nothing but
a pariah if you went against your mother. So up we gets
and duly puts on our Sunday best and takes to the
streets like little gentlemen, to stop up the mouths of
Reaction, to put a stop to the bosses. Because all the
years your mother dandled you on her knee, she fed you
on grovelling to the bosses. We'd wet ourselves to obey.
Obey orders, do what we're told. Talk about Party
discipline, that's not discipline at all, it's crap. Proper
discipline now, that calls for judgement, you've got to
know what you're doing. We never had nothing like
that. It didn't take a lot to make us crack, or bugger off
when nobody was looking, make a balls up and then try
to cover up afterwards. We'd wet ourselves to believe.
And we do believe too, like me to tell you for why? To
get a bit of peace. So we can settle down and take things
easy. It only needs for times to change, and we go to
pieces. Always blame the other fellow. Like what happened to Zachariadis. While Stalin was alive they sat up
on their hind legs and begged. Then Stalin dies, the
scum floats to the top and everything falls apart. Our
own lot jumping on the bandwagon, the same people

that started the flag-waving for Zahariadis, they were the first to ditch him too. That's the sort of people we are. But to really believe, can you imagine what that's like? It's a ferret that gnaws at your vitals every hour of the day and night and keeps putting you to the test and never lets you go. Not just spouting half-digested garbage like a lot of these namby-pamby ideologues, party secretaries maybe, still doesn't mean they can't be wrong. Because if all those people had crept out of the woodwork at the beginning and stood up and said enough, we wouldn't be in this pickle now.

I stared at them transfixed, the endurance etched into their faces made a profound impression on me, but inwardly I was seething. As though their features had been branded with the innate sanctity of the persecuted, something that for years now has been an inexhaustible component of communism and its lore in Greece. I don't know if other peoples have so come to associate the endurance of the martyr in the face of arrest and torture with the idea of communism. But it was the first time I had encountered this blend of abject fatalism and fierce, unwavering determination, these people aroused in me sorrow and anger together, I was at once fascinated and repelled. One moment I'd be won over by their fortitude, the next I'd begin to despair of their wretched condition.

From Dimitris' mother I got to know the story of her life under the Occupation. She showed me the white streak in her hair and told me how it had changed colour one night in the Averof prison, how afterwards she'd taken to the mountains and how she'd spent her childhood years under canvas. With nowhere to go they'd made a pitiful progress out of Piraeus; the first

103

night they pitched camp, she remembered, it was pouring cats and dogs, we children carried the bundles on our shoulders, Mother went in front, the bottom of her skirt all caked with mud as thick as your finger. She had the baby in her arms and from time to time kept raising her eyes towards heaven. Father came last, with his greatcoat round him, coughing and stumbling, we lost him after a month, from consumption. Me and my little sisters, bundled up in rugs made from old remnants, the rainwater dripped on our noses and we'd no idea where we were going — with the wrath of the Lord over our heads and the bundles of clothes bumping our shoulders. And when we'd made our camp and put Father in the ground, then we tried to pick up the pieces of our lives.

As I listened I was reminded of the story about Alexis and my mother. For Alexis and my mother had been in love. But Alexis had been a communist, while my mother had been brought up to take an egg raw for breakfast, by aunts who never ceased to enumerate the beneficial effects of the egg upon the skin, the voice and the eyes; in those distant days when my mother used to worship Hans Jarray in the *Diary of a Girl in Love* and wanted terribly to be like Lily Darvace. Alexis had chosen to tread a path of his own, where my mother was incapable of following. He departed for the mountains, leaving her to read novels and brood until the time came when she would meet my father. And my father would recite verses to her. And carve their initials on a royal pine tree at Kifisia — but on the evening when she'd introduced him to Lucy a star had fallen. Could it have been Alexis' revenge? my mother would often wonder bitterly in her own diary.

104

7

I LAY IN BED reading. I wasn't enjoying the book, but it's a habit with me, once I start, to read something to the end. This was kitchen sink stuff. In my overtired state I couldn't bring myself to turn over the page, but sleep wouldn't come either, though I knew I'd have to be up again at crack of dawn. To type leaflets before the start of classes. I put my hands firmly over my eyes and tried counting, but before I'd got to thirty the faces lined up in a hazy void, a gelatinous substance was being applied to my stomach, the bathroom tap was dripping. And above all Angelos. Who said he'd be better typing it himself, with that dry laugh of his, and all because I'd got the line spacing wrong. What if I'd had any greater responsibilities! And what did I think I was doing sticking in lines of poetry? These were serious leaflets, weren't they, not a girl's album. I retorted had he perhaps heard of the national poet Solomos or did he prefer Tsitsanis and the songs of the down-and-outs, the *rebetika*? For he was always humming them under his breath and I'd never liked them, I felt they polluted my soul. But Angelos had a way of making me feel small. Every time as I typed the cyclostyle sheet I was in terror of making a mistake, I couldn't bear it when he ticked me off. I'd curl up in despair, as his eyebrows met in the middle and a frown puckered his forehead.

I had fallen into a stupor that wasn't quite sleep, when the doorbell rang three times. It was our signal. I got out of bed crossly — these late-night visits had become a habit of Fondas'. Who then bored me senseless, for Fondas on top of everything else was a poet. And would drop in to recite his poems to me, all vibrant with passion. When I could bear it no longer and told him what I thought of them, he took it badly and complained that I didn't understand poetry! But unfortunately for me I gave him what he wanted. I took pity on him in that state, as though I were the one who had written those poems. For a moment I considered not answering, but he rang again, more urgently this time, and I felt apprehensive.

Fondas stood in the centre of the room, the harder he tried to maintain his composure the whiter he became as he stood beneath the bare bulb, and I braced myself with thinking, Courage in adversity, comrade, and tried to summon up the fortitude of Dimitris' father. Fondas was flinging his arms about in an effort to order his thoughts, as though winding himself up. My knees turned to jelly, my last ounce of spirit was seeping away through my feet and I had a momentary vision of my spirit flitting about the room like a moth, it was a notion of Calliope's that the spirits of the dead come back as moths to beat in frenzy against the lights on a summer's evening. We had to go and empty the flat, destroy every trace of our presence there. For heaven's sake sit down, I said to him, and let's plan rationally, tell me what's happened. He stared at me, but without looking at me, his eyes were fixed in terror on *Guernica* behind my shoulder. They've arrested George, he said, his sister told me an hour ago. Four men in plain clothes had burst in and taken him. They'd turned the house upside down, searching for weapons, pulled the stuffing out of the mattresses and hit his mother in the stomach with a rifle butt when she tried to intervene and stop them taking him away, the woman had slumped to the floor as George had been bundled out. Who was George? Angelos of course. A chill ran down my spine, to think that not until this moment ... I was livid with him.

It had never occurred to me that we could be caught. I knew about the tortures carried out by the Security Police, I knew the jails were full, but that some day it might be my turn had never really entered my head. Only in exalted moments when I used to square up to them mentally with impunity, whistling forbidden marching songs under my breath. But not once had I asked myself in all seriousness, how would I behave if I ever found myself on the notorious Fourth Floor? I listened rooted while Fondas talked on. We had twenty-four hours — that was how long he reckoned George could hold out before he talked — twenty-four hours to clear the flat and go into hiding. But oh dear what an unlovely boy was Fondas, if only he'd had a sense of humour. I'd never once heard him crack a joke, he only ever said things that frightened me. Going into hiding meant a slow death by asphyxiation. Like being buried underground and breathing through a reed, like the Viet Cong I'd read about last year. I was ready to scream as he stood like that with his arms flailing, as though breasting a sea of his imagination and trying to push me to shore. He said he'd taken his dad's car, but his dad didn't know, we'd have to hurry. I threw a coat over my shoulders. A light rain was falling and the slippery surface of the road glistened.

While we were packing up all our papers and tubes of printer's ink — it had been just the other day I'd bought our latest batch of clandestine equipment — our overriding concern was what to do with all this stuff. I felt the greatest pang of all for the rubber stamps that Dimitris had carved out with a shoemaker's awl. They'd come out very well, but they'd cost him the skin off his fingers getting them right. There was nowhere to hide it all. The typewriter was another problem. I suggested taking it with us. I don't know, let's sort the room out first, then we'll see. We took the stuff down to the car in the suitcase, we'd find a place. Not likely, he said, have you gone out of your mind? Best thing's to chuck it all down a manhole, I know of one a couple of streets away that doesn't have a grating. We were falling over ourselves in our agitation, we could have been sworn enemies. His neck had somehow got longer and he reminded me of the stuffed crane in the house at Kifisia. How I'd used to hate that bird when I was little, I'd never miss a chance to tweak out one of its feathers when nobody was looking, it scared me so. And the more objections he managed to think of, the more determined I became to hang on to our stuff, and determination gave me courage.

Before he started the engine he drew me tightly to him. Well, we've made it so far, he said. I threw my arms round him with relief. I could hear his breathing and mine, we briefly kissed. But then I thought, with a pang of vexation, it had been an easy chance, he was taking advantage of me, and I pulled back abruptly. As he stared at me, hurt and embarrassed, my head began to clear — come on, this minute, we've got to warn Dimitris. He started the car. The local taverna was beginning to spill out into the street and we heard a raucous chorus from inside. I realised my eyes were moist. I said, couldn't we wait a bit, Dimitris has to get up at five anyway, do we have to burst in on him when he's asleep? I was sorry now for being abrupt with him. He looked at me — but what could we do for two and a half hours? His hands clung limply to the wheel. In his mind's eye Dimitris was going to save us. We could find a hiding place for all this, I suggested. Shouldn't we have had somewhere ready all this time, for this kind of emergency? I daresay we should, he hissed through his teeth, and a lot of other things too. But what mattered now was to get the car back. If his father found out he was capable of going to the police. I started to count up the friends who might take us in and realised with impotent fury that there wasn't a single one. I'd never time to wash my hair for having so many friends, but at a time like this there was no one I could turn to. Then Fondas spoke, his voice light with relief. He'd got it. We'd try his Uncle Stelios, and he put his foot down.

As we went he told me about his Uncle Stelios, who'd been a political prisoner once and been through it all himself. In the end he was saved by losing his reason. When they'd let him out he'd had to spend two months in a psychiatric clinic. His relatives, the better ones anyway, had gathered round, one had found him a job, another a wife. They'd taken care of him and supported him when he'd not a spark of life left himself, he'd had nightmares of the prison camp for years, the blue sea of the island: curse the sea for a whore, and the screams of the prisoners mingled with the howls of the guards. That was why we could count on his uncle. He'd always been one of us, though of course practical necessity and

109

his obligations to the family had kept him rather out of things, Uncle Stelios had always been one of us; you only had to say USSR and his face lights up. And Fondas could remember when Gagarin flew into space, and the celebrations had lasted for a month at Uncle Stelios'.

I sat and waited in the car, my eyes intent on Fondas' silhouette on the frosted-glass door, praying that all would be well. Lights came on in the house, Fondas disappeared inside. I counted, to make the minutes pass more quickly. I watched him come down the steps with his tail between his legs. Without a word he got in beside me. I waited for him to tell me, and began to tremble all over, it was obvious his uncle had refused. The house was plunged back into darkness, as though swallowed up by the depths, like a ship breaking in two. For the last few minutes I'd been staring fixedly at the light, expecting it to herald our salvation, just as though we'd been adrift in mid-ocean, it served me right for giving way to that sort of thing. But now the lights were out once more in the house, its people returned to sleep, Fondas wept in impotent fury against his uncle, and his father's jet-black Mercedes with the doctor's sticker on the windscreen, became a coracle tossed this way and that in the storm.

His uncle had accused him of political immaturity, his principles would not allow him to help us. Because, and Fondas ought not to forget this, he'd cocked things up badly. What were all these Party squabbles, libels, denunciations? So listen to me: go away and read *Dialectical Materialism* with care, maybe that'll help to sort you out.

His voice in my ears became a kind of deafening thrumming that engulfed me, how was this possible?

Paul's crying came back to me, on the eve of the coup. But now Fondas! When all was said and done, he was the one who'd taken on the role of instructor in our group, and he couldn't listen to Elvira's Fotis without changing colour and bristling all over. I felt myself launched suddenly into space, what were we doing here rushing about in the middle of the night? With a catch in his voice he rambled on: OK so I haven't taken sides in the split — does that make it *my* fault we've now got two Communist Parties? And he denounced his uncle as a Stalinist lackey. My temples throbbed, he made me feel like a performing bear, led by a ring through the nose at fairgrounds, whoa there, give us a trick, and afterwards thankee sir ... thankee kindly as the hat went round.

Then he pulled himself together and we started off. I was surprised to find he knew where Dimitris lived. Later it turned out that Dimitris' mother had worked as a char in Fondas' house. We sat ourselves in the little kitchen while the coffee was put on to boil. Poor Olga made a great fuss of Fondas, stroking his hair and calling him her dear. She had caught on at once and launched into anecdotes of the Occupation to boost our morale. Even when Dimitris came in she kept this up and got on his nerves — give it a rest Mother, it's the middle of the night, all that religious stuff has gone to your heads, give it a rest can't you! Then he asked us what the trouble was, his manner brooked no nonsense. His hair was all tousled, fresh from sleep, I thought he was going to let us have it. But no. He caught my eye and I felt better. Throughout the time Fondas took to tell the tale I could detect a twitch of mockery on his lips, but he listened patiently. He accepted Fondas' conclusions and conceded we had done the right thing, though rather hastily. Since we'd no means of knowing what had led to George's arrest — supposing, for instance, they'd had a tail on him, then we certainly would have been behaving like prize idiots in going to the flat, we'd have walked straight into a trap. Since that hadn't happened, probably George had been the victim of a tip-off, which meant that for the time being we were safe, but it still wouldn't do any harm to lie low for a bit. As he spoke he sipped his coffee almost calmly. No question that he might go into hiding. Fondas argued, irritable with anxiety. Dimitris turned on him angrily, whose shoulder did he propose to lean on then? As a unit we were disbanded. There was no underground network capable of protecting us now. His father was in a bad way, his mother was at breaking point, she'd taken him to one hospital after another. What were these people to live on? On the pittance Irene earned? As for us, we should keep our eyes open around the university and the student haunts, it was sticking out a mile, that's where the rot must have started.

It was time for him to go to work and Fondas didn't dare insist further. Dimitris persuaded us finally that there really wasn't any need for him to go into hiding. We worked out how to keep in contact, and numbly went our ways. He left first on his motor scooter. The noise died away at the corner of the street, I was full of vexation. If ever I asked him to accept something from me he'd refuse as if I had the plague. And once he'd said, patronisingly, wasn't it enough I'd thrown in my lot with the Left, let's not become the philanthropist as well. Later he'd apologised, he hadn't wanted to offend me. It was just that he didn't much care for that sort of

112

thing — it doesn't suit you love, better chuck it down the drain, if it gets on top of you.

Day was breaking as we drew up outside Lucy's house, still burdened with the suitcase that I obstinately refused to empty down a manhole. Mary her maid showed us into a room. She was unwilling to wake the mistress at once, she'd had to take valium to get to sleep. She put some milk on to boil and offered us biscuits. She smirked with a knowing air, God knows what she imagined. When we were alone Fondas started up again, was my passport up to date? We'd have to get out, before our names were posted at the airports and frontiers, we'd have to escape abroad. The more worked up he became, and profusely sweated, the more I found myself wondering what I was doing mixed up with him in this escapade. I even felt sorry for him, but I was repelled by his panic. Could he be doing it on purpose to create an atmosphere between us? As though he were acting out a crisis that had long ago taken shape in his imagination.

Lucy's reception of us was as I had anticipated. Her house was ours, she declared. She would take it on herself to notify Fondas' parents. I made her promise not to say anything to mine, but only to Calliope to say that I'd gone off on a trip and hadn't had time to say goodbye. She agreed of course; and contented herself with reproaching me for having been out of touch for so long, from home OK, that she could understand, but not to keep in touch with her ... that she found heartless of me — too unkind, my pet, and sighed.

Lucy, I realised with hindsight, had always had a way

of pulling the wool over my eyes. I lay as if hypnotised under her tragic, enigmatic spell. She had a way of firing my admiration for everything about her, often with the greatest of ease, by the simple expedient of taking my part in every eventuality. It flattered her to think that she alone was capable of understanding what made me tick. And so naturally enough this cast her in the role of fairy godmother — who else could come to my rescue with her magic wand and a selection of garbled maxims, mostly culled from Freud? I don't want to belittle her, but there really had been a time when I had clung to her skirts. Then as I'd got older and grown away from her, increasingly it had taken all my energies to resurrect out of the ashes of my past love for her something vaguely bittersweet.

Alexis' portrait gazed down at us with tragic severity, poised you'd think to break out of his frame and scold us roundly, as we floundered about to play our farcical parts. He had been still at school when he joined the Party and later as a student at the Polytechnic had declaimed, *Not from the womb of Fortune hurled, but Maker of a brand new world* ... before departing for the mountains. Lucy, albeit never actively involved, in her affection for her beloved brother had never been far away either. One evening, after the liberation, there had been a knock at the door, the two of them had tripped over one another breathlessly on the stairs to reach it, and there stood Alexis the guerrilla hero, the light of the world. And that October evening their mother had played the piano for the last time. At daybreak Alexis had left; he'd disappeared without trace. Until they learned he'd left his bones on the peaks of Grammos.

114

From Lucy's point of view it was as well that the family had private means, she had been able to gather up the pieces without the pressures of earning a living as well. She always did adapt easily. Though it's possible that if she hadn't had money she might have managed better. Alexis had never been able to make her see this. Together they'd once visited a shanty town on the outskirts of the city, she couldn't remember its name, only that Alexis had had some Party work there and had taken her along. For those had been the days, before the war this was, under the dictatorship of Metaxas, when he'd still had hopes of converting her. All the way back he'd kept explaining to her about capitalism and the ruling class. He'd gone on and on; until suddenly he'd felt she was miles away and broken out, deathly pale, with all manner of accusations. And when he'd calmed down — you've got it all wrong, she'd said to him, you've got it quite wrong. She wouldn't mind losing all she'd got, she could live in one of those shacks, so long as she could find happiness. She could adapt, she declared, she could adapt even to having nothing at all, no she wasn't scared by poverty, I swear it Alexis, I could live on air, just so long as I knew happiness. But Lucy had seen, to her consternation, that instead of being mollified by this — she still felt bitter about it after all those years — he'd gone off at the deep end and called her an idiot, bring on the airy spirits a great panacea that was, and he'd jeered sarcastically at her for the rest of the way home.

Later it had all worked out to take your breath away. She got engaged to a lawyer in the right-wing National Rally who'd had a sheltered upbringing. She'd been keen to marry him too, despite their ideological differences, she'd been making some hard resolutions and

115

was determined to make a go of her life. Those had been glamorous days, trotting from one embassy reception to another, Lucy had shone in those circles. But just when she'd begun to muse philosophically on the impossibility of true understanding, man's great support in adversity, and to console herself that she'd find peace at last by the side of her lawyer and the pain over Alexis' loss was beginning to ease, she learned from a cast-iron source that her fiancé was on the payroll of the CIA — and that had been more than she could take. It had been just at this time that we returned from Paris. And no doubt my father had exerted his influence, too, to make her break off the engagement.

Now she was telling us with a distraught air of how she had been dreaming just now of Alexis. Actually it was his photograph, the one hanging there on the wall. She had reached out to touch him but had been afraid the yellowed paper might disintegrate. Then she'd heard his laugh, she went on, an icy laugh, and she'd struck at the walls and the walls were suddenly made of glass, empty mirrors. Then he'd appeared as he'd been that night when he came to say goodbye. His left knee had started to sag, the weight of his body had followed, with its crossed bandoliers. With a screech of the wooden floorboards, the double doors had opened wide and then closed and the photograph still hung there, laughing ferociously at her.

Fondas listened spellbound. Now and then he shot me a meaning glance, as if to make sure I shared in the magic aura that enveloped him. It was Lucy's eyes that

116

held my attention, they were like the eyes in a child's tracing when you try to bring out a dreamy expression. As I was staring, I caught a whiff of incense and thought it must be her mother with the censer at the icons. My mouth went dry, this house was haunted. The stillness got to me, the kind of stillness that lies in wait for you just before the shriek of terror, before the ghost in broad daylight, when every creak of the door is a warning to be on your guard. Mary the maid went past with a disembodied air, as if communing with apparitions.

Fondas seemed to feel at home in this ambience. I got up and kissed Lucy, I put my arms around her with an attempt to be bright and tender. But as I did so I felt afraid some unpleasant memory would return at any moment which, if it did, might help to lift the burden from my shoulders. And this vague sense of threat began to solidify into a pang of loss; suddenly I felt the pain, like a physical mutilation, of missing my mother's hand — without warning a picture out of the infant-school reading book shot into my mind, of a child nestling on its mother's lap while she tenderly strokes its hair, the whole picture came vividly to life for me, as I remembered my own mother panting in the lap of Franz. Later when Franz had gone, I lay in wait to see how she would take it. And here I vindicated my father at last, in his preference for impeccably upper-class women. Women who knew how to preserve their mystique. The alternative, he used to say, is like making love to a consumer catalogue. He could never stand my mother's pathetic weakness for buying things, her craving to amass handkerchiefs, perfumes, trinkets, for all the world as though the wretched woman had taken a vow against renouncing her lower-middle-class origins.

And it was in this that Lucy most strongly resembled Ava Gardner, not just in the dimples of her cheeks. My dad used to say that from the colour of a woman's knickers you could tell everything about her. Lucy's knickers were transparent and flesh-coloured. My mother went in for the most expensive lacework. Not that I took my father's witticisms too much to heart, but I'd been able to see for myself from an early age the pathetic absurdity that lurked in the various boxes and parcels that kept turning up in the wake of one of my mother's shopping sprees. It was with a strange sensation of anticipation mingled with embarrassment that I'd watch her try on her newest dress in front of the mirror. I knew my father would scoff, and the certainty of it made me tingle. While Calliope, like a Jezebel by her side, pursed her lips. To win her over, my mother kept making her little presents, she'd hand her down now a skirt, now a scarf, hardly worn, as good as new. But it would have taken more than my mother's castoffs to bridge the gulf between them. Because Calliope was determined that my mother had usurped her own prerogatives, scornfully she used to say: All very well, I mean, for Telly, he's too kindhearted to want to keep tabs. It's her money after all. From the rents of her suburban house that's been knocked down for flats. Week in week out the rents come in, fair enough, and where does all that money go, you may well ask? — bless my soul if she doesn't spend it all on lipstick!

So when Franz disappeared from the scene, I had lain in wait to see how my mother would react. Every morning on the phone to Liza — my mother was still in the first flush of enthusiasm for her new bosom friend. That had been when I was studying for my entrance exams and it had cost me an effort to endure the way they twittered on. The sound of her voice made my gorge rise, like the taste of mare's milk on my tongue. I struggled to solve an equation and felt a wet rope tightening round my head. Oh what a mixed up person was my mother! Like a prism, not one to be pinned down. Pity welled up in me, as I heard her hoarsely saying: I don't take things lying down, you know Liza. Out came the old tale of woe, duly filtrated by neurosis and her reading of fiction. And maybe some day she'd tell her the full story; that was the refrain. Liza for her part suffered from an artistic temperament and enjoyed using to excess expressions like *experimentalism* and *the masses*; she would listen and sigh, wistfully hinting at hidden troubles of her own that were scarcely more easily to be borne. Only then would I replace the extension where I'd been eavesdropping, and lock myself in the bathroom to cry tears of mortification; it wasn't that I didn't care about her — the trouble was that I did.

After that they'd gone off for the holidays to Skiathos and by the time they returned she had taken up with a gigolo, so I didn't have to worry any more.

I found it hard not to feel anxious about George, his eyes haunted me like a childhood memory and I had to make an effort to bring them to mind. Even the air I breathed I felt I owed to George; trapped in insignificance I consoled myself with the thought, what a difficult thing is comradeship; I'd great qualms about this, was I worthy of such a mythic moment, when two people come together who are strangers and yet bound absolutely to

the same cause; qualms of remorse too, because in the
beginning I hadn't liked George, it all seemed so futile
now and anyway I was always afraid of getting things
out of proportion — I could put a modest face on it, but
only I knew what tendrils of creeping pride held me inwardly in their thrall.

Two months passed in complete inactivity, never-
ending hours in the back part of the house, cooped up in
a little cubbyhole like a small veranda, I used to try to
read. But I easily wandered off into daydreams, drifting
softly, imperceptibly into self-pity. I'd recite verses or
sayings to myself, and gradually came to nurture my
delusions. But behind the self-indulgence and mockery
were banked up sobs and tears. I'd never been so much
affected by dreams. They used to linger in my mind, too,
with crystal clarity and I felt confused: had these things
really happened once and I'd forgotten? I was smoking
with my Grandmother Myrsini and the two of us were
giggling, our faces luridly made-up, as we sat in a hud-
dle on the stairs at Kifisia. A gypsy woman came to tell
our fortunes, as she came up to us she laughed, her
mouth was full of gold teeth, then she went away and
left us holding out our palms and crying pitifully. My
Grandmother Myrsini I knew only from photographs,
those that had escaped my grandfather's ire. And I
feared her as a threat and an evil portent within me.

Usually after the first ten pages I found I couldn't read
any more. The classics bored me, and of those there was
no shortage at Lucy's. Fondas regarded this an imper-
tinence on my part, a kind of shallow arrogance. He
used to stand beside me and threaten me with the
lighted end of his cigarette if I didn't recant. I had the
impression he was watching his chance to take my

hands in his and touch my breasts. Little Woman he used to call me, and threw up his hands to heaven, as though calling the immortals to bear witness. But on one of these days in the dead period after lunch he didn't quite manage to throw up his hands but held me pinioned instead. For once we hadn't been bickering about Shakespeare or Molière. This time it had been which was the greater writer, Dostoyevsky or Tolstoy. Fondas backed Tolstoy, because he found him positive, a rich distillation of the great human values, much better than the murky world of Dostoyevsky who was so piecemeal and inconsistent. I said to tease him: Human values, comrade, are manipulated every time by the ruling class in order to serve its own ends, i.e. corrupted. This was the moment when on past performance he should have flung up his hands like a suppliant at the altar and denounced me as a Pharisee of materialism, but this time he launched himself at me instead. I didn't resist at first, then gently I moved his hands away. I couldn't easily have defined what I felt. I was troubled by the suspicion that he was doing all this with almost surgical detachment, with an effort, as though trying through me to overcome some defect in himself. And whenever he came really close to me, I don't know how it was, but he seemed to create empty spaces between us, to generate a silence that left us further apart than ever. That afternoon he drew back without a word, and avoided me for the rest of the day. He always exasperated me because he never said what it was that he wanted from me — if he'd wanted sex, couldn't he have come out with it and said so?

We relied on Lucy for our contact with the outside world. What she told us was always pretty depressing, and pretty much the same. She had contacts with people in journalism. She even encouraged us to think that her trip to London with my father had been somehow connected with the resistance. Her morale thus boosted, she allowed her hopes to soar. I stared at her as she said this, and thought to myself, if you're talking about a poem by Seferis she can certainly be intelligent, but in matters of politics the best you could say of her is that she's bird-witted. She really believed that the democratic countries of Europe would kick out the Junta. At times like these I used to remember Elvira's Fotis and concede that he hadn't been so far out after all, though I could never bring myself to agree with him entirely. My annoyance with Fotis was personal rather, he talked too much and was vain, but then Lucy it turned out, by contrast, was plain stupid, of course she loathed the dictatorship, at the level of cockfighting: let's see an end to this Papadopoulos, nincompoop of a jumped-up colonel, that sort of thing. Once I could stand it no longer and said to her, Look I don't give a fart just to see the end of Papadopoulos and Co., I'm talking about the whole *School of Dictators.* What was that supposed to mean, she enquired sarcastically, and I flung at her, beside myself, the whole bloody Greek Parliament, that's what it bloody well means. Her mouth opened wide, revealing a gold-filled molar. But she's quick on the ideological draw, the penny dropped at once, Cohn Bendit you mean, the Almighty preserve us, what a load of claptrap! and she laughed indulgently. Fondas intervened to make peace, for once he tried to show me tactfully that I was in the wrong, no doubt he was afraid that if he preached at me he'd only drive me further in the same direction and he was no fool, he knew he couldn't put

122

one over on me any more. So he tried to wheedle me round, but even this annoyed me. He got on too well with Lucy, and as a result had become more verbose than ever. I sat and stared in wonder at the two of them, how could they? — it was like playing patience to pass the time. So I left them to it and followed Mary the maid into the kitchen — since my political awareness was on the level of those people I found I could most easily sympathise with, who had never in their lives read even the *Communist Manifesto*, and this for the simple reason that they had never learned to read.

Mary the maid was the spitting image of our own Calliope, with the single but significant difference, that while Calliope could never forgive those brigands of the Left because they had killed her brother, Mary's grievances knew no bounds, beginning with the Asia Minor atrocities that had cost her a husband outside Ankara, and from there to the Jews that had put Christ upon the cross. There was a look of insanity in her incessantly darting eyes as she warned me of the wiles of the antichrists, she could smell demons and their snares everywhere about. And never ceased ranting on, with the look of someone casting spells against the evil eye, about the navel of freemasonry, by which she meant America. Mary the maid was an Old Believer; she had fallen victim to the apocryphal obsessions of Lucy's mother Julia, who that particular month was reliving the martyrdom of St Eudocia of Makrembole. Propped in her wheelchair: she had never walked again after '49, it was to be the penance she'd laid upon herself after Alexis' death. The story goes that when Alexis came to say goodbye Julia, instead of giving him her blessing as a mother, had read him the riot act, wasn't it time now that we were liberated to start taking his studies seriously? But Mother, he'd replied, how can you be so blind, can't you see that now's the time the worms are going to turn and raise their heads at last, at this moment the struggle for our cause is only just beginning. Julia had retorted, he'd no right to assume the mantle of the Messiah, such talk was blasphemous and she hadn't nurtured him to go forth to some calvary. Until the news had fallen like a blow, and she'd never recovered the use of her legs, but lived from that time since in perpetual atonement, with saint succeeding saint in her devotions.

One day Lucy told me she had been talking to my father about me. At first he'd affected indifference, but then had bared his soul: it was like having the sword of Damocles hanging over his head, I was a constant thorn in his flesh, and more of the same melodramatic sort. From her manner of speaking, lips pursed, I realised she wanted to scold me, her eyes had taken fire already. I was more surprised than anything else, because for years she'd been adept at handling this particular situation. For quite a lifetime they'd been coming together and going their separate ways as though they had all of eternity before them. And the sword of Damocles hanging over our household, from what I remembered, had always been their alliance. We all knew that when they went off somewhere at the same time, supposedly by coincidence, they went to renew their affections. And we awaited their coming, to see if normal life would resume once more; that was how we lived, from one temporary breathing space to another. Until the day came when my mother ceased to care — on the surface anyway. I was always quite pleased, if anything, to hear of my dad's little flings, as though they served to postpone the final break. But it was not to be postponed forever. And my mother would commit suicide, every detail of her death planned and relentlessly rehearsed. But I anticipate, at this time Lucy was hiding me in her house. And I used to marvel at the love that bound them, like the blinding untrodden snow. I unleashed all the romanticism of my nature to try to vindicate or at least to comprehend them, though I didn't delude myself that their romance was of the glossy, and essentially trivial, variety that you read about in fashionable magazines, the sort of tale where lovers drool inconsolably in the dazzling glare of the Aegean. And there was something cloying in her manner that I found irritating — how could I possibly fail to get on with such a terrific man, anyone would envy me a father like that, look at Fondas.

For Fondas' parents had been sending messages via Lucy that dire steps were imminent if he didn't present himself at home. Dire steps meant going to the Security Police. They were appalled at his neglecting his studies. If he had done wrong, in their book, there was nothing for it but to make proper amends. His father, who was a famous surgeon, exceeded the bounds of mere conservatism, he exalted the prewar dictatorship of Metaxas to the heights of metaphysics. While his mother was a society lady who dissipated her energies among tea parties and royal foundations in aid of various charities, and had a brain no bigger than a chickpea. Fondas had kept them at arms' length for a while now, they barely greeted one another in the morning. But now he was really worried. He thought them capable not just of going to the Security Police but even of demanding, themselves, to see him punished. He confessed that it had been his father who had denounced his Uncle Stelios too, all those years ago — and the frightful thing was that he had done it not to curry favour, but because he really believed in his heart of hearts that a man must pay, must suffer even torture, in order to regain his place as a citizen.

We imagined all kinds of things about George's arrest. His elder sister was in regular contact with Fondas and told us how his interrogation was progressing. George was standing firm, they'd smashed his ribs, but he hadn't talked. So we began to plan: once he was sent for trial we would come out of hiding. I had the feeling that if I let myself go, if I gave free rein to the pity and the self-pity I felt, I would gain some relief. But I was inhibited by a gnawing sense of awareness of how wretched we were, I felt particularly disappointed in Fondas — and I wasn't strong enough to accept him for what he was. Instead I began to feel quite hostile towards him, as though he'd reneged on some great promise and let me down.

8

THE GUARD WITH the gold teeth and flower print shirt kicked open the door: you're wanted upstairs. I hauled myself to my feet, propping myself against the wall and taking the weight on my heels. And chuck some water over that filthy face while you're at it, he added, his jaws seeming to snap as he spoke. I grasped the rim of the concrete sink; a mouse ran out between my legs and disappeared down a crack in the flagstones. Black flagstones, black tombstones, I repeated to myself, I had a sense of all the cells breathing together within me. In the basement courtyard everything was quiet. The women had been herded into the little room, I could see them, heads bowed, with face to the wall. The men had been taken down to the dungeons. The iron door opened and we went out. In the cubbyhole beneath the stairs the teaboy with his coffee pots and teabags, his face jaundiced and hair sleeked back, smoked furiously.

The week before they'd taken me up to Tourkovounia. I'd seen the moon sailing between clouds, I'd been stripped and beaten. The moon sank down in the sky, later when I'd opened my eyes I'd been back in the cell. My teeth were chattering violently and I vomited. I concentrated on making myself as small as possible, huddled up in my corner in the shape of a hoop, I was shivering and the soles of my feet were on fire. The slant-eyed one with the shaven head had shoved a filthy rag into my mouth. I choked on my vomit and retched. This would go on until I told them everything I knew. The torturer bares his fine teeth in a laugh: how would you like me to chuck you out of the window? The other with the clipped moustache says he'll pull out the hairs of my bum one by one. My blouse has gone stiff and chafes my shoulder. Before they took me up to the terrace the policeman with the fine teeth and clear blue eyes had brought his cigarette up to my eyelids. The smoke seared me, if I blinked the ash would blind me. I bore it until the tears rolled down. Each time they took me up to the Fourth Floor, I was terrified I would break down and talk. And each time I'd held out. They filled the room with such menacing hatred that it sustained my anger as a weapon against them.

Half fainting, I saw my father rise wide-eyed to his feet. He caught me to him and I dissolved into sobs. A dull wave of bitterness washed over me bringing more pain in its wake, the next moment I passed out in his arms. When I came round it was to see a broad smile on the face of the torturer with the clear blue eyes, fine rodent's teeth and American crew cut. The Chief, his shoulders hunched, began to wave his arms about. My darling, cried out my father. Then the three of them began to babble at once. When they were sure I was listening, my father took his cue: there was no need for all this, I'd been led by the nose, I was an impressionable youngster, and so on. The Chief nodded in agreement: it's our belief she's basically sound, she's not the sort to have any truck with communist swine. — It stands to reason, with her family history, why should

128

she get mixed up with that scum? If she'll just tell us all she knows we'll let her go. — Such a shame too, having to miss her classes. — Tell them all you can my love, they know it all already. — Oh yes, we have the full facts in our possession, the written statement is only a formality. — Think what all this is doing to your mother. — Miss Panayotou is an intelligent young lady, with a brilliant career to look forward to. — Come on my love, just tell these gentlemen what they want to hear and let's get it over.

I looked from my father to the others and back again. Eventually they tired of this barrage. It left them played out and breathless, gasping and sweaty as though I'd caught them jerking off. Upon the instant in blew my Uncle Joachim, the General, like a tornado. The two policemen leapt to the salute, but he took no notice of them. He strode up to me like a peacock in his finery, his puffy jowls and medals dangled over me. He gave my ear a tweak and turned to the policemen: Gentlemen, I shall undertake to be responsible for this young lady. They had no objection, but first of course I would have to sign my confession. My uncle the General ordered me to sign. I don't know how it happened but the thought took form in my head: you prize shit. I grinned and that seemed to shake him. He would sign for me as my guardian, he was taking over my father's authority, he had other bright ideas too. He was taking over responsibility for me, and anyway my signature had no validity in law.

There followed a series of bowings and scrapings, entrances and exits, whispers, sardonic grins. At last they lifted me up bodily and carried me down the stairs. My father turned to me with a despairing look, ready to collapse in a heap. They put me in the back of the car and off we went. The reassuring shop windows were as they always had been with the carefree populace stretching their legs beneath the awnings, a silent herd that loudly proclaimed its complicity.

My mother wept buckets, my darling we're so sorry, we're so sorry. Calliope fell upon my neck. Then they froze as they heard Joachim's decree: either I signed and told them all I knew, in which case they would let me out, or back I went to rot in jail. My father cast abject, doleful glances at me. This was the limit of my parole; then back I had to go. Outside the apartment block an unmarked baby Fiat was waiting. But I had the feeling I'd gained something by my brief outing. Now that I was so much at home in my cell, with the secret signals that communicated with the cells on either side.

I stayed inside for another thirty days. July came and went, I'd been three months in the hands of the Security Police. For the last week they seemed to have forgotten me. I reckoned that soon now I'd be transferred to jail, that was the usual thing. One evening the slant-eyed one with the crew cut had come in; casually he'd forced my mouth open and stubbed out his cigarette on my palate. It wasn't the worst thing, but if at that moment they'd hauled me in for interrogation, I'd have been ready to write down everything. But he left me to scream and charged on to the next cell. The next day I'd been taken to a dilapidated old building in neoclassical style on Third September Street. After twenty days, who should I see there but the Chief, with his hunched shoulders, and my father.

My father had not been idle. At first the sly old fox, the General, had tricked him into acting the raving anti-communist, with that put-up scenario of letting me go. After that episode he'd had a kind of nervous seizure and broken off all relations with his uncle. A further reason was that the General had literally seized the disputed piece of land in Attica. When he'd got over the shock a week later, my father had started rushing hither and thither from one influential contact to another. Red Cross, Amnesty, Civil Rights, he tried them all. And all of them had said yes, well, we'll see what we can do. As a result I received soluble Vitamin C tablets and for my birthday a cake. The guard in the flower print shirt held it out on its cardboard base and flashed his gold teeth at me. By the time they'd finished with it, it looked half- chewed. Many happy returns, and mind you behave yourself from now on, the guard roared with laughter, lounging against the door for all the world as though expecting to be offered some. That was how I spent my twentieth birthday, at Security Police Headquarters. Until finally, who knows how, someone hit on the bright idea. When it came to the crunch, the comrades weren't going to be too pleased if they thought Miss Panayotou had ratted on them, they'd ostracise her, before long the young lady's enthusiasm would dampen down — that sort of thing. I had to go over it again and again in my mind, when I was called to account for the fact of my release. I used to go pale and my face would crumple when they accused me of cracking, I'd spewed up all I knew and more and that was why I'd got off almost scot-free, no military tribunal, no jail sentence. The spectre of these accusations haunted me for some months afterwards.

That morning when I'd decided to risk a visit to the flat — there had been some clothes I'd wanted — I'd found them waiting for me. We had heard that George had been transferred from Security Police custody, which meant they wouldn't be likely to torture him any more. We added up the pros and cons, and concluded there was no need to stay in hiding. We'd had it up to here anyway, we couldn't go on like this. It was just the mood I was in that morning, I thought I'd go to the flat and see what was what.

On the bus I stared at the other passengers with nostalgia, it was a wonderful feeling, finding them still there, jostling up against me, as though I'd escaped from a terrible nightmare. With a sudden pang I was reminded of the canary I'd once had. Of enfolding it and refolding it in gold wrapping paper and digging it a grave beneath the loquat tree. Tears of justification welled up in my eyes; even in the dream that had prefigured its death I'd felt a weight of guilt.

They moved too quickly for me even to cry out, and hustled me away quietly, to Headquarters. The first people I suspected were Fondas and Lucy, I had to, it was a way of imposing some sort of order on events. I was also shocked at the shamelessness of my invention. How ready I was to disown my nearest and dearest! Even the thought that Fondas was a good friend didn't weigh with me. It came quite naturally to see him at that moment as a stool-pigeon or informer or whatever else — it didn't matter, anything to keep my brain on even keel. The picture of him rushing to the phone and dialling the Security Police the moment I was out of the door, and telling them I was on my way, was the one that worked the best. But from the questions they put to me I gradually gained confidence; they seemed to know almost nothing, only the vaguest generalities. And even there my family background made them wonder. In any case it was as well I realised in time that whether I held out or not rested in my hands alone. They'd nothing to pin on me, except for what I might tell them myself. This gave me courage. In the beginning I pretended complete ignorance, but they didn't swallow that for long. It began to emerge that they knew about me through the university. And though they pressed me hard, I still found ways to wriggle clear, until at last the shit hit the fan and they sent me up to Tourkovounia. From that moment on, each night from the beginning, I would give myself short breaks, a little longer, just a little longer. And then my father came.

I discovered afterwards that they had waited on tenterhooks for me to reappear. When several hours had passed, convinced by now that I'd been arrested, they had wondered dully what to do. Lucy was all set to phone my father, when the doorbell rang and there he stood, looking quite demented. He'd had a phone call from the Security Police. Shell-shocked, as he put it, he'd come straight round to Lucy's to ask her advice what to do. They'd had to tell him the whole story, and when he'd finished bawling them out and had subsided in exhaustion, they'd made their peace and agreed on a course of action. Lucy would leave for London before I cracked and the arrests began. As for Fondas, he could do as he thought best.

For him, this meant the same nightmare as before. He gathered up our apparatus and threw it down the manhole he'd had in mind all along. Then he determined to flee the country. He went via his parents' house to ask for some money and pack a suitcase. He was ready to face them calmly, but his father put him on the spot. At the height of their quarrel he told him it had been he who had tipped off the Security Police and given them my address, it had been the only way he knew to unravel the thread. Fondas screamed at him that he disowned him as his father, and threatened to soak himself in petrol and set alight to himself in Constitution Square. No question now of fleeing the country. And so it came to pass that the famous surgeon went to Security Police Headquarters to plead that it had been all a mistake, I was in no way involved, and so on. He had even gone so far as to threaten them with statements to the press.

There followed a difficult time for Fondas, as he tagged along, now with my mother, now with Calliope, on their visits to Headquarters to take me parcels. He was always asking after me — a lamp always burning for your sake, poor lad. My mother sighed, how the poor boy seemed to worship me. He told her how he'd got to know me at the Faculty, how he'd first set eyes on me in the laboratory, and afterwards I'd plucked him by the sleeve, something he can't stand as a rule, but with me it was different, like a timid child that needs to cling ... and whoosh came my mother's tears in floods, she had to admit she was susceptible to sensitive young men with a touch of the feminine about them, unlike the ones she used to know before the war, stiff upper lips all of them. Even my father had developed a soft spot for Fondas and was tickled to discover that even for a wild untamed thing like me a man could be found who seemed to care. By the end I was going to find Fondas practically installed as my fiancé.

I was lifted up by the Chief and my father, and we arrived home. But I would much rather have been held for trial and come before a military tribunal. I wouldn't have cared whether or not I was acquitted. All I wanted was to gather up the period of my captivity, and close the account. For hours on end I'd drawn up the lines of my defence for the tribunal on the trapdoor of my cell in Bouboulinas Street. I set up a comical and dignified courtroom, I moulded the military judges out of bread crumbs and set them on high-backed chairs made of paper bags, and the proceedings began. Try as I might, I could never manage to complete a sentence, I'd go back to the beginning and revamp my words in ever more highfalutin variations, exalted to the skies by the brilliance of my oratory. I was swept off my feet along swirling drains, but I held on, then I was an egg, a hen clucking in the straw strained to hatch me. My cell expanded vastly, there was something pounding at me, I reached out to grab hold of the trees that floated by me, swimming like proud horses, I could hear Calliope as she patted me and my head was delivered like a tiny egg, I was gasping for want of breath until Solomos the long-dead poet came to my rescue with butterflies over the lagoon at the siege of Missolonghi. The public gallery is full and my defence prepared; like the old heroes of national independence, with the banner of the cause draped about me, I launch into the praises of my own deeds and from the bottom of my heart despise the still waters running deep of General Makriyannis, God-fearing hero of national liberation who came by wisdom with his runner beans behind the Acropolis. In his place I prefer to worship the arch-brigand Odysseus Androutsos, who was hurled off the Cyclopean walls. Can you state an opinion on Makriyannis? It had always been Duty Number One in the Youth Movement, to read Makriyannis: the futile voice of the lower middle class in Greece. I preferred an uncompromising stand and quivered to clasp the knife of the poet Varnalis, that thrusts, that twists, that turns to light, that turns to mind.

But later I awoke and all around me were hollow promises. I was the child brought up to ease and luxury untouched by the shoddy castoffs of American capitalism. Enamel cups of powdered milk with school meals. Mothballs for the destitute administered by the Red Cross. Dollars from the evangelicals for widows and orphans. New Testament and Star of David. Collaborators with the enemy every one of them, Gary Cooper and the rest of the good guys. While here in Greece with every day that passed they sold out Makriyannis to the foreign embassies that line Queen Sophia Avenue.

At all hours of the day my mouth drooped open, I couldn't chew properly, my only sustenance was milk and almond-flavoured chocolate. I sucked at my chocolate and took in the fact that other people had the firm sharp teeth and untroubled stomachs to devour whole sucking pigs if they felt like it. I was light as air, like the comical little bird I was watching as it pecked about the weeds, in my imagination I was flying through a wood while the hunt was on, the hunter fired at me and some time later the hunter's children chewed and sucked my tender bones. I remembered the days when I had practised ballet and been universally admired for the proportions of my body, the teacher had said she would make a prima ballerina of me, and held me up as an example to the other girls, observe Myrsini's legs now, notice the control in her joints! All very well, but I didn't have any joints in my head.

I spent the rest of that summer at my parents' house, convalescing. I had some abscesses on my feet, one of my toenails was missing. My father called in a succession of doctors to check me over, but there was little any of them could say. I would make a full recovery but it was a matter of time. When I was definitely on the mend my mother suggested going somewhere quiet, to one of the islands. They both showed their consideration and were gentle with me in a manner that seemed to say, the child is sick, or, the child needs looking after.

So we went to Naxos. It was perhaps the first, at least as far as I can remember clearly, and also the last holiday that we ever spent together, just the three of us. For my mother it was as though the anxiety she had suffered over me had given her a new lease of life; it was her Indian summer. She was as gentle and loving as the mothers in children's books. I was much impressed that she knew whole poems of Cavafy by heart, and what's more, not the edifying ones about Ithaca or Thermopylae. She'd quote the lines at a moment that seemed just right, with the easy-going familiarity of casual conversation. Even my father was charmed by this; several times I could sense his surprise and delight. One evening before dinner, we were sitting on the waterfront, drinking ouzo. He laid a hand softly on her shoulder, then hesitantly slipped his arm round her, and she lay back against him. Not far off an old man was muttering about Mandilaras whose body, bearing the marks of torture, had been washed up by the sea. I strained eagerly to listen, but at that moment my prayers were for my parents. I'd have liked to believe in miracles, but I knew that my father was on the phone every night to Lucy. As he sat sipping ouzo in the moonlight, he was suddenly overcome by a shaking fit, as though he were stifling. He laughed it off, saying the still air was getting to him, oh for a breath of wind he said, but no breeze blew and the sea was like treacle. For a while he fidgeted, then subsided into silence. I concentrated my efforts to keep a hold on those hours, that I knew would never come again.

This time there was no fuss when I left home. They'd got used by now to the idea of our living under separate roofs and we remained on the best of terms. I came to see the years that had gone by like green branches that are difficult to burn and fill your eyes with smoke, but even after you think they've gone out, keep on smouldering out of sight; and so I came to terms with them.

With my father I could talk; my mother called me her best friend. And among her confidences to me, accused my father of neglect. I saw with alarm how quickly she was ageing and asked myself who will be left to comfort me: her memory would skip over recent events to dwell obsessively on memories of her youth, the same ones over and over again, and in this way she seemed to feel herself younger. Sometimes on those peaceful afternoons my flesh would creep, as though already I could hear the breath rattling in her throat. My father had indeed neglected her for a great many years, and this with a peculiar delicacy all his own — as his trips to London became more frequent. After Xenia we heard of nothing more, it seemed there was nothing to hear. He busied himself with his papers, he was determined to write a book. But books were all very well, what about the here and now? It was one thing for my father to believe that with parliamentary government his shares would go up, and quite another for Dimitris sitting around unemployed for months. I never forgot that. I bought them flowers whenever I went to see them — and in this way I kept up with my family obligations.

My mother complained that I'd no business acting the nanny to the family bastard. But Xenia's little Catherine was the greatest family support I had. And Xenia looked on me as the seal of legitimacy and paternity, she told me she owed it to me that her future was no longer such a worry to her. Why so? Well, in due course I could count on being a very rich woman — she saw me as heir presumptive to Victoria and the General as well as my father — couldn't I pass a little something on to her, just so she could make ends meet, now she'd got the baby and all? What a change from the bright young thing that had so got up my mother's nose. Now she'd got to watch every penny, she often broke down and cried, she couldn't bear the uncertainty of it — what she wanted was marriage, not so much for the sake of the thing, it wasn't that, she needed the stability, she couldn't stand it any longer. I knew the story well: her father had had the largest textile business in Crete but had had the misfortune to go bankrupt; her mother had died young, from cancer, leaving her and her brother to the tender care of their stepmother.

Apart from the moral and purely personal vindication of having stood firm under torture, I lacked any visible or invisible means of support. I had a fine line in self-pity too, but that wouldn't do. It was a long while, alas, before I learned to make a distinction between ideas and the people who hold them. What upset me was not so much the ideological problems themselves, as the way we used to go about resolving them. I was repelled by Fondas' messianic posturing — he'd found himself a captive audience by now in some of my old schoolfriends, raw recruits to the cause. Unutterably bored by the lives they led, they were ready to sit at Fondas' feet and hang on his every word. It disturbed me to watch the facility he had for turning everything into abstractions which then became fixed constellations among a set of heavenly ideals, until little by little you began to lose your grip on real life. He managed in this way to detach you from any personal pleasure in what you were doing, to enlist you in the service of an ideal, as it might be of brotherly love, or sainthood, or any other aberration of religious freemasonry. In other words Fondas had the capacity to drive you to joyous self-immolation or to utter revulsion. I found myself torn, since I knew him so well but had a very limited tolerance for this kind of thing.

We used to talk for hours on end, and all to no purpose. When we went to the cinema we'd spend days afterwards discussing the film we'd seen. From Paris Urania had sent me some literature on May 1968 and the Prague Spring; these were the burning issues that occupied us. There was gossip too. Elvira always had the latest thing. Some hair-pulling in Paris, what a fool our people had made of themselves in Rome. Andreas Papandreou had said something or other, Theodorakis had changed his line again. We learned of new tortures inflicted on Panagoulis, would-be assassin of the dictator Papadopoulos, and so it went on. During this time I began timidly to forge a line of my own. Fondas accused me of being blinkered and inept. Secretly I was rather proud of myself and it always gave me a warm glow whenever an idea that had occurred to me independently cropped up later in some book I was reading. It was about the only way I had to indulge my self-confidence. Still, I kept myself on a reasonably tight rein, and always held back from being openly bossy, a weakness to which I recognised I was prone. Whenever I felt myself going over the top, I'd suddenly but quite deliberately change gear until I'd got myself enough under control to escape a charge of being hard-line or dogmatic. Today this no longer worries me, I know that I'm neither of these things, at least not for the reasons my accusers would have had in mind. But in those days it was a consuming passion with me, to be branded a hard-liner would have been the ultimate humiliation. Probably because, with the split in the Party then at its height, we tended to equate a dogmatic hard line with the courage to form an opinion and to hold on to it, with the strength of mind never to change or abandon a position without putting up a fight, not even when we were insufficiently prepared, or perhaps inspired, to defend it seriously. I never saw the sense in this antagonistic approach. In those days we were proud of ourselves if we could put our comrades' backs against the wall — it was known as ideological conflict. As for me, I'd already got my back against the wall, and even splayed across it, for no other reason than to deprive them of the satisfaction of putting me there themselves.

9

WE WERE CLIMBING Lycabettos, the better to talk with the backdrop of Athens spread out below us. It had been Urania's idea, and we hadn't liked to deprive her of the chance to admire the view she'd missed so much, it was the least we could do. I was fond of isolating every little thing and blowing it up to gigantic proportions. I was still mulling over the bargain jacket I'd found. Mullein and tangerine and hyacinths and the crumbs of honey biscuits in my pocket, that sort of thing. Fondas was frowning into space, obviously irritated by Urania's effusions of the last hour: how incredibly stale and provincial we were here in Athens. I'd been rather put off too, her manner had the air of speech, but all she did was to shower us with her saliva.

We ordered ouzo and waited to get our breath back, before picking up the thread again. Fondas had been rather quiet lately — he'd immersed himself in his university work, he was taking his finals that summer, and the spectre of his military service after that was understandably preying on his mind. Perhaps even my behaviour towards him had had something to do with it, but for the moment he seemed to have fallen under Urania's spell. It wasn't as if I'd ever made him any promises, I'd always treated him pleasantly enough. Even when we'd had rows I had always been the first to concede a grin and we'd make it up. The idea had begun to take root in my mind that my friendship with Fondas was determined by forces beyond my control, and I told myself that this was precisely what true friendship is.

We were hearing now of new forms of torture at the Headquarters of the dreaded Military Police. George had been brought before a military court and been given eight years. While the trial was on, Fondas and I had lots to do, Dimitris too — the excitement and the tension held us together. But when George was transferred to the island of Aegina, the friction started. To begin with, Fondas didn't like the idea of my getting engaged to George, we'd absolutely nothing in common, he insisted; he knew us both well enough to be convinced it was nothing more than the glamour of the political prisoner that moved me — I'd live to regret it one day. In the end I'd ignored his advice and this had hurt him. Because in his anxiety to shake my resolve he'd told me a lot about George that had betrayed his dislike for him, and now felt cheapened.

Dimitris on the other hand, perhaps because he disapproved of us on principle, never commented directly, I found his tact heavy-handed and clumsy, as he began to put a distance between himself and the rest of us. Now he'd friends of his own, a different set of contacts. His manner became overblown, as he used to discourse about the Party, full of fiery parables out of the New Testament, stuff about husks and chaff, or goats and sheep. For one reason or another we no longer got on. Of course we still saw quite a lot of one another, but only at the cancer clinic. It was there that Dimitris' father was destined to end his days; and it was in this sanctuary that I took my final resolve to give up studying

Medicine. The morning he died and I'd seen his body wasted from prostration, I'd gone out to wait in the corridor, when a doctor went past in a cloud of Paco Rabanne. I said to myself that's it, I'm not going to be the innocent cog in the system and reminded myself, *you can't have good doctors unless you first have a decent society* — I don't know why, the moment seemed ripe and I didn't care any more about reason or logic, it got to me, the preening way he walked, this pompous shit of a doctor reeking of Paco Rabanne, as he sauntered down the corridors of the cancer clinic, for all the world like someone walking his dog in the park, and I heard Irene cry out and said to myself, so far and no further, I won't be the innocent whore, and that's the end of it.

But my real motive lay elsewhere; our cell had been disbanded, we would never again do clandestine work together. We were vaguely aware of the way each of us was tending, but our discussions were always very general. If wasn't even any fun to talk now, it was as though we despised one another. Fondas was incensed by Dimitris' hard line, couldn't we just be ourselves without going overboard to kowtow to the Sovietophiles? I don't know that Dimitris really was a Sovietophile, he certainly had a lot of time for the Party but didn't altogether identify with the official line either, at least some of the things he said would have been enough to get him expelled. I kept aloof from the split. I viewed both sides dispassionately, to my mind they were all in the same boat and it could sink with them for all I cared. They called me a Trotskyite, which I wasn't. I didn't know either what I was or what I wanted to be — I used to read about the liberation movements at the end of the war, I read *A Partisan in the Mountains of Roumeli*, and contented myself with the yellow shirt of Mayakovsky. I'd been excited by a pamphlet on the Tupamaros, translated by Vasilis Vasilikos, that Urania had smuggled back for me from Paris.

Urania had changed a great deal since the days when we used to whistle Theodorakis under our breath on the way to evening classes. Each time she came back she had a different bee in her bonnet, one time it had been poetry, another psychology — only last year she'd wanted to know what I thought of Rilke, I'd never heard of him and she threw up her hands in horror. Inconceivable, how could I possibly not have heard of Rilke? She knew I liked to ape the manners of the working class, but I only succeeded in making myself ridiculous. And true enough, I had my faults.

There had been a time when my father, to show his interest in me, had taken to recommending me books; I remember staring at him as though he'd been talking about viticulture. But it went deeper than that, the time had passed when with Cavafy and Seferis tucked under an arm I too could play the intellectual; the empty form annoyed me beyond belief, but I hadn't any time to spare for the real thing. The modern Greek classics were enough for me — Solomos and Papadiamandis. Later, when I'd found myself in the hands of the Security Police, one of the fixed points I established, to keep my mind steady, was to wonder what nationality this Rilke might have been. But this year Urania had returned a

Marxist-Leninist, so no sooner had I reminded her of Rilke than her lips curled with scorn, the trouble with you my dear is, you actually *enjoy* provoking people with your nonsense.

All this time a fly was buzzing about my head, Fondas was cleaning his nails with his keys again, the picture was frozen as if time had stopped. I was exhausted with Urania's passion for clarifying our ideological positions, for three weeks now she'd been pestering us with this refrain, soon she would be leaving and none of us was any the wiser. I felt an itch all over, as though we'd come to the top of Lycabettos at midday on the day of Epiphany for no other purpose than to rid ourselves of lice. With Fondas, if she'd wanted, she could have reached an understanding; as for me, I'd warned her from the start not to expect too much. And it bothered me to be there between them, as I suspected she wanted nothing more than to humiliate him in front of me before she left. She turned her smile on both of us and launched into a profound peroration on the Greek light, the gist of it seemed to be, you had to be deprived of it before you could notice it properly. I caught Fondas' eye and we both grinned. Urania caught our look and decided, wisely, that it wouldn't do to take offence, so she turned a spectacular somersault instead and catapulted us straight into the Paris Spring when the gates of heaven had stood open. And by way of heaven right into the *events* of May '68. The scenes she described were familiar to us by now, but she loaded them with such significance that it was as though she flaunted them before our eyes. She came out with a range of ideological conclusions and was generally above herself. I had slumped back in my seat, as if to watch the news on TV,

147

idly following the words as they came from her lips. But now Fondas shifted his weight in his chair, put down his keys on the table and launched into such a tirade, you'd have thought his male pride had been threatened. This response was so unexpected, and so out of keeping with his normal self — normally he could juggle arguments endlessly until you wearily raised your hands in surrender, it wasn't that he'd persuaded you exactly, more a token of his perfect success in boring you rigid. He glared at us and his face was pale, his lips had gone dry and beads of sweat stood out on his temples. I was quite alarmed, I wondered if he had a fever. I put out a hand towards him, but he waved me away. With a deep breath he plunged on, quite beside himself by now, little hussy, he called her, here goes then, all right let's clarify our ideological positions, where do you want to start, with feudalism in Greece? I signalled to him to go easy, but he rounded on me instead. This got me on the raw and I told him if they'd come up here to sort out their personal problems that was fine by me, but they might at least say so straight out and not try to shunt the problem off on to something quite different, you can't blame the *Thoughts of Chairman Mao.* Urania, shocked into silence, thrust a toothpick into her mouth and gave all her attention to the panorama of Athens. Then she turned to face me, what did I mean, personal problems? *Personal* problems, with that head case? That had programmed and regulated his life till all it was good for was chucking in the dustbin? It went like clockwork: now I'm going to eat, now I'm going to fuck, now I'm going to read. He'd poisoned the air she breathed, that Christmas. As he got to his feet, there were tears in Fondas' eyes. I ran after him and caught

148

him up, he pushed me away roughly, he called me another of the same, and went on clattering down the steps.

A couple were watching us, as though eager to see murder done. We left the money for the bill and got up to go. On the way down we stopped and she began to cry. It wasn't that she'd meant to hurt him. But he'd never leave off softening her up and being patronising about her political opinions, it made her feel degraded. When they made love, she went on, he'd press into her with all his might and then say right, come on now, what about the *Thoughts of Chairman Mao*? No one but him was allowed to know anything about Marxism, no one but him could have a personal opinion, least of all the girlfriend he was screwing. I tried to explain that yes, Fondas had his faults, but we oughtn't to forget what he'd had to live with for the past ten years, what struggles had turned him into such a dry old stick, and left him so touchy about the slightest thing. As I listened to my own voice I was taken aback by the string of commonplaces I was able to produce without believing them, or at least, I'd never before thought of any of this as extenuation for Fondas. And I trembled with emotion as it came home to me for the first time that he mattered to me. I felt it as an obligation to defend him, I could do no less after all he had done for me — never mind that I hadn't wanted him to and had never given him much encouragement. But I did feel a certain compunction about him, coupled with a vague notion that when I'd first met him the happiest time of my life had begun. I remembered how listless and bored I'd been in the labs, before that. I couldn't stand any more of this and burst into tears, I told her Fondas was like that, it was all the

149

fault of his upbringing. And when it came to ourselves, we might kid ourselves we'd fared differently, but actually we weren't a jot better than our mothers, just as devious, just as impotent. And as my thoughts reverted to my own degree of responsibility for bringing us to this pass, of the sterile and tiresome friendship I had encouraged, my voice became choked with sobs and I had to stop. Urania was taken by surprise, she gave me an uncertain look, then she dissolved as well. We wept in one another's arms, the clouds came down and I felt chilled to the bone; as if my tears had washed me clean. And I imagined a gentle rain that would penetrate me through and through, and wash away everything that was superfluous.

When we'd stopped crying, we went down the rest of the way in silence; I was looking for an opening, I wanted to ask her back with me — but she got in first. What she couldn't understand was that neither I nor Fondas would openly take up a position, we seemed to get high on the drug of our short-term response to the dictatorship. I let out a long breath, I was so aghast, all right, I said to her, to you it's a drug, but how high do you suppose you get being tortured by the Military Police? She rebuked me, in gently patronising tones, for over-dramatising. Of course that wasn't what she'd meant, but how did we manage to be so indifferent to something as big as the invasion of Czechoslovakia? If we were to take a truly responsible line, surely we had to come out into the open and adopt a position, instead of simply carrying on the game with two packs of cards? Adopt what position, I asked her dully? And who am I supposed to be? Am I Sartre or Aragon to take up a position and be quoted in all the papers?

150

I remembered holding the newspaper in my hands; it was midday and I choked back tears because it had never seemed possible to me that Soviet tanks could occupy a socialist country. In my mind I re-traversed the length of Amalia Avenue. The white traffic lines on the roadway and the stocky soldiers, in full battle dress standing stiffly to attention in the middle of the road, and a little old man waved his stick at them censoriously. Then one of the soldiers pushed him over. The man bounced back like india rubber and waved his stick again, taunting them: go on then shoot me, Judas. The soldier turned a blind eye, a woman took the old man by the arm and led him away. I walked on and the helmets shone, I imagined the scene if only Hadrian's Arch would topple over and crush the tank parked in front of it, but the arch did no such thing and nor did I, a year later, have the casuistry to offer a *Marxist* explanation for the Soviet invasion. Instead I consoled myself with collecting cases of torture for Amnesty. That had been the first time I saw the marks of the bastinado on the soles of the feet. Later the invasion passed into the lore that fuelled our hollow debates, with each of us taking a stand according to his particular viewpoint; it had ceased to hurt.

I wanted to tell her it wasn't so much the pros and cons of the invasion that mattered, it was our wider attitude to the events that had made it inevitable. And I wasn't interested in tidying up my position with this or that argument. But I allowed her to judge me, I sat back sweetly and submissively and took her diatribe like a crucifixion. And my silence only roused her to greater vehemence, she would never have thought it of me that I could be so blind. I surprised even myself with my

151

forbearance. I listened to her with bowed head, as if ashamed to admit to myself that there were times, depending on my mood and in any case only in my most private moments, when I couldn't have given a damn about the Prague Spring. Not that I went along with the pro-Soviet hard-liners. But once the first shock of the invasion had passed, the event itself lost most of its significance, it became part of a mythology and what did I care for the metamorphoses of Zeus? Fondas on the other hand was explicit in his condemnation. But his ideas were quite settled or quite conventional — and it may have been this that had provoked Urania, with her passion for being redder even than the reds.

She kept wheedling me to tell her what resistance group I was working for, she wouldn't let go of the subject. Without waiting for an answer she concluded that I must be in the Communist Youth. Curiosity now got the better of her, and she stopped scolding me, but her newfound intimacy got on my nerves, I wasn't under interrogation. For the umpteenth time I told her I'd no illusions left, I didn't want to get involved again. Can't you see I'm drifting? Then there was the surveillance, sometimes when I went home to the flat I'd find a summons waiting for me, from the Security Police; they'd rant at me and make threats, next time I wouldn't get off so lightly just because of some General. A gleam came into her eye, I'd given her the handle she'd been waiting for. How come I'd managed to avoid a court martial? Lots of people had told her I'd cracked and blurted out everything, that was why I'd got off. Not that she believed it herself. I was her friend and she trusted me. I thanked her for her trust. She looked at me quizzically and wanted to know why I had dropped out of university, it wasn't because I'd been sent to Coventry was it? I hardly knew what to say — oh, I said, there was a move that way at first but it didn't stick; there was Fondas to speak up for me you see, they all trusted him as a hard-liner and then he's got his scholarship, the students listen to Fondas. Oh I see, she said, that's what I thought too — that you dropped out because of that. She had heard about it even in Paris, she went on, people had been asking her, what manner of creature is she, and drawn comparisons with the generally suspect stance of my father — d'you reckon she's as soft-centred as he is?

We went on down, stepping round a mêlée of five or six pedigree poodles, and parted coldly. The time was past when we used to whistle Theodorakis and share our anxieties how to find the *right way, the true.* Old friendships were breaking up, beyond hope of recall, and we would all accumulate many scars yet, enough to cut off each of us from the others in our chosen exclusion zones.

Which side was I on? That was the first thing Anestis asked me. I listened as he talked excitedly about the split, and wanted instead to talk to him about George; about his smashed ribs and the letters he sent me in his trouser hems. In jail each of them tailored the Party to suit himself. Today you'd laugh and crack jokes with so-and-so, tomorrow someone else would give you the cold shoulder. You tried to be friendly to the second, then the first starts to scowl. That was the kind of ideological ferment they had in jail, it left him no opportunity to settle his own thoughts and adopt a position. It was a small, inward-looking world, in prison. Your fellow-prisoners might descend on you one day like a cloud of locusts, poisoning your mind with cheap taunts: Take Aris now, Aris Velouchiotis, great communist hero wasn't he. Aris was a traitor, Aris was a poof, that was the sort of thing they said, just so they could watch you reduced to tears. It was petty, it was cheap, each man cared only to vindicate himself. They sounded old and embittered to him, as they shat on their own lives and struggle, picking over the efforts of so many years without a trace of self-respect. It took the winter of '68 before they even dared open their mouths. And then one blamed the other and all of them claimed the dead for their own. George, as he told us in his letters, would stretch out with his face to the wall, and breathe deeply through his nostrils.

But I never did say anything of this to Anestis. I could never manage to put my feelings into words. Whenever I tried I would feel afterwards somehow diminished, cut off from a part of myself by the false and trivial response that I saw my feelings arouse in the eyes of others. This even happened with my father, when I told him I was getting engaged to George. He guffawed as if it was the joke of the year. I've no anxiety about you my love, but what about the poor boy? was all he could find to say. And made a candid offer of advice: think it over before you make up your mind. I felt humiliated by his sarcasm, like a bucketful of cold water poured over my ardent enthusiasm. So I clammed up and told him merely that I was getting engaged to George so that I could visit him in prison, a contract of convenience for the good of the cause. He sat quite still staring at me for several moments, then rose to his feet saying only, I don't understand your morals.

I wasn't entirely clear myself. I had persuaded myself I was in love with George, but wasn't entirely certain that what bound me to him was quite that. One morning, back in that dungeon on Third September Street, by an oversight of the guards as they escorted me to the loo, I'd come face to face with him. It had given me a shock, as I'd thought he'd already been transferred. At that moment, as our eyes met, I felt as though all my future lay transparent before me. I'd managed to smile numbly, and felt subliminal stirrings within me, like the movements of a snake charmer's fingers. For the rest of that day I was sunk in a reverie of bright colours, late in the afternoon the feeling overwhelmed me and I burst into song. The guard kicked at the door, shut up you slut. But at the same moment that he began to swear at me, came George's voice singing in answer from the neighbouring cell. It was a song of such happiness that all the cells laughed too, even the two guards were laughing. Three days later my father had come to take me away.

It was George's view that a man becomes emancipated only when he has thrown off the fetters of economic dependence. He wasn't greatly impressed at my merely leaving home, he thought I ought to work to support myself. Otherwise I was going to remind him of those well-off American kids who make revolution with poppa's bank draft in their wallets. My stand against my parents meant nothing for as long as I still looked to them to support me. George kept up this tune, and as the dialogue was not easily carried on — what were we going to put down first on tissue paper and how much was there time for through the grille that separated us — I came close to despair, it all sounded so ascetic, or so at least I felt at the beginning, he might have been urging me to shut myself up in a nunnery. I had always taken it for granted that my parents had a duty to maintain me. And come to that, a portion of my Great-Grandmother Flora's estate was already in my name. I tried to explain this, but I don't think he understood, he just conceded the point and so took the wind out of my sails. He realised he was taking a hard line, perhaps the reason was that he'd suffered a lot himself, even as a child he'd worked for a pittance to bring in a bit extra for his mother. What's the point, he wrote to me, of putting ourselves under restrictions? When we're already bound by a whole set of moral strictures of our own making? Often his letters made me feel ill with the debt of guilt they gave me, mostly this had to do with the traumas he'd suffered in childhood. But what all his prescriptions and powers of persuasion couldn't bring about I came near to effecting myself, because my life had come to depend on an inner resistance I'd set up, a resistance first and foremost to the safe and solid way of life. And this moral compunction, which George understood as arbitrary self-denial, to me meant despising the process that reproduces betrayed revolutions. And since I had the example of Guevara before me, there was some point in my trying too, with every day that passed, to live a successful revolution. It wasn't just an empty gesture to renounce my worldly goods, I was determined to start with myself, only then, it seemed to me, would I have a share in the great revolution, when first I had won the thousands of little revolutions that came in my size. All this I used to say to Elvira's Fotis, who dismissed it as so much sawdust, just like the rest of bourgeois culture. My father said I reminded him of those colourful Russian chappies in the last century, who'd had not dissimilar disaffections. Fondas would merely laugh and egg me on, with a hint of mockery. As for George, I was very doubtful if he had understood what I had written to him and suspected that his insistence on my finding a job was prompted rather by the notion that I was callow and sheltered and needed a baptism of fire to bring me into line. The gist of it seemed to be that he'd no time for what he called *revolutions in the first person.*

But I shouldn't be talking so much about myself. I was all at sea at this time, practically in a panic. And revolutions in the first person were no more than a matter of talent: I had to be on the watch for despair like a disease, and make a correct and timely diagnosis. I knew that if there was a spark in me, it came from risking everything from a position of safety. My head was full of bindweed that twined inexorably round the solid certainty of my family's wealth. And I caught myself idly weighing up various handy calculations: I could deprive myself and be forced to manage, but there was a lot of money stashed away that I could fall back on; I wouldn't be caught short, now or whenever, I was free to reject capitalism but it couldn't ever turn on me in retaliation and strike me down or maim me. This was the reason, when I dropped out of Medical School, that I felt so proud to be cocking a snook at the bourgeoisie by depriving it of the chance to exploit me. Fondas went wild. Such a decision, he said, was at best reactionary, and when it came to the bit if everyone thought and

157

acted like me we'd be put back centuries, to the age of the troglodytes. On a previous occasion he had ranted on about how the popular movement needs fighters, not professional people. I explained to him that it wasn't any of these attitudes, which in the nature of things come and go and get their lines crossed and change, but sheer disgust that had made me give up Medical School. That in the end I didn't need even to practise the profession to know that I'd made the wrong choice. Meaning? An unholy alliance of my father and Fondas pressed me to explain what I meant precisely by the wrong choice. But they already bored me more than I could say, I could hear them chanting already in unison: dreamer, airy-fairy nonsense, and all the rest of it. I'd had enough of their good intentions and straight path to success. A path that would fill Fondas' room with the empties that had helped him dodge the memory of the honourable art of medicine. They don't give you a chance, he was to slur in days to come. Or maybe he should have shut himself up in his ivory clinic; compassionate and caring in his small surgery, receiving his patients. And when they were poor not taking any money. And prescribing them the best of medicines. Talking over their problems with them gently and philosophically. Later towards evening he would do his rounds. And never sleep with the phone off the hook. Always eager, always ready to sacrifice himself for his patients. Who in their turn would look on him with admiration — our wizard. But Fondas had not the patience to wear himself down by degrees, like the good doctors of yore who when their hour came used to yield up to the Lord a soul inured. And did their duty the way a candle burns down before returning to the eternal pap. Fondas was ambitious and progressive

158

beyond the call of duty, and he paid the price. He wanted to introduce order and justice into hospitals. Until he took to drink, and no more was heard of irresponsible doctors or bastards of administrators. All the problems of society he transposed to the bottle, and he doesn't even write poems any more, only drinks.

10

THROUGHOUT THAT FIRST YEAR his mother and sisters, perhaps because they were embarrassed by the need to show some sort of gratitude to me for sticking by him, maintained towards me a somewhat constrained attitude of polite subservience. Even George himself used to irritate me with a certain look of entreaty from behind the grille, that seemed to be setting me up on a pedestal. When we dared, in the few moments remaining to us at the end of each visit, to imagine the days that would follow his release, such a tremor used to come into his voice that I was quite shocked. He used to say I gave meaning to his life and more in the same vein — it wasn't what I wanted or could even bring myself to hear. It scared me to think that his happiness depended on me, and I began to be afraid I was nothing more to him than a heaven-sent prop to lean on for the duration. I would even have preferred it if he'd looked at me with straightforward lust.

Until, without my realising how it had happened, we swung to the opposite extreme. My devotion to him was now taken as read, and even, perhaps, irksome to all of us. He became dogged and hectoring, he would badger me to explain myself, the least thing was enough to set him off threatening an end to our engagement, accusing me of being wilful and irresponsible, with one thing and another I came to find myself in the ludicrous position of continually having to plead with him, without even knowing precisely what for. Then his mother began to complain: if I came along for every visit, that meant she missed out on talking to him for two minutes longer. From Piraeus where I used to join her and throughout the hour-long boat trip she would scowl, in the end we agreed to split the visiting hours between us. When I dared to voice my sense of hurt to George, he held forth to me about mother-love. And accused me of being in no position to understand an unhappy woman, a woman of the people, his mother. To make matters worse I also had her constantly keeping tabs on me. Euthymia, that was her name, would ring up every evening after nine to make sure I didn't go out at night. Because I was her son's fiancée, that meant I'd no business to be out after nine. I said to George this just wasn't on, there were spies enough all round us. He turned pale, I felt he was capable of slapping my face, if the bars of the grille hadn't been between us. The suspicion came to me that it was he who set her to keep an eye on me, he'd given her so many prerogatives already. So I swallowed back my rancour as the unhappy feeling settled upon me that I would for evermore be having to excuse myself for im-agined peccadilloes. I came to the conclusion that I could never make him happy with me unless I could first win over his mother. But for all my efforts to be polite and obliging towards her, there was always something in her manner that held me at arm's length. Even at the stage when she used to call me her little daughter, whenever I ate a meal with them she would artlessly needle me with one thing or another: our glasses aren't cut crystal you know but you mustn't think the worse of us for that, we're good decent people and that's the most important thing — and her lips would purse with innuendo. And I seethed inwardly at the wasted effort of putting myself out for this complete stranger, and of letting her get away with things I'd never have put up with from my own mother.

I fared little better with his sisters. At first I was quite relaxed with them; I even found I liked them. And the important thing was that being with them made me feel nearer to George. I got them to tell me all about him, they let me go through his things and I felt the solid bulk of the actual objects that used to surround him as a counterweight to his absent self. But I soon wearied of that. The effort it took me to make myself pleasant to them became a dead weight. The elder sister in particular, Aspasia — I was afraid of her, the way she talked and talked without stopping. Sometimes she turned on me directly, I was free to come and go while her brother was rotting in jail and had been ploughed in his studies. I recognised the truth of this. But that was what hurt me most: her attitude to social class, her facility for making me ashamed because my father wasn't a manual worker. With the younger sister, Helen, I got on better. But in her case it was her incorrigible innocence that repelled me. She certainly disarmed me, but at the same time she drove me into a sort of maternal tenderness towards her that in time became a heavy burden to bear, it was as though I'd involuntarily shouldered the responsibility to protect her.

I sustained myself, deliberately, on illusions. I spent six months trying to find a job in a factory. Try as I might, I find it impossible now to recapture my state of mind at that time; I only wonder how I ever managed to do it, every morning going the rounds of the clothing factories and coming back in the middle of the day with nothing achieved and half dead from weariness — it was sufficient reward that I'd tramped the streets of the industrial zone of Athens. George said I reminded him of a melodramatic film, trying to make the working class my dupe, and he flew into a rage. Christ what a hopeless catalogue of near misses and wasted efforts, he went wild and a vein beat blue in his forehead. Then he relented and his eyes filled with tears. He looked at me tenderly and pleaded, why didn't I find private lessons, do cramming sessions for school kids? Surely I could see it myself, the working class isn't a foreign language you can pick up just like that. But I didn't like him trying to control my thoughts. However great the shock, I would have to realise on my own the error of my ways. For me those months were a time of regrouping my forces. Since retreat was unthinkable on the one hand, and on the other the chances of finding myself a plausible billet receded, I acquired a rhythm of my own in trudging from factory to factory. And if I made him think of a melodramatic film, he made me think of a personnel manageress.

She sat behind her desk and smiled without a dimple in her cheeks. Pustules marked her chin where the hairs had been plucked, the upper eyelids curled faintly downwards and her eyebrows didn't match. She could have been a Byzantine empress or a Sunday school teacher or an accountant absorbed in her work. What

163

she was, was the personnel manageress of Softex. She showed me politely to a chair. She held my ID card in her hands. Why did I want to work in a factory, she asked, and I replied, I need to live on something. Then she asked me, why didn't I go to a big department store like Minion? Why should I want to work in a factory? I'd be better suited at Minion or Lambropoulos. She went on to ask about my father's job, how many brothers and sisters did I have, and so on. I told her my father was a cobbler and I was the eldest of six children. She stopped fiddling with my ID card and looked carefully at my particulars. She asked me where I lived, and stared at me disbelievingly. I explained hastily that the permanent address was out of date, now we lived round here, in Egaleo. In the old days my father had had his own shop, but we'd fallen on hard times. I could scarcely contain myself. She asked me could I read and write, had I had a job before? What about my mother? She was in hospital, I said, with bile. Her lips twitched again with disapproval. And then she went into attack. It was swift and deadly. At first I stared at her humbly as my defences reeled. She was talking, this spinster, about my pullover: wasn't it rather expensive? My mother had brought it back for me from London the year before last, she was spot on. Oh that, I tried, my granny knitted it for me. She did, did she, and how old was my granny? A thousand, I snapped back crossly, what does it matter how old my granny is? Ah ha, so I was impertinent too. With a lift of her eyebrows she gave me to understand that Softex was not for me. I should go as a salesgirl to Athenée or one of the other department stores. Factory work wasn't a merry-go-round, I should realise. But that was the trouble in this country and why we were

164

starved of progress, why we were still an underde-
veloped nation. How could we go forward when every
Tom, Dick and Harry off the scrapheap thinks he can do
a real job by signing on in a factory? We might think it's
a joy ride. But the factory worker is something sacred.
The cornerstone of our society. I made a move to get up,
but she waved me back into my seat, she hadn't finished
with me yet. She said you're badly brought up. Her
plucked chin hardened and the black roots of the hairs
showed. I'd never before experienced such anger. I
couldn't understand what it was that so incensed her, in
the end she peremptorily ordered me out. I snatched
back my ID card and made myself scarce. As I passed
down corridors full of machines, the working girls
stared at me with curiosity. Outside the gates a conversation had started up in the queue of unemployed people
waiting their turn. What kind of a life was this, they
said, queueing up just like the workhouse. They asked
me how I'd fared and shook their heads over me. A girl
came up to me, wanting to know every detail, with such
passionate intensity she could have been asking about
the questions in an exam. She seemed even to be pleased
that they hadn't taken me, as if her own chances were
thereby improved. I looked at the other faces and raked
their features — what did they have that I didn't?
Perhaps I didn't look hungry enough.

So my pullover had bothered her, all out of shape and
faded as it was! Exactly, was all George had to say when
I relayed the encounter to him. In order to convince her
I ought to have worn a garish new cardigan from the
street market or off a barrow. It was just this about me
that reminded him of a melodramatic film. Like
workingwomen in a glamorised love story. The woman

165

had been perfectly right. There I had been, with my affected scruffiness, trying to fool a personnel manageress who knew her job. What did I think she was paid for? Then seeing me on the verge of tears, he tried to take my hand between the bars and comfort me. He understood how I must feel, he said, it moved him to see me so persistent, but I had to face up to it: that kind of thing wouldn't do nowadays. I lowered my head to hide my tears from him. Deep down I understood. Lately I'd begun to feel the weariness of despair, that for as long as I refused to come to grips with it gave me no peace. I often found myself identifying with the unemployed, as they scrimmaged from the crack of dawn outside the factory gates. At these times a sense of suffering would overpower me, paralysing even my speech. To the point that I caught myself wondering what these people found to hope for in their lives, how was it that they didn't just sink? Then of course I'd recover my senses, and feel relieved as though awaking from a nightmare. This made it easy now to share in the plight of the unemployed, full of vibrant commitment way over the odds — and this was the cause of my extreme exhaustion: that I could never quite avoid the knowledge that I was fooling others and fooling myself, the knowledge that nothing was going to turn me into a working-class girl, not even the gaudy cheap cardigan from the street market of George's jibes.

At the last remaining moment of the visit he begged me earnestly to raise my eyes and look at him; do put an ad in the paper offering private lessons for school kids, he said. If I could only hold on until he got out, everything would come right, he was sure of it. He would certainly do all he could. And so we parted. Looking back from the boat I watched the lights go out one by one on the island and thought of him wakeful, listening to his heartbeat in the darkness. Time passed with agonising slowness, it hardly seemed to pass at all; sleep took hold of me and I ran in a panic up and down the prison dormitories. All night I dreamt of the Aegina prison, and breathing down my neck was the personnel manageress.

Just as the man from Epiros had prophesied, one by one they began to slink out of the manger of their anti-communism and bleat that they had been duped so on and so forth. It was difficult for me to realise that I had no part in any of this: if the victims of anti-communist purges had chosen to shake hands with the ideologues of the extreme Right, the humiliation was theirs, not mine. But this afforded the occasion for a sparring match with Anestis. Had it not been for Aunt Victoria looking on and chuckling at the spectacle of two strays rabidly licking their wounds on the dung heap, I'd have spat in his face. Anestis had a lot to say about the traumas undergone by the Greek people. About the torture and the suffering that had seeped drop by drop into the inmost recesses of the national soul, but would rise at intervals to the surface in one form or another, now as blank despair, now as hot blood, heroic deeds, great sacrifices. But to my mind all this, despite my own stormy perplexities, was no more than a grandiose pretext for throwing in the sponge.

My father on his latest return from London had found two plainclothes men waiting for him at the airport; for a week he'd been held at Security Headquarters, but had been released thanks to Aunt Victoria who as time went on was turning into the belle dame of the junta's admirers. Her life had become so full, she couldn't keep track. Theodore had long since jettisoned her, but then after an unsuccessful attempt at suicide she'd got back her old vitality. And gradually she'd become an admirer of Colonel Papadopoulos, whom she described as a man with real muscle, a brilliant statesman, in short a personality — and Victoria had always gone for personalities, before the coup hadn't she admired old George Papandreou's son Andreas? Oh yes she'd properly revered him then. So, even though her relations with my family had cooled, she exerted herself to get my father off, though needless to say, not without strings. He was obliged to support the government abroad, over civil rights. I never learnt precisely how he handled it. In any event his resistance to the dictatorship became progressively confined to heavy innuendoes, a joke here and there about bald Colonel Pattakos or Papadopoulos' wife Despina, now and then he'd whistle a forbidden song under his breath, and propound the theory that nothing can be done, you're wasting your time even lifting your little finger. I said to myself that even before this, his grand tirades had borne much the same message. But with the difference, then, that he had still believed in his scorn as a force to be mobilised against the junta. And now he encouraged us to be of good cheer, he even tried it out on Calliope, the barometer of public opinion, common and bastardized though it was. I observed her responses whenever he provoked her to debate, and they were invariably of a most platonic kind, until she drove him to despair and then he would yield tipsily to black forebodings. The people were conservative, he would sigh, but why? He might have probed more deeply there with his scalpel. But who ever was afraid of my dad's theoretical blades?

Dimitris on the other had lost his cutting edge in the fight to survive. I went to his house one afternoon and found his mother in a dreadful state, gulping back tears as she had done while laying out the corpse of craft-master Gregory. Dimitris had snatched from her very arms her hand sewing machine, to sell in the Monastiraki flea-market. The sewing machine that was to have made a dowry for Irene, all that she had left, she'd nothing else. I tried in vain to console her. She beat her breast and prayed aloud to die rather than see all this. I asked her where Irene was. She looked at me as though she couldn't remember who I was talking about. Gradually her grief began to lessen, her sobbing subsided. She went up to the table where the sewing machine had stood, by the window. I went to her and stroked her hair, this started her off again, invoking death, but in a low voice without passion or intonation, like someone chatting to an old friend, and I felt suddenly frightened. She called upon her dead husband, how could he do this to her, after all the ups and downs they'd been through together, couldn't he have taken her with him? It was more than she could endure, she'd rather die and be with him than see all this.

It turned out that Dimitris was emigrating. He'd resolved on this as the only alternative to the hell of unemployment; and, in order to pay his way, he was ready to sell not just the sewing machine but his own soul. Before they would let him have a passport he had had to denounce his father at the local police station. Throughout this time he had clammed up completely.

169

Only in his eyes could you see the pain it cost him, like the wordless protest of a suffering animal. All my efforts to get through to him failed. He avoided me on purpose. At the very last moment he phoned. He left his sentences hanging in the air, he was defensive and touchy as though I had been the one to blame, or as if he owed me some kind of an explanation. Shaken I told him that it isn't the things we do that stick in our conscience, so much as our inability to face up to them and explain them for what they are. But even while I was speaking I felt ashamed of myself. I knew perfectly well what he wanted to hear from me. And I knew too that if I were in his shoes I would be reacting in much the same way. I saw nothing wrong in his preferring to go as a guest-worker, rather than go on forever beating about all over the place trying to get a job and then having the threat of the sack hanging constantly over his head, though Fondas regarded it as an easy way out and Fotis muttered about broken spirits caught in the toils of Capital. What saddened me was just that I wouldn't have wished — this on a theoretical, perhaps a mythological, basis — for men of the Left to have to take decisions of that kind — not men like Dimitris, who from the age of fifteen upwards had given himself body and soul to the cause. Not even the signature at the police station disturbed me, since one thing led to another in an inevitable chain reaction. That was what I tried to tell him, that the real thing would be if he could break the chain. That it would be wrong of him to yield to self-reproach or to succumb to the rat-race, precisely because he'd once tried to break free of it — even if this meant he had to sell his mother's sewing machine and denounce his father to the files of right-wing patriotism.

I was close to tears and stammered out some well-meant clichés. Only when I heard him put down the phone, and the thread was perhaps severed for good, did my voice come free, but by then it was too late. I was left in such a state of confusion, it was as though the objects in the room were revolving round me. I cried, then I ate some salted sardines, and drank iced water all night. By morning, the time when Dimitris would be crossing the frontier, I was experiencing the limp relief you feel after a moving book or a memory out of the past. From Munich he wrote me a letter which was as sentimental and melodramatic as I'd feared. I wrote back, avoiding moral or party pronouncements. A postcard followed in which he paid tribute to my fine soul, the 'soul' twice underlined and the ink smudged as if he had wept or spat over the word. From that time on we sent mutual regards by way of Irene. I found it impossible to go on writing to him.

The only person who truly cared about Dimitris, I mean who really felt for him, independently of his political line, was George. And it was only thanks to George that I came to recognise the grudge that I bore inwardly, as though Dimitris by his action had toppled the pedestal on which I had set the entire working class.

But the wheel goes on turning, the years went by and events with them. Democracy returned to Greece, and so did Dimitris, modestly affluent by now. He bought a two-roomed flat for Irene as a dowry and found her a husband. Later, with what was left over he began a partnership with a friend and opened a machine shop; in a matter of months he was doing good business. By this time he was wearing collar and tie. He was a person of some standing and was offered a position in the Party, an important post, with responsibilities. Dimitris became an exemplary Party official, when others went off to the bouzoukia he'd be manning the office with the comrades, and the first to know what was going on — what's our line on Cyprus? what's our line on the Middle East, on Portugal and any other burning issue of the day? When the office closed they might all end up in Plaka, listening to wartime Resistance songs; the only trouble here was that Dimitris was to get himself engaged to a good woman with a dowry, and she was a great fan of Bithikotsis, he's one of us no matter what, he sings the old Theodorakis songs, like *Romiosini* and the *Axion Esti*. And it was then, many years later, on the anniversary of the Polytechnic massacre, that he accused me of being a *Chinese box*: he couldn't believe his eyes as he watched me spewing up all that stuff like something that's learned its manners in the gutter. This because I'd contradicted him when he'd claimed there was nothing to prevent the pro-Chinese groups from being infiltrated and taking their line from the Security Police — poor Dimitris, I'd turned to him and said, what does it matter to you, when there's so little left of your own great expectations? And he was furious; Chinese box, he hissed after me as we parted. I bit my lip and was reminded of that demonic passion of his as he rummaged through the papers and apparatus of our cell in the resistance group, in the days when we used to print proclamations. Then he would rush about, eyes bulging with excitement and why, I asked myself, did they glisten so, was it the fumes of the duplicating ink that brought tears to them, or was it those miraculous powers of endurance, when he'd recount the blows that fortune had struck at him, but always blended with

172

matters of ideology that he never allowed to sink from sight? He had been the most insubordinate of the three of us when rulings had been handed down from on high, and as a result they'd often been accompanied by an exhortation to comrade Stefanos to pull himself into line, but bullshit, he would say to us, what did he want with absolution from a pack of priests? Fondas at that time used to remark on the lumpen aspects of Dimitris' personality, and would expatiate on how his ego had been deformed by the role-models of bourgeois hero-worship which begin by arousing the imagination of the oppressed individual to extremes of defiance and self-assertion ... on this Fondas would crabbedly deliver a whole scientific discourse, but Dimitris was the most consistent of us all.

Even today Fondas will discourse tipsily on Dimitris' efforts to justify the various compromises that had accompanied his progress from labourer to machine foreman, until he made his pile and managed to set up in business; it takes a lot of courage, Fondas will assure us, to let yourself go so utterly and so systematically, a man gets tired to his very soul — that's why Dimitris needed the prop of his unswerving devotion to the Party, and made his peace. The trouble for me in all this was that, when I'd prayed that Dimitris wouldn't reproach himself, it had never crossed my mind that his atonement would take such a form — absolution from a pack of priests.

People at large watched television, followed the soap operas and cared for nothing but that we should win at Wembley. They talked of a time *Before the Revolution*, when they meant the coup d'état, but they seemed to have forgotten the difference, and with equal enthusiasm commemorated the anniversaries of historic events, revolutions and coups. Somehow or other life had to go on, and we watched news bulletins and turned over the pages of newspapers when we'd had enough of art cinema weeks, but crowds of soldiers sweated in the dust of the Old Olympic Stadium to celebrate the military prowess of the nation. At the same time we were appalled by some of the unexpected tints appearing among the Left. Still licking the scars of older persecutions, they now reached out in a gesture of down-at-heel national solidarity to the opponents of the dictatorship of every hue and shade, while the said opponents of every hue and shade responded with calculated radical noises. And so the days passed; we read the statements put out by prominent Greeks abroad and nursed our insatiable appetite for resistance.

For myself, I gave nothing away; I wasn't prepared to think in clichés, but what better did I have to offer? It seemed that the student movement was getting off the ground at last. But beyond the university precincts, absolute calm prevailed. There was no obvious way, there wasn't even any organised policy, to widen the struggle beyond the student sector. There were some efforts made, but they never went beyond trying to inform public opinion. Was it that we actually wanted to ignore other sectors? This was my own sticking point; with the way they tried to make the movement take off in reverse. We were banking on there being people out there, biding their time, and that somewhere at some crossroads we'd again join hands with the crowds that had turned out spontaneously in their thousands for the funeral of the poet George Seferis.

I was asked if I wanted to join such and such a resistance group, or perhaps I'd given up too? I didn't like being written off as the little rich girl who ran away when the going got tough. But I didn't want to make the same mistakes again. To sit around drinking coffee in the streets round the university and kid myself that this was resistance, or to trot out the current smears against rival groups. In any case I could have agreed with all of them, more or less, but I wasn't going to go along with any of them in practice. For a while now people had been saying it wasn't worth it, for a handful of proclamations, if you were caught, to spend up to fifteen years in jail. There was something in this too, except that in our muddled arguments it often led to resignation. Not from indifference, far from it; but the resistance groups had nothing to offer more eloquent than the lessons their members had learned from bitter experience. As a result, with their in-built failings and ideological inadequacy, they often ended up robbing you of the tiny spark of confidence you'd had in them when you took the plunge and joined. And then you could go around with a smile of angelic bitterness on your face, that declared you had made your contribution and done your best, you could do no more. The way we saw the situation in those days, when we discussed it, was this: from the moment of becoming an active member of a group you had six months before you; after that the noose would begin to tighten. At the same time we knew that if it hadn't been for informers and surveillance, the Security Police couldn't have done a thing. We were brave enough at demythologising the dictatorship in

175

theory — but in practice we were impotent, and ended up, whether we liked it or not, by deifying the external forces that kept the Junta in power. The prevailing inertia we tried to account for each in his own way. We were neither radical enough nor strong enough to rid ourselves of the traditional models of revolutionary action. We'd be churning out the same stuff for the rest of time: item, causes of the dictatorship in Greece; item, the works of Lenin plus also now *Socialism with a human face, socialism with the handcuffs off.*

High noon on Solonos Street and Helen was staring at me in disbelief. I lost the train of what I was trying to say in the effort to be frank with her, I didn't care if it wasn't what she wanted to hear. And I found myself wondering at the indefinable colour of her eyes, now copper-green, now the paler tint of sea and olive-groves. I wasn't trying to persuade her, I only wanted her to understand. Then I stood back aghast as she rounded on me with: *the children of bourgeois families end up in anarchism and nihilism, just two of the masks of Reaction against progress and democracy.* Couldn't I get excited for once with all that had been happening lately, instead of trotting out hoary old clichés? The street clashes had shaken the whole city, while I sat back and did nothing. She was talking rubbish, but I knew myself well enough to hold my peace. She wasn't being fair to me, it wasn't as if I hadn't been involved too. And I wondered why it was so easy for people to get the upper hand with me. One minute I'd have George tearing me off, the next Fondas would patronise me in his supercilious way, now here was Helen, and worse than either of them.

I had put her in touch with someone I knew at the Law School. This had been in April 1972. She'd phoned me and we'd arranged to meet in town, at the spot where Petroulas had been assassinated. I'd been taken aback by her frivolity, here's hoping, I said to myself. She'd been waiting for me, wide-eyed with enthusiasm; that had been when I noticed the extraordinary expressiveness of her face, it may have been due to her jet-black hair, the way the light caught in it and spread an aura like hoarfrost about her head. Anyway I kissed her ecstatically. She was breathing so fast I could scarcely follow what she said; she wanted me, now this instant, no matter what, to introduce her to a resistance group, she wanted to do clandestine work, she owed it to her brother and to all the other political prisoners. In other circumstances I would have been content to calm her down. But she had caught me off guard and so I'd agreed. It was the first time I'd put someone in touch with a clandestine group and it scared me, I felt I was leading her to her doom. It was worse later, after she'd been arrested and her mother kept on at me.

Now she obstinately screwed up her face — our morale and our faith must never weaken, the cause demands it. My attitude was unacceptable, my whole manner was pathetic. Couldn't I understand that everything I was doing only served the forces of Reaction? I laughed irritably and said I supposed the next thing would be, she'd be accusing me of collaborating. But the more I tried to mollify her the more abusive she became. For a moment I caught sight of the two of us sitting there on the park bench, for all the world like mother and

177

daughter. I said as much, hoping to defuse the situation, but instead she went off the deep end. There was nothing for it; if she wasn't going to quarrel with me I'd have to try to explain to her why I wasn't actively involved in the resistance. In the end I snapped back that what she needed was a bit of restraint and self-knowledge. She'd no right to call everyone who disagreed with her an anti-communist. But I immediately regretted it because she tossed back her head and laughed in a way that was the spitting image of myself when I wanted to get Elvira's Fotis on the raw. And suddenly I felt an overwhelming tenderness for her, as I saw how implacably she had set herself against me — I could see how far apart we were, and felt the sorrier for my placid, easy-going self, with an effort I held back tears and found there was no way I could dislike her. We had simply travelled by different roads. She'd started out the hard way, I'd had it relatively easy, until we'd found ourselves whipped along by the current behind the prison bars of bourgeois dictatorship or democracy. She determined, and I refusing, to affirm that what we were fighting for was the better world that Marx had talked of — though we'd rather lost sight of Marx in our pursuit of the masses.

All the same, I had the feeling at this time that we were whistling in the wind. If I remember rightly, it was after January '72, when the first mass meeting took place in the Law School, that a series of court actions had begun with the aim, as far as legal means would allow, of promoting democratic procedures in student affairs. I wasn't much moved by this — not that I didn't care, but it struck me as politically uninspired. When student elections were duly held that November, government appointees *prevailed* of course, but the majority of students recognised only those student committees that had been elected in the lecture halls. At that time too, regionally based societies began to spring up: societies made up of students from Epiros, from the Peloponnese, from Crete, the Dodecanese. We used to stroll in the sun past the Museum, at any moment the police were liable to pounce. We'd take to our heels with the sirens wailing in our wake. We'd go down under their truncheons, then we'd pick ourselves up and carry on, our chant splitting the air as we ran: *Fascists out, they shall not pass; no draft for students.* That was what the student movement amounted to. As I knew well enough by now. I believed that a similar surge would have to get under way in other sectors, in work places for instance. In factories. These were the places where the political parties and the resistance groups ought to be making their presence felt. Nothing like the personality cults and old party lines of the bourgeois resistance. And one question, a naive one admittedly, continued to bug me: OK, but whatever became of all those people who flocked to support the United Democratic Left in the days before the coup? Where had all the voters gone?

11

I WAS LEANING OUT of the window, the news agent opposite was pegging out the afternoon papers by the front
of his shop. I whispered the banner headlines aloud to
myself, with a strange feeling of foreboding; before me
were the faces of my mother and my Grandmother Myrsini superimposed, I'd given them the slip and was
walking on a carpet of camomile. The night was unend-
ing and I dreamt of vast open spaces. Dancers in glitter-
ing circus costume were getting ready to mount a glit-
tering spectacle. I felt fluid, as though I were floating in
warm water, and laughed happily with the crowd. Then
the walls of a cyclopean fortress loomed in the distance;
a papier-maché tragic set and one by one the dancers
disappeared as though they'd stepped on the secret trapdoor leading into the fortress, I awoke with the clammy
sensation of a dark tunnel pierced by lingering groans
that reached all the way into my room.

I got up to answer the door. It was Lucy. Something
was up; without so much as an apology for my interrupted siesta she breezed through the flat in a cloud of
Madame Rochas. I'd been avoiding her since the time
she'd given us refuge; I don't know what it was, but I'd
begun to find her cloying susceptibility affected my
stomach. The latest I'd heard of her had been that she'd
taken up with an entrepreneur out of the society pages,

and literally swept him off his feet. They were spending late nights smashing piles of plates at the old-time bouzoukia of Tsitsanis and Bellou.

She was so full of herself, she didn't notice how cross I was. The first thing I said was, I was in bed with a temperature of a hundred, she might as well not have heard me. Actually it was only up a couple of points, but I wanted her to leave me in peace. She didn't even show concern, a rare lost opportunity as she'd a penchant for that sort of thing. So I concluded something of truly tragic proportions must have occurred, as she sat there crossing and uncrossing her elegant legs. She asked me sweetly if I wasn't going to offer her something? I said grumpily, only aspirin and water, aspirin's good for you, I added. Good idea, she bounced back, I've a terrible headache. I brought her an aspirin and cursed the old cow for calling my bluff, couldn't she see the mood I was in? As she still didn't tell me what she'd come for, but continued to stare at me with her dimples deepening, I began to fret with suspense, what could be coming? But I didn't ask, I sat down facing her and waited, affecting unconcern.

Then she broke the news, and it was truly shattering. My father was getting a divorce so that they could marry. She wanted to tell me this herself, she didn't want me later on saying they hadn't considered me. She launched into fine excuses in the best soap opera tradition, what a hard time they'd had for so many years, and they'd only kept up appearances for my sake, because my father wouldn't have me growing up in a broken home. I looked her straight in the eye: a more vulgar irony I could scarcely have imagined. She went on in all seriousness, I was grown up now and had left home, it

181

was high time they made something of their own lives. She put such artless emphasis into her words, I began to feel I was the one who ought to reproach myself, for being such a long time in the growing. I said so to her face. She replied placidly that she hadn't come here to pick a quarrel and that from someone like me she didn't just hope, she *counted* on my understanding. How kind, I replied, that was too flattering. I thought of asking what she'd done with the entrepreneur, but I could hear already the injured tones in which she'd retort, what a perfectly beastly thing to say. And anyway does anything ever come for long between two people who've been in love for close on a quarter of a century?

She was so pathetic it was almost funny. She seemed to believe everything she said, and suddenly she began to cry, what a mistake it had been, only cussedness, only a quirk of fate had kept them apart. And what makes it so tragic, she went on, is that you don't often meet someone you can love truly until death.... As she continued in this vein, I began to feel quite shaken. She wept, huddled in her chair, and bared her soul to me. She'd given her whole life to her love for my father and the awful anguish of uncertainty. She'd come to feel like his shadow, and despair had often turned her thoughts towards death. She kept repeating that a great secret bound her to my father, and sought to justify herself: anyway his marriage with Natalie had been on the rocks for years now and I wonder, you know, could you say that Natalie ever, really, loved him? You couldn't — you could be sure of that from the way she behaved, I'd be hearing a few home truths about that in due course. I said, I don't want to hear my mother mentioned again, if I start on that you won't know where to put yourself

182

for shame. She pulled herself together and apologised. She hadn't meant to give offence, but she'd always admired my courage in facing up to the truth, that was why, as much as anything, she was taking me into her confidence now.

I listened to her with my hands half over my face. By degrees her mood began to lighten and she went back in her mind to a morning in Constitution Square. What a thrill it had been, she'd been browsing round the shops in the centre of town, when she'd seen him standing before her, it had been like the answer to a prayer. They'd gone for a walk arm in arm, happy beyond words. They'd wound up at the Zappion gardens and sat down at a patisserie. He'd said to her, let me read your palm. She asked him gaily what he saw. Telly had pursed his lips and kissed the hollow of her hand, I see a great love, he'd said with a tremor in his voice. But at that very moment whom should she catch sight of but Natalie in the distance, in her starched collar. Then she'd remembered with a feeling of dread that Alexis was fighting with the revolutionary army. She'd been reminded of his last farewell, when he'd asked her to send his love to Natalie, tell her she's in my thoughts and one day if I'm lucky and come back from the front ... But Natalie had been content to copy out poems about love at close quarters and there was beginning to be a danger she'd slip through your fingers if you didn't keep a lookout. Lucy had thought of her brother tramping through the snow. With a sudden flush she'd risen from her seat and excused herself with almost unseemly haste, but then her steps had faltered, she couldn't bear to leave them together. She'd paced up and down under the trees, with the touch of love still tingling on the palm of her hand, she'd been ready to fling herself down on the grass and cry. So she'd circled back, keeping herself out of sight, hidden by the branches she'd watched them in one another's arms and suffered agonies of humiliation as it dawned on her that Telly had brought her to the Zappion for no other reason than that he already had an assignation there with Natalie. From then on she'd refused to speak to him on the phone. Then she'd heard of their wedding and flight to Paris. Hard on the heels of the first blow came the second, her brother's tragic loss, and the two griefs together had brought her a kind of peace. But not for long — no sooner had we returned from Paris than their old love took wing once more. From that time to this, despite all the strain and the frequent partings, they'd always stood together. As for me, she'd used to take a pride in me, she practically worshipped me while I was growing up, I was the child *she* would have had by him, if things hadn't turned out so tragically.

She was beginning to regain control of her voice, she took out a hanky and wiped her eyes. Oh yes, I said to her, I hope you took an equal pride in Xenia's little Catherine and Nancy's little Agis as well, did you know about that? She shot me a pleading glance — that's different, she said. It's not the children's fault of course, but those girls are just plain tarts. I saw the jealous rage that twisted her face and felt sorry for her. I asked, to change the subject, did my mother know? Of course she did, they could hardly have kept it a secret for so long. Could she be pulling my leg, I wondered? I explained what I meant, did my mother know of their decision? — as far as the bond between them went, of course she knew, we all did, I'd grown up beneath its aura. When

184

she went on to say I was the first to hear the momentous news, I made it clear I wasn't prepared to play the part of messenger in this ancient tragedy. She begged me not to be sarcastic. I looked critically at the wrinkles on her face and compared them mentally with my mother's. There they were in their mid-fifties, acting out their lives like a Punch and Judy show. I'd have liked to tell her that the trouble was in *them*, in their special genius for messing up their lives, and not in the tear-jerking romances they concocted. But I let her be and got to my feet.

I went to the window, and glanced down once more at the banner headlines in the newspapers. I felt boxed in by the hardness, the air of passing judgement, that they drove me to adopt for no other reason than so as not to become like them. With all their bullshit they forced me to be wary, like a hunted animal. To peel off reality in layers and sift through every little detail, though the only result was to cloud things further. I found them constantly between my feet, obstructing my path, inside my head, claiming me for their own. From all sides they came at me, there was nowhere left to me to muster my own resources. And the harder I tried to ignore them, the more I longed for a straightforward personality, like Helen's.

I turned back to face the room, imagining her, legs apart, beneath my father, and wondered curiously what they still managed to get up to together — apart of course from languishing sighs. Before she went she came up to me and kissed me. I kissed her too. The moment I was alone, I burst into tears. My father had been unwell lately. His features were swollen from cortisone, his eyes bulged, I grieved to see him in such a state.

185

Calliope had told me how he'd immure himself for hours in his study, surrounded by his books and papers. What does he do it for, there's nothing he needs, why couldn't he sit back and relax a bit poor man, couldn't he take his siesta like everyone else but no, always these papers of his and heavens above you should see how his hair's gone, he's almost got nothing left on top! Calliope was greatly agitated by all this. I'd dropped in the other day to visit him at the newspaper offices, and found him in deepest gloom. I made as if to go out again, and it disturbed me the way he begged me to stay, he needed to have a talk with me, he said.

He began with Nancy, she'd got her claws into him and he couldn't get rid of her. The two of them, aunt and niece, had set their hearts on ruining him. I had known that Nancy was Xenia's aunt but had always remembered them being at daggers drawn, they were always squabbling over something. And my father wondered sadly how he'd ever got mixed up with such a pair of baggages. Did I realise that Xenia was blackmailing him? With every demand she upped the stakes, where would it end? She'd even tried to get him to make over the house at Kifisia to Catherine. As he went on his manner became more confiding, a long time ago in Paris he'd slept a few times with Nancy. That was all. He'd been sorry for her of course. She was a sad case and couldn't sleep with a man without burdening him with the whole sorry tale of her life. Dammit he *had* felt sorry for her, but no more than that. They'd lost touch after Paris and it had been many more years before they met again, in Athens this time. She'd opened a beauty parlour, and seemed to have sorted herself out. He'd run into her by chance in Victoria Square, they'd sat down to drink a cup of coffee and before he knew where he was she'd managed to cry all over him about how she was lonely, she was near to despair, and so on. He didn't know quite how it had happened, she'd got a way with her the bitch, no doubt about that, the next thing had been they were in bed together. That had been the first and the last time in Athens. But it had proved fateful. Because she'd fallen pregnant if you please. Amazing how luck was so often against him, it seemed he couldn't sleep with a woman without getting her pregnant. And she, blackmailing little bitch, had had a little boy, the spitting image of Grandfather Agesilaos. What d'you make of that? At first he'd hoped the situation would go away, but in the end he'd given in to pressure. It touched him, in the end, that he had a son. But that had been his undoing. Now she milked him regularly. As though she'd struck a bet with the other one, to see which of them could sting him for more.

I could hardly contain myself; the room was spinning in front of my eyes and I was afraid that when it stopped I'd have lost control of my mind. He got up and stood close to me, tenderly he murmured that I was his firstborn, his one true child, he wanted me to understand and forgive him. And while we held one another in this embrace there came a quiet knock at the door. We were still entwined when we saw before us a young cripple. The struts of his crutches were wrapped with stinking wads of cloth. His eyes were deeply sunken, his cheeks hollow; at the sight of him, like a ghost, I came abruptly to myself. Something similar must have happened to my father, for in a moment he was back on the other side of the desk, his manner wholly professional. The cripple spoke up, would Mister Panayotou please excuse the liberty. My dad stared dubiously at the disabled man's brows where they met in the middle. I'd have put him at no more than twenty-five. He wanted nothing special, he said, it was just that last year he'd lost a leg, down the Mineral Mines. What Mineral Mines, my father asked irritably? The young man explained which Mineral Mines he meant. We were both of us appalled — so far as I knew we'd no very serious connection with the Mines, OK my father had inherited some shares, but so what? The cripple stared at us, provocative in his wretchedness, then dropped his eyes in embarrassment. He went on tonelessly, as though he'd learnt it all off by heart. And would we mind him taking the liberty? A whole year now he'd dragged himself round like an invalid, no one would take him on. So if we'd excuse the liberty, he went on, Mister Aristotle Panayotou is a good man, he's got shares, he writes in a newspaper. Perhaps a job as a door-keeper or a night-watchman, you're the man to help me, Mister Aristotle sir. My father heard him out with a hangdog air. How come you know about me, he asked. Oh Mister Aristotle sir! he cried out in tones of veneration and lapsed into silence. His eyes darted about the room. It was from Calliope his aunt. He'd been on at her, of course he had, couldn't she put in a word for him, but she was that stuck up, not a chance. Oh no you don't, she wasn't one to beg favours, she couldn't bother her Master Telly over a thing like that. What was he to Master Telly indeed, to go bother him about? He should have been more careful, that's all.

My dad let out a long breath of relief. He offered him a chair and cigarette. So that was it. Good for Calliope, what a Cerberus! But you mustn't blame the poor woman, she does it to protect me you know, there's a lot of injustice in the world, and we newspaper men are always in the limelight. I was sitting like a cat on hot bricks, I got up to go, but I wanted to hear the scene to the end, to see how my father would deal with it. His manner was quite different. He spoke easily and well. Not a trace now of the ageing figure who had made such a mess of his life. The cripple stole sideways glances at me, my father noticed, and explained that I was his daughter. He acknowledged me with a nod of his head. I got up and shook him by the hand — it gave me an excuse to change position, I couldn't bear to sit facing him. My father continued his rigmarole, so that was it, Calliope had a nephew ... Why of course, you must be Olga's son. Fancy that now, it must be thirty years since I last saw her. We lost touch when she married your father. And all those years she and Calliope weren't even on speaking terms, but what can you do with the female sex? The cripple had settled himself as best he could in the armchair and was listening carefully. My father asked him about his family and he replied, until the subject was exhausted. Olga it seemed had been placed with a legal consultant at the Mineral Mines, then she'd fallen for a miner and married him. Before long she was a widow. And now here was her son, another victim of the Mines. But Calliope, with her well-known weakness for reflected grandeur, at some point had fallen out with her sister and they'd never spoken since.

An awkward silence followed. All of a sudden my father was desperately busy, he began huffing and puffing, he was overwhelmed with work, and of course times were hard. But he'd look into it, if there was a place he could give him ... just at the moment there was nothing he could think of, we could hardly throw someone else out on to the street just to make room for a friend of the family, but never fear, something would turn up, if he'd like to leave his phone number, we could let him know. The cripple explained that he didn't have a phone number, but it wasn't any trouble to call again next week. My father took fright: why waste your time — nothing may have turned up by next week? I'll tell you what I'll do, here's my phone number. The cripple raised himself from the armchair, drew his crutches a little towards him and put his weight on them. He made as if to say goodbye, but held his glance unwaveringly on the room. Then father in the manner of a man with something on his conscience or maybe just because he'd weighed up how little he stood to lose, he paused and spread out his hands before us, something between supplication and the way you cast the evil eye, take a look, he said, take a good look at these hands, they're not a lot of use to me now, are they? But with these same hands he had touched the very bowels of the earth. And he reeled off the names of rare minerals: anazonite onyx, lemonite, iron pyrites that people call fool's gold — mineral upon mineral. And now he'd no job. In his anger and humiliation his face had lost its colour. It was all right for us, he laughed. Thank you very much, he said, much obliged. And left with a frozen smile. We heard the hollow tapping die away down the corridor. Then my father burst out, he'd see to the hall porter all right, letting in just anybody off the street like that. Drunk on ouzo again, no doubt, did he think he was paid to sit there like a bloody Buddha?

Then suddenly he seemed to remember my presence

and broke off. He turned to me wearily, what was he to do for him, he wasn't fit for work? Dammit, there're unemployment offices, what d'you call 'em, insurance schemes, surely he'd come under something like that, they'd give him a pension wouldn't they? I said nothing, and got up to go. He said where are you going, aren't we having lunch? I made an excuse that I'd fixed to meet Elvira, I couldn't keep her waiting. What about tomorrow? He said he'd phone. Then he sighed that his day had been ruined, how was he going to get the sight of the cripple out of his mind? And what about the reality? I asked him in surprise. My ears were thrumming as though a great wind were blowing. And of all the minerals he had reeled off, like whiplashes across our cheeks, my imagination had been caught by the one he'd called fool's gold, I could almost feel a scaly hand laid against my skin, as I remembered the diseases of the VD hospital, the metallic, scaly skin of ichthyosis.

The sunlight was too bright for me, I felt myself on fire all the way home. The next day I waited for him to phone, but he never did. And now today came Lucy, to announce their decision.

I phoned to find out what was going on and got Calliope, incoherent with grief. Last night they'd shut themselves in Telly's study, and talked and talked. Telly pounding the table with his fist, Natalie crying and pouring out the scores of a lifetime. Calliope was dying to give me a blow by blow account, but I cut her short and said I only wanted to know the upshot, what had happened? Well my dearie what do you think? First thing this morning my mother had packed her suitcases and announced she was off to London. She had left a letter for me, continued Calliope, she'd been sorry she couldn't say goodbye to me, but it wasn't possible, it was all explained in her letter. And now what was Calliope to do, should she bring the letter over herself or would I drop by and pick it up? I told her keep it and I'll drop by. She'd cooked me fish soup, would I like her to bring it to cheer me up — you're all skin and bone dearie, with eating nothing but yoghurt.

I put down the phone irritably. The next second it rang, it was Helen to tell me the Law School occupation was on, I'd better get a move on, they'd soon be putting up the barricades. I flew into the street like a cavalry charge. As I dashed about looking for a taxi I was in a whirl of impatience, they mustn't put up the barricades before I got there. The very air seemed to echo with the slogans, *Hands off the students, no draft for students.*

The morning had started all topsy turvy, my head felt heavy. Dust and cobwebs followed me about the room. Outside the sky was bright. Inwardly I could feel the fever raging through a glaring void and the white-washed icon-screen came back into view. Not far off from a little hut I could hear the secret comings and goings of people in hiding, or people far from home — like sailors whose ship has weighed anchor leaving them behind in a foreign port, the pier slippery with spilt oil, later a cool breeze from behind the mountain would clear the air. On the rocks were pinned photographs of wanted men, soft weeds were draped over them, and a tremor took hold of me as I decided they must be gravestones.

The days that followed the Law School débâcle were a difficult time for all of us — some were in hiding, some lying low, others on the wanted list. All the ones who'd been against the occupation were able to congratulate themselves quietly that they'd been right all along. And the papers were asking: how long can three thousand students keep up a hunger strike? My attention was fixed on Helen, who was all for carrying on. I enjoyed listening to her, but she couldn't convince me that we would be able to hold out and make them rescind the law on student conscription. Because the bloodletting of the Polytechnic on 14th February may have brought the centre of Athens to a standstill. Tempers were roused to some extent, but beyond the doors of the Law School not a tremor ruffled the bland face of compliance, the talk was of waiting for maturer conditions. Look, one speaker insisted, we're just not prepared for a long-term occupation, the building isn't suitable, there have been cases of people passing out in the crush, and he added that not all of us barricaded inside were equally of a mind to persevere, he pointed to some pregnant girls sucking lemon-rinds, the speaker was fond of the sound of his own voice, and finally hadn't the Vice-Chancellor himself promised them a bloodless exit from the building? So the decision was taken and hands raised above our heads we stumbled out into the early afternoon sunshine to be greeted by a crowd of thirty thousand. I found myself in a knot of students running up Academy Street, with the fuzz hard on our heels. Thus ended a year of campaigning for democratic student elections. But we had the experience of an occupation behind us now — we had something to build on for next time; that was Helen's conclusion, and I agreed.

The arrests began that same day. We lay low — which meant that we didn't sleep in the same place each night. Not that we gained much; three weeks later Helen was dragged from her bed. They kept her at Security for a week, then handed her over to the Military Police — the tortures inflicted by Security paled into insignificance compared with what went on there, it was said. Her mother had a kind of seizure, she lay stiff and rigid on her bed and raved. When she came to her senses, she nobbled everyone she'd ever heard of who came from her own part of the country in a position of authority, to try to enlist their help.

For George this was the final straw. Well, what sort of a way was that to organise a sit-in — like the naval yard at Kronstadt? And things had been starting to settle down too! He accused us of losing our sense of reality. Then his mood changed and he clung tightly to the bars. If only he'd been outside with us. It was like being elbowed out of history. He could imagine the streets of Athens littered with bloated corpses. On other occasions he was severe with me. I had been responsible for his sister. Couldn't I have kept her out of it, what was the good of her getting mixed up? Even in the army they didn't let two members of the same family serve at the same time. Did she have to be sacrificed as well as him? Then he'd say he was sorry. But I had my work cut out keeping up with him. When things were bad he had the habit of raising his hands in the air; my own despair, when it took a grip, was quite different: just give me a machine gun in my hands. During the years he'd spent in prison he'd got used to nitpicking over things that for those of us on the outside had long ceased to matter. Perhaps because if you're on the move you haven't the

194

time to watch your own movement, still less to look over your shoulder as your impetus carries you forward.

But what did that leave for me? I was afraid of offending him, and the prison ambience couldn't have helped. Once he got out, it would be easier to find our feet. I'd so many friends of both sexes, but a friend I could call my own in good times or in bad, a friend I could talk to about anything under the sun, without either of us fearing to risk looking a fool in the eyes of the other, someone I didn't have to agree or disagree with, I didn't have; only George. I went over his features in my mind and trembled to think that our love might founder in all this pettiness. I counted the days until he was due to be released, but I couldn't imagine what life with George would be like. Without the grille and the warders. The pistachio groves of Aegina and the little ship that took me there. The seagulls and the flying fish. The wizened mothers of the men inside and the little benches beneath the eucalyptus trees, where we waited for the visiting hour. The cries of the children from the school nearby. And afterwards the pain of the return journey, the sea choppy, portholes caked with salt, cigàrette butts and the stench of vomit. Behind us Aegina would float serene on the Saronic Gulf, while I sat huddled up, gulping back saliva, as I tried to find a sense of proportion. Now resigned, now raucous and cheerful, in sympathy with the mood of the other women, I'd indulge to the full my penchant for soaking up the prevailing atmosphere. As though hypnotised by the sighs of the mothers, sounding in a shell. George, a man exalted to the divine, ran a hand through my hair, bent and whispered the words of Solomos, *Hail sister! the pallor of thy countenance is passing fair*, but never as I slept had I dreamt of his embrace. Always in my dreams he gazed down at me severely, frowning, like the Pantokrator from his dome in church. Then the awareness of poverty would go through me like a knife — I'd only to catch sight of the thin plaits of an old woman's hair, the carbuncle on her ear or her worn fingers, and the visions would fade.

At moments like these even the songs of the top twenty would bring tears to my eyes, I felt I could sigh for all the rest of my days over the down-at-heel shoes of Thomas' fiancée. And suffering stirred like an octopus in the depths, as you heard Thomas' fiancée tell her story, and you saying where are you now Makriyannis, hero of national independence, the two of you should weave together in your *Memoirs* the story of a little girl thrashed, and the secret mingling of her outraged honour with your own tears in a deserted church, when your fellow-countryman beat you within an inch of your life — why don't you say your prayers together, maybe you could intercede for her a little with the Lord?

George had often asked me — what do you know of the people? I used to lower my head sorrowfully. What *did* I know of the people? Nothing at all. Macho men all dressed to kill, broad print ties in pursuit of a destiny of distant dreams: those I knew and feared. Well-bred ladies, a smattering of manners and a smattering of culture: these I knew and feared. And something else: mothers fetching butter from the fridge — a creamy mixture made from every kind of froth. A silent film with Laurel and Hardy falling down and getting up again among the custard pies.

What could you do but weep and clap your hands for Charlie Chaplin?

12

AFTER THE DIVORCE, my mother moved to London for good. Even I hadn't expected her to take it so hard. But Athens held nothing for her now. We talked on the phone almost daily. She kept begging me to join her there, even if only for a short time, couldn't I find myself a degree course or something, and come and live with her? What on earth did I find to occupy my time in Athens, how could I bear to live in that dreadful city? I said I'd love to see her, but I couldn't travel, they wouldn't give me a passport. She thought it quite ridiculous. I kept explaining patiently why, but she never seemed to listen. She would already have passed on to *them*. By which she meant my father and Lucy. I swore I kept them at arms' length, I hadn't gone to the wedding, I didn't want to know, I'm on your side, I told her. But she preferred not to believe me. She'd tax me with how hard I'd been on her, how I'd always loved Lucy more than her. Her recriminations would run on without pause for breath, then suddenly she'd put the phone down and I'd be left with the sound of her sobbing echoing in my ears. With my father things were little better. From what I could see he'd gone through with the divorce without enthusiasm. Lucy had somehow caught him off his guard and pressed home her advantage. Because he may not have loved my mother, but the two of them had evolved a way of life together that had more or less worked. Now Lucy made him change many of his old habits. Every Saturday lunch time, for instance, she'd drag him off to Kifisia to spend the weekend in peace and quiet! And it was rather comical — I'd gone along with them once, and could barely stop myself from crying and laughing as I watched them.

Meantime, the famous secret that had bound them for so long was finally revealed. I wasn't in the least surprised, I'd almost expected it. Alexandra, the ten-year-old they now formally adopted, was their own, all their own, and they'd had her brought up in London. Lucy, after all, could always be relied on to keep up appearances. This primness was yet another reason for me to dislike her. At least Xenia and Nancy made no bones about what they were. So Alexandra was duly adopted to complete the picture of the holy family. Which with me made a happy foursome. It crossed my mind to take on the management of this bordello, crack the whip and make them belly-dance before the crowds, and pass the hat round at street corners. My father was unamused by my perverse sense of humour, as he put it, but never fear, you're my firstborn, you're the most precious of all. And launched into some spiel about love and being liberated so that each of us can find love where he will. Come off it, I said, I've heard that before. I was riled by his defeatism. It was always the same, whenever he started holding forth about himself, I'd be borne along by his theorizing and his confidences. He knew how to spike my guns, he only had to tease me for being strict and puritanical. I'm fed up, I shouted at him, with this soap opera, can't you just leave me out of it? But by now he was well away. As I listened to him I asked myself was it possible, in all sanity, that he believed this crap he was talking, could they really imagine the shreds they'd made of their lives had anything to do with progress and liberation? Could he really be so obtuse as not to see how irresponsible he was? He'd always blown with the wind. Out of sheer pity I let him parade his eloquence before me. And heard him accuse me of not being any fun.

Until the day came when my mother committed suicide. Every detail of her death was planned and relentlessly rehearsed. The story was told to me by Liza, when we had a few moments together after the funeral, of how that morning she had woken in good spirits. She'd whisked her egg in the mixer, full of the joys of spring, her future an open book before her and so on in cheerful vein. Liza had been overjoyed, she'd begun to tire of nursing her. On the spur of the moment they'd decided to invite some people in, to celebrate. They set to with a will, to make their preparations. My mother was to phone round their friends, while Liza did the shopping. But when she'd got back, she'd found my mother listless. What could have happened while she was out? She'd experienced a moment's worry, then thought no more of it. She'd prattled on, determined to restore my mother's good humour. But it was no good. Her cheerful mood of the morning had evaporated. She returned to her favourite mumbo-jumbo about Alexis. It had become an obsession with her recently, that Alexis before he took to the mountains had laid a curse on her, from childhood he'd had an envious, spiteful streak, and he'd cursed her so that she would never be happy again. And had haunted her dreams with the face of a vengeful saint. What more could he expect of her? Now that she'd had to give up even her husband to his sister, couldn't he leave her in peace at last? Liza had done what she could to calm her down, and put her to bed. That had been her mistake. She'd been busy with getting ready for the guests, and by the time her anxieties revived, people had begun arriving and were knocking on the door of her room: no response. From there matters had taken their course. She'd been rushed to hospital, but by then it had been too late.

To my mind this woman had gone to such extravagant lengths to get her own back at me for failing to become the prima ballerina of her dreams. She was flown back in her coffin and they all dragged me along to the cemetery where they vied with one another: Lucy sobbing, Calliope with whooping gulps, Victoria weeping buckets. They shot menacing glances at me as though they felt my presence cramped their style. I wanted to cry but nothing came. The sky was white, my breath misted the glass lid on the coffin, I felt choked by the gladioli. In turn they went by and kissed the glass, making the sign of the cross over it. When they lowered her into the grave, Lucy's sobbing reached a crescendo. Her manner was altogether that of the pious matron mourning a close relative; while my father's tears flowed unrestrained. The spectacle they made cancelled out my misery. Next we stood in line and accepted condolences. Then came the time for drinks. My father said the brandy they doled out at funerals was beyond the pale. He became maudlin with the reflection that he was here to mourn his former wife. I stared out of the window with the line by Elytis thrumming in my head: *The cypress trees point like clock hands set to midnight.*

200

During the days that followed, I began to haunt the Athens First Cemetery. In a daze I circled round her grave, I couldn't come to terms with the sight of her face, dead in its coffin. And I roamed in a daydream among the gravestones. Idly I inspected the inscriptions and the photographs of the dead. Within me something hung in the balance — perhaps it was my links with the living. I'd reached a suspended state, a kind of frozen serenity. I counted on my fingers how many more I'd have to see dead and buried before I could walk the earth as my own mistress absolutely, if only I could have been brought up in an orphanage. And so I made my peace with death — six or so feet beneath the ground, standing outside the iron railings that enclosed my mother's grave, where one by one the other members of our family had turned to dust, I sat and watched the birds among the cypresses without emotion. My sleep was haunted by the same dream continually. I'm going with George, a gentle breeze caressing my ankles and the chill of fear upon me, to a sleazy hotel in a darkened city. In the doorway of the hotel sits a woman who reminds me of someone, but I can't remember who, and she starts to tell us the story of her life. We go on past her and frantically try to find our room. The woman's voice follows us, her shadow overtakes my feet, until it starts to solidify and turns into my mother. By her feet is a pile of long white bones that gleam. She bends down to gather them up, but they elude her grasp. With a pang of certainty, I recognise the bones of Alexis; I badly want to help but all I can do is pretend not to notice. I shoot a sideways glance at George, as though I'm ashamed of her and don't want him to realise who she is. He returns my look with a penetrating stare that frightens me. I close my eyes to hide the radiant awe I feel for Alexis. All of a sudden I'm lost in an expanse of sand. There's the glare of a summer's day and I catch sight of Lucy's and my mother's sun hats, cast aside on the sand, and my father sunbathing, sandwiched between the two of them. Then a sudden quirk of wind snatches up the sun hats and whirls them far away in a brilliant waltz, etching their progress like wrinkles on the heat haze. My mother runs after them, then seems to weary as her hands flail hopelessly, she's sinking into the sand, there's sand even in her mouth, but she catches them. And when she rejoins the others, smiling broadly with the sun hats in her hand, what will she see but my father looking into Lucy's eyes and pushing back the hair from her forehead? That had been oh so many years ago, as my mother would write in her diary. So many years since my father had first met Lucy. All the winds of the firmament might blow but never, never, had he reached out a hand to push the hair from *her* eyes. And with the bitterness of this reproach she had swallowed down the pills and her darkened form stands staring now, as Alexis' bones cascade without a sound and scatter like so many feathers, to all eternity she'll weep and flutter after them. Then I'm with George in the sleazy hotel. We're still trying frantically to find our room. We turn down corridors that echo with my mother's grief, and push past fleshy, dark-leaved plants. When we find it at last, we open the window that looks out onto a courtyard, and hang out our socks to dry. George is staring at me with an austere look and his toenails gleam in the darkness. I'm constantly shivering in my sleep, I never did dream pleasantly of George. We'd always be soaking wet, something would always come between us, we'd always be trying to find something and when at last we found it we'd be like strangers waiting for something to happen; and at that point I'd awake.

But in the light of day my memory was unimpaired. I knew how the pages of Mother's diary merged into one another — and found it natural that they should merge also into my own life. I'd analyse myself and feel my nightmares formally registered, as if by doing so I could freeze them into a harmless narrative, into something that the brain could control. I could even propose aesthetic functions for them, and tailor them accordingly on grounds of taste. The one thing I couldn't manage, and this went back some way now, was to sort out my feelings for George. I had set out to convince myself that I was in love with him. I used to think of him in the prison yard, with the bitter taste in his mouth in the aftermath of each visit, his loneliness at night. In just this way I had once visualised Paul in hiding. But when it came down to it, who thought in that way of me? I was always at sea among fantasies of other people. The very next day after my mother's funeral, I'd gone to Aegina as usual. Under the spell, I daresay, of the seductive narcissism of grief. When he saw me wearing black a shadow darkened his face, I began to feel sorry for myself too. But then when he began asking me all about it, I felt irritated. His condolences got on my nerves, I didn't like his way of showing sympathy, and I could manage without it. I tried in vain to remember when it had been that the touch of his fingers through the bars no longer gave me a thrill. Whenever he wasn't near me I felt I needed him, but as soon as we were together I found myself almost disliking him, the smallest thing would put my back up. I began to feel I had suffered a great deal for George, that distance had finally put too great a strain on our love.

My father was worried about me, but there is always a degree of posing about my dad's anxieties, everything depends on the right pitch of theatricality as he lays bare his soul for the umpteenth time, the necessary pall of gloom, and now he'd Lucy to provide a disingenuous accompaniment to his self-doubt and recrimination. Together they would relieve their feelings with stormy tears, they'd bemoan their lot and in due course calm down. After two months it was as if my mother's suicide had never been, a dense cloud had scooped her out of the land of the living. I'd given up my visits to the cemetery too. I'd read her diary which Liza had given me. I read it many times over until I knew all of it by heart. Then I burnt it page by page in the sink. The air in the kitchen was thick, I turned on the extractor fan, and then the tap. The charred shreds whirled about and stuck to me. Then the phone went and I jumped, I felt as though I were emerging from the effects of a drug. It was Urania, were we going out for a meal tonight? I told her to meet me in the square.

I turned off the extractor and the tap. The sink was choked with black flecks. I got a cloth and wiped it up carefully, as though to leave no trace behind. My heart was pounding. Next I took a shower, put on scent and a white blouse that smelled of detergent. So ended the period of my mourning. I felt I'd done enough. As I headed downhill towards the square the Easter breeze struck me full in the face and I felt better. My dream came back to me, with my mother running and chasing the sun hats and then trying to gather up some old bones. And already I felt quite cheerful with the rationalised version I was going to give to Urania. I found her sitting in a café with Fotis, Elvira and Thodoros. They were pleased with my transformation. I ate well that evening and belched at the end of the meal. I even tried to smoke a cigarette, but that was too much for me.

Some days later Anestis asked me to lunch at their place. I wasn't much excited by the prospect, but he came himself to collect me. He looked curiously round the walls of my room, and came to a halt in front of the shelf that held my books. I felt powerless, as though my whole life were being probed in front of my eyes, with that playfully casual air a certain type of visitor adopts. He turned and said each generation had its own things to stick up on the walls. He scowled, I suppose in disapproval, at Guevara and remarked how difficult it must be for the young to resist the trend, be they never so discriminating, I was a good example of what he meant. Still, there we were, he concluded resignedly, something's bound to rub off from the system. Then he chose to comment on my meagre library. I bore it patiently, telling myself that Anestis was a hard old nut, the trouble with Anestis was there was nothing in the centre. This casual sniping began to get on my nerves. He went on to say that the young of today were content with simple certainties; even if they read all the books in the world they were still just wasting their time. What they lacked was any sense of culture. They'd no idea how to ask questions of their reading; they'd either swallow it whole or decide they weren't interested, they couldn't penetrate beneath the surface, still less assimilate anything. They'd been corrupted by television. They could barely express themselves any more. He looked at me and laughed — how about you for instance, hacking away with a blunt instrument in your hands, you're in too much of a mess to decide what it is that really matters to you, something you can make your own and really work for. That's why you've so little sense of purpose, so little to say for yourself. Not once, he continued, had he heard me explain fully and clearly what I believed about a given subject, however straightforward. He'd often wondered what it was that made me tick. He laughed again, with an air of great good humour. It didn't seem to matter what I said. We spoke different languages. I listened to him tight-lipped with vexation, what right had he to put me on the spot? Then he came up to me and grasped my chin to turn my face towards him. I pulled away from him in annoyance. He wanted to know if he'd upset me talking like this, I wasn't to take it to heart, he went on, and drew me closer. That's what I like so much about you, he concluded. The blunt instrument in your hands. He bent down and kissed me on the cheek. He said again was I cross with him and I muttered that I wasn't. I was surprised to find myself so spineless. Then he lapsed into fussy bonhomie. Time to be on our way, Zoe would be waiting.

I ate with difficulty, I had the feeling that at any moment I'd dissolve or melt into thin air. I kept thinking of the smell of nicotine on his fingers. And as I watched them I found I liked them, so dry with the veins standing out. Zoe was pregnant and sat like a saint with a halo, while Anestis anxiously anticipated her every wish. Quite the happy couple, I was irritated by their ex aggerated show of affection for one another. Throughout the meal Zoe caressed him with the teasing femininity of her voice. And he responded with fatherly solicitude.

I was trying to work out how long it had been since I'd made love. Not since Paul. And even then it had given me little pleasure. I concluded I was badly deprived. Deprived and stale. Elvira had often harped on my complete inexperience in matters of sex. You can't live on fantasies forever, it's what you *do* that counts. She was quite right. But I was repelled by the idea of making love with another man. I wanted to wait for George. While I waited I found relief in masturbation. I told Urania this and she ticked me off, you'll make yourself potty in the head, she said. I wasn't impressed. But gradually I came to dislike the idea of making love even with George. It began to seem like incest. And anyway I'd always been put off, when I used to go with boys in the old days, and they always seemed in such a hurry, even Paul had cared only for his own pleasure. Only the scenarist, when I was very young, had asked me how it felt, what did I feel when he kissed me, when he held me in his arms, what did I feel until I felt sick. And that had been pretty short-lived too: a month on Mykonos. When I'd seen him again, later, in Athens I'd thought what a creep, I couldn't think why I'd agreed to go to bed with him.

A penny for them, Anestis broke in on my daydream. Zoe began to rib me too; why surely, I was thinking of my young man *behind bars.* The way she said it, it was as though she'd guessed what I was really thinking and meant it as a rebuke, especially the way she stressed behind bars. I replied that I'd been thinking of my mother, and how unfair it had been; I was unashamed by the lie, as though in that moment it had dawned on me that I had, quite truthfully, been thinking of my mother. Anestis looked at me sadly and said I really must let it go, after so long. It had been the hand of fate, and what was done couldn't be undone. I was alarmed. Imperceptibly desire for him was taking hold of me, I was finding him sexually attractive again, with all the closeness I'd felt towards him once before, when he used to visit my dreams. I was content to let my imagination roam, at the end of the day I felt blameless and innocent, indeed I felt quite powerless before the self-confidence with which they raised their forks to their mouths, and the firm champing of their jaws. A surge of euphoria brought me closer to them still, from my exalted height I cast my blessing upon them. After the fruit I said I had to go. Anestis insisted he never took a siesta, if I wanted we could sit out on the veranda and talk, just the two of us. I excused myself and said my farewells. Out in the street I stumbled blindly, I was in such a state of turmoil, the glare affected me too, I got home in a state of high excitement.

The next month passed in a steady hankering for romantic sunsets and weepy novels. One moment I'd be swearing with impotent rage, the next I'd conjure up a pantheon of hugely chubby angels. In under a week I'd covered the records of Bach sonatas with scratches. I couldn't even bring myself to visit George, it didn't seem to matter that I'd waited for him so long. The heartthrob Kazantzidis sang from the barrows of the street vendors, *Every girl is just the same*, and the barrow boys took up the refrain, *Every girl is just fair game*, as I walked past and old sad songs of yearning echoed in my wake; Thomas' fiancée looked at me sternly as she walked up the hill to Aegina prison, proud to be wearing the talismans of lifelong fidelity under her bra-strap, next to the skin. And there was Helen, in the hands of the Military Police. I said this to myself and a lump rose in my throat, I couldn't forgive myself. I'd never been laid-back enough to hang about in bars — and never wanted to either. But as I looked in at their apathy I felt I had lost forever, even for a moment's pause, the right to stretch out in a chair without a care in the world, while time dallied idly about the pavements; I would sigh that I'd been fated never to rest upon this earth.

Fondas was doing his service in the Navy, he'd ended up on Salamis. We hardly saw one another now, or it might be truer to say that I avoided him. He had got involved with a girl called Katie, a trainee doctor. From what I could gather, he'd taken her home to his parents, they were going to get married after his military service. She was doing her stint in a rural practice, somewhere in the direction of Corinth; they'd do all they could to meet as often as possible. We met once, when Fondas called to offer his condolences for my mother, and she seemed a nice girl. We spent three hours in one another's company and found nothing to say. Katie was rather jumpy and seemed to be watching me warily. A day or two later she came to my flat and told me to my face not to try to see them again. Because whenever he saw me, Fondas got ill. No, he didn't let it show, but I'd been very bad for him. I was appalled by her manner. How dared she talk to me like that, I said to her. She explained curtly that she loved Fondas, that was how. She'd no idea what had happened between us, but it had obviously been something pretty unhealthy. So she was asking me to leave them alone. I promised her I would.

George's mother was on the phone, where had I got to? George had been asking after me and what was she to say? For the first time in my life I felt sorry for her. She controlled herself with an effort, if I'd given her the slightest sign she'd have begun pleading with me — I couldn't leave her only son and walk out on him, could I? Even so, she half said it. Not now, when everyone was saying there was going to be an amnesty; I'd kept it up for so long, surely just a little longer till he was out of jail, I could do what I liked after that? Typical mother-and-son! She'd go down on bended knee, I could walk all over her, but George mustn't be made to suffer. I put it down to my mother's death, but she didn't fall for that. I was only making matters worse, finding excuses. The idea had got hold of me and I began to be afraid it would become a millstone tied around my neck that I had let a whole month go by without a visit to Aegina. And all the months before would count for less than nothing.

Standing there on the doorstep with three orchids wrapped in cellophane in his hand, he cut a ridiculous figure. I thought of Zoe's burgeoning abdomen, you dirty old man, I said to myself. Or so at least I tried to quell the tumult within me. He parked himself on a chair and began to talk about nothing in particular. He couldn't say exactly what had given him the idea of paying me a visit. But what on earth did I do with my life, holed away here? He didn't take exception to my room, this time, or eye my bookshelf critically, he didn't even scowl at Guevara on the wall. He seated himself with an affected air of ease. Trying to play the lad, I thought, and felt a pang of pity for him. He said in so many words, I was turning into a real good-looker, each time he saw me I'd changed. What a lot I'd grown up these last couple of years, and what a lot I'd been through. He began to talk to me about his own student days, about the German Occupation, his work for the Resistance, his years in prison. Then he asked me to make him a cup of coffee. I've only got Nes, I replied. No, that wouldn't do, it upset his stomach. I'd nothing else to offer and he asked me how did I manage to live in this place? He noticed the dust everywhere, you'll be eaten by cockroaches, he said. I gave an awkward giggle. Then he said why didn't we go out somewhere? We could go down to the seafront; all right, I agreed. I was very curious to see how the evening was going to turn out. He seemed to have come for no other purpose than sex. Perhaps he couldn't do it with his wife, and his thoughts had turned to me. The surer I became of this, the more hurt I felt. I didn't so much mind the sweet nothings he was murmuring, as the innuendo I detected in his voice, the impatient desire that seemed to inform his movements, as though he were dying to make a grab at me.

As he drove he talked to me about Zoe and the child they were expecting, in a way I found quite touching. He loved his wife very deeply, he said. But what *is* love? he wondered with a turn of his head towards me. Every time we stopped at a red light the engine stalled, then the car would jerk forwards as he swore at the other drivers to right and left. What did *I* think about love? he wanted to know. I thought of what it was that had bound me faithfully to George for more than three years now; and told him. He looked disappointed: that was a shallow attitude to have. I'd rather be shallow, I said, maybe then I'll be able to see deep water ahead. He winced, let's not be too clever, he said.

I was curiously unnerved to find him so unscrupulous, I'd never have thought of him putting on such an act to get a girl into bed, I was unhappy about what it was he'd suddenly seen in me, for the best part of a lifetime I'd thought of him darkly frowning beneath the weight of the world's ills, morosely pensive — and yet I recognised something in myself too as I watched him, guessing in advance his every gesture, that reminded me of the cliché gestures, the predictable smile, of Xenia's brother when once he'd tried to have his way with me. And all this I began to find amusing — the eternal game, I mused to myself and wondered, do I play or not?

We stopped at a small taverna and faced one another across a table. If I moved my legs at all they were bound to touch his. There was a warmth between us. He began to tell me that he'd become rather tired of life with Zoe. I noticed that for the first time he pronounced the name without his usual tenderness. At first, he continued, he'd been overly jealous, the fear of losing her had given him sleepless nights. Then suddenly something had changed, something had snapped inside him! Of course he loved her still, but he'd ceased to be jealous. He ordered whitebait, sour greens, fetta cheese and retsina from the barrel. He filled my glass and began to look at me appreciatively. Bet he tries to make me drunk, I thought to myself. He commented on the beckoning slant of my eyebrows, the texture of my hair, my green eyes. In the tones of a a reciter at a social gathering. He lit a cigarette and offered me one, he was surprised not to have noticed before that I didn't smoke. He asked me

212

why was I so quiet, what was on my mind? But without waiting for me to answer he carried straight on, as he looked at me something seemed to cry out within him, you're so beautiful! A slight hoarseness, the touch of a drawl, came into his voice, I reminded him, he continued, of American college girls playing volleyball and leaping up in the air till all you could think of was how it would be to have them in bed, just supposing they'd take any notice of you of course. He left the phrase hanging in the air and immediately began to fuss, he hadn't offended me by saying that, had he? It was just this ability to speak frankly that he admired so much in my generation. To call things by their real names and not beat about the bush. He laughed as though to congratulate himself and asked again if he had offended me. No, I don't mind, I told him. But what are you trying to get me to do, fuck with you? Say it then. His jaw dropped; when he found his voice again he said to me was I aware what I had said? I was a complete disappointment to him. I said, so was he to me. We sat in silence. He stubbed out his cigarette and lit another. He had drawn himself up in vexation. No doubt he'd have been flattered if I'd said tremulously, with a husk in my voice, that I loved him. But all the while the love that had so unnerved me earlier was ebbing away into the soft lapping of the sea on the beach. I was full and disembodied as my thoughts followed my gaze out into the Saronic Gulf, towards Aegina.

I heard him let out a long breath. He looked old and pathetic, I'd broken the spell that he'd been at such pains to create. I wanted to tell him I'd been in love with him ever since I was seven and that for years I'd carried the imprint of his lips on my cheek, the time he kissed me congratulations for getting full marks in my school report. It had been my first kiss of love. But what was the use? That had been seventeen years ago and everything had changed since then — only memories remained to pull me backwards and bring the past to life, memories that slid like grains of sand slowly through the cracks, like random grooves on the surface of my being; I said to myself there it is at last, the point of no return, there's the young Karl Marx, and there am I sitting across a taverna table from Anestis and struggling to recall properly the first page of the *Eighteenth Brumaire of Louis Bonaparte*, at the same moment remembering that when I was small my parents never used to ask me anything directly, in the second person, such as how was I, was I feeling all right? The question would always be framed at one removed, *how is Myrsini*? as if they hoped that gradually I'd change into someone else, and though I knew quite well whom they meant and duly answered, I'd always cast a glance over my shoulder — I got used to seeing a shadow there and grew up with the idea of a double.

I said I was sorry, as I said it again I reached out for the palm of his hand. He stared at me without seeming to see me. I sat and listened to the sea and decided I didn't care if I'd hurt his feelings. I felt his presence as no more than a bundle of bones: I could leave it to my imagination now to put him together and take him apart without effort. After a while he spoke. The fault was his, he said. He was grateful to me for bringing him down to earth. He'd made the mistake of thinking he was talking to an adult. He'd been wrong and he begged my pardon. I smiled just as though nothing had happened, with a wide-eyed look of wonderment. He was certainly annoyed. He beckoned the waiter and paid the bill. The food on our plates was scarcely touched.

On the drive back neither of us spoke. When we drew up outside my flat he turned to me and said, what happened tonight, that's between the two of us, OK? But of course, I replied. All right, he said, but won't you let me into the secret now? What did he mean? I asked him. Just this: who was it sharpened the point of my blunt instrument? he chortled and whistled down his nostrils. I'd have liked very much to tell him, but I didn't bother. Even the pity he aroused in me made me dislike him the more. I said goodnight hurriedly. Back in my room my eye fell on the orchids, and I burst into tears.

13

WE SAT WAITING FOR HIM under the eucalyptus trees —
the eucalyptus, they say, is so voracious it won't let
anything else grow near it. They say a lot about love too.
But words are easy things and the toils of love immense.
I was sitting next to his mother and trying to control my
impatience. At any moment the door would open and
he'd appear. Several nights in succession recently I'd
gone to sleep with the image of this moment fading from
my eyes. How often had I tried to imagine what it would
be like: him setting down his suitcase in the roadway,
and gathering me up in his outstretched arms, to whisk
me off into meadows full of poppies. I'd fallen a willing
victim to the clichés of romantic love; as I sat worn out
on a stone bench waiting for George, not a word came into my mind that wasn't secondhand. You've gone white,
his mother said, and squeezed my hand. I was touched
by her gesture, it wasn't like her to show affection, not
even to her children.

The door opened and when I caught sight of him, I was
the one I was sorry for; after all the grille that had
separated us had also been a protection. I remembered
an evening at dusk, long ago. I'd been waiting for him
outside the Museum, we were to go and type leaflets, I'd
been feeling relaxed and cheerful, at one with the world

as I sat placidly slumped in my café chair, ready to make peace even with the tourists. I'd seen him in the distance and caught the swift appreciative glance he darted at an attractive woman going past. That had been the first inkling, as I suddenly yearned to see him look at me like that, that I might, just conceivably, be in love. As though a great tide were ready to burst its banks within me. Ever since then I'd been ruled by this same trembling anxiety. Whenever the mood broke, it would leave me torpid, in a state of docile idiocy.

He came to a stop on the pavement, but he didn't put down his suitcase as I'd imagined him doing. With composure he put his free arm round his mother's neck, kissed her on both cheeks, and let his head rest fleetingly on her shoulder. I hadn't been prepared for this. I tried to smile, but that wasn't easy either. His own smile was razor-sharp, as if to say to me, from here on, if we stay together, it's to be on equal terms. I took this as a threat. I went up to him and put my arms round him, as though I'd have liked to pick him up and set him down somewhere else. He hugged me to him, my love, he whispered with a tone of surprise, almost of annoyance. It was as though he hadn't wanted the word to pass his lips at such a moment. As though he'd planned something different for our first meeting and I had somehow tried to get in first. Afterwards we joined in the general celebrations, and all made our way together down to the harbour. The tourists gaped at us from under the café awnings, while waiters scurried about to fetch their orders. All the way back on the boat he held my hand tightly clasped in his, and talked to his mother. I eyed the two of them, as though under a spell. It was the first time in several years that our bodies had been so close. And all the while that he seemed to ignore me beside him, his touch whittled me down to nothing. Before my eyes I conjured up expanses of virgin snow, and pine trees clothed in icicles. My mind roamed across the sea; I thought of Fondas' uncle who'd been on an island concentration camp, the blue sea and the screams of the prisoners, curse the sea for a whore, the salt sea.

We came to Piraeus. I said, well, I suppose it's bye for now, we'll talk later, on the phone. Neither of them made a move to restrain me, it was quite the most natural thing in the world, they seemed to say, that I should leave them alone together. With an effort I held back tears. Well, bye then, I repeated, and George said what time would I like him to ring? His words sounded strangely in my ears, though his look gave me some assurance. Whenever you like, I said. They drove off in a taxi, leaving me to walk to the Underground station. I walked in a daze, I scarcely had control of my feet.

I took a shower and felt better. I became very reasonable and very mature, it always made me feel sorry for myself that I could so easily understand the way people behaved, but at the same find their behaviour so hard to stomach. Yesterday I'd filled all the glasses in the flat with sprays of jasmine. And as I went to change their water I was struck by my air of helplessness; I threw the lot in the dustbin and started to hum a tune under my breath. But I couldn't keep it up. I moved the phone onto the bed and curled up next to it, as if willing it to ring.

It was quite late before he rang. He called me his girl, said he wanted me to come out with him. He was celebrating with some of his oldest friends. Before he hung up he said, do hurry, I can't wait to see you. I spent a long time in front of the mirror, I'd decided to tart myself up. I put on a dress my father had brought me from London, that I'd never worn all the time that I'd been ashamed to be seen in posh clothes. Then I stood back and inspected myself dubiously. But my doubts went no further than appearances. I'd only daubed myself so liberally with creams and rouge in the certain knowledge that I'd go straight back to the bathroom and scrape it all off again. I gave up looking in the mirror, and as I moved, my shadow rose like a giant bear to the ceiling. Like the time I'd turned into my own ghost and learned self-assurance. I'd had a passion then for dressing up in sheets, hiding behind doors and turning the electricity off at the mains. I enjoyed the fits I gave Calliope and my mother, occasionally even my father would cry out in alarm. But this I found more humbling than I could bear, as I saw him vulnerable and powerless to protect me. And in this way I'd learned that I would have to come to terms on my own with terror.

I arrived late in Peristeri where they lived. George's mother was darting hither and thither at fever pitch, and I was touched. Aspasia had had her hair done, and looked her best. Most of George's friends I had met in the old days. They were standing when I arrived, still undecided which taverna to go to. They thought we might eat somewhere locally and then go on to a *boîte* in Plaka. Stelios, Aspasia's fiancé, said he knew this *boîte*, it was fantastic, he said, the songs there really had something to them. All this time George kept me close to him. What's the matter? he asked, your eyes are all puffy. His mother gave me a funny look. She'd never much liked my taste in clothes — my dear girl you'd think there wasn't a decent dress to be had in the shops, that you have to wear that baggy old thing, just look at the way it's falling apart on your shoulders. George answered, with his arm protectively round me, that that was how he liked me. Well if he must know he wasn't a lot better himself, she scolded, only half in jest. In the end we settled on the taverna at the corner. Afterwards we'd take it from there.

During the meal they all had their say about the political situation. George whispered to me, what a bore they were, he'd much rather have gone off with me, just the two of us. It was a shame, he said, but we could hardly get rid of them. They were the old gang, you see, he wouldn't like them to think he'd thrown them over for a woman. I was rather put out by this, but I told him to forget it, it's quite enough for me to be out with you after all this time. He put his arm round me and popped a piece of meat into my open mouth. He was so glad I understood. Helen was talking about torture. She had lost weight while she'd been in the hands of the Military Police, and looked haggard; but she was still in the front line. Stelios questioned her and she answered him rather condescendingly but also, as she realised herself, all too graphically. Then Stelios began to get carried away and got on his high horse. The rest of us fell silent and listened to him. He'd an enormous admiration for people like George and Helen, they were heroes, but it would be a mistake to think that everyone can be a hero like that, it depends on stamina, on spirit. Either you've got it or you haven't, in your heart of hearts, otherwise there's no point. I saw George make a face. Aspasia was digging Stelios in the ribs to make him lower his voice, people might hear from the other tables. But he was well away. He banged his fist on the table and shouted, Here's to you George you're a splendid lad, and to you Helen, my in-laws to be, long life to you both and strength for battles yet to come. Helen held herself in check for as long as she could; at last she burst out. There's no such thing as a hero, she said to him. Have you any idea how many people have been locked up and tortured these past few years? You must have. Perfectly ordinary people, people like me. What's special about me? I was caught and I was tortured, as simple as that. Just because I didn't give in to them, that doesn't mean I'm any different. If it happened, who's to say you would give in to them either? It's the most reactionary thing you can do to set the individual on a pedestal, apart from the whole; that's bourgeois thinking, are you with me? In this struggle of ours, there must be no pedestals. It's up to each and every one of us to do his utmost, no more no less. If we start saying not everyone can be a hero — what'll it be next, not everyone can join in the struggle? And can you imagine what that would mean? It would be like sending them home. Like threatening them with isolation. When all's said and done, like sending them off with absolution, of all the irresponsible ...

Another of the group spoke up — give us a break, you're driving us round the bend, talking off the top of your head like that. Could anyone deny that Panagoulis was a hero? Not everyone could throw a bomb at the dictator's car. And what about Guevara? Or Aris Velouchiotis back in the civil war? Are you trying to tell us that everybody is the *same*? No one's ever said that, not Marx, not anybody. Helen went crimson and threw out her chest. He was missing the point, she told him curtly, do you have to be so literal? What mattered was to set our people free from the remnants of a slave-owning, feudal, bourgeois morality, and from there she moved on to the leadership of the popular movement. Revolutionaries aren't made in heaven, a hero may be one thing, a revolutionary something else again. A true revolutionary is first and foremost the voice and vanguard of his time, but as for the awesome tragic qualities that are supposed to make someone a hero, they're nothing but a psychological safety-valve for the oppressed masses, cunningly manipulated as they are by the ruling class in order to weaken the popular struggle ...

Everyone had frozen. Stelios was aghast and didn't know where to put himself. Aspasia turned ferocious glances on Helen and, with her hair fixed in a rigid perm, she looked absurdly out of place. George burst out laughing. Sakis, who had interrupted Helen before, insisted: what else could you call Panagoulis, if not a hero? Helen replied that Panagoulis himself had surely no such idea in his head. *You* make him into a hero so as to make an alibi for yourself. Sakis exploded and demanded to know exactly what she meant. Helen gave a laugh and this incensed him further. He hammered the table with his fist, no he wasn't having it, would she please explain herself this instant? Was she trying to suggest he hadn't taken part in the struggle? Did we have to listen to babes in arms now spouting their opinions? George intervened and told him to take it easy, it was only talk. But he wouldn't let it go. Beside himself now, he rose to his feet and shouted that if she'd been a man he'd have settled this outside, as it was she could thank her brother and the skirt she wore. Got that? Then he flung some money on the table and walked out. Aspasia turned reproachfully to Helen, big-mouth, she said. It was as well that the other three members of the group took Helen's side. They'd had enough of Sakis, he's paranoid. Good for Helen, he'd had it coming to him, it wasn't as if no one else around had done their bit in the resistance. Gradually our high spirits returned. Helen began making up to Stelios, she stroked his hair and teased him. He paid no attention at first, but then he yielded and called her a little minx, trying to get round him with her charm, you're a one you are, for having your cake and eating it ...

George whispered to me that Helen had done a good job on Stelios too. Because they hadn't had time to get to know one another yet, but he'd tried the same sort of spiel on him too. He'd gone on for hours about his idea of a hero — it sounded like a kind of excuse for not hav-ing been to prison himself. And he'd made a clean breast to George, as it were modestly, of all he'd ever done for the resistance, how he'd helped people in hiding, how he'd given some money and so on, and all this quite ob-viously in order to raise himself in George's estimation, though George had no reason not to think well of him, the more so as he was going to take his elder sister off his hands. Anyhow, George went on, Helen was getting on his wick, she'd changed out of all recognition. All through lunch she'd harangued them. He was pleased in a way, but all the same she was driving him insane, come to that what had happened to her, this was more than hysteria, she hadn't turned neurotic had she? And how could she talk like that? You'd think she was ad-dressing a crowd. Had I noticed? We weren't a mass meeting. I was at a loss for words. For myself I was more hurt than offended by Helen's tirades. I don't know how it was, but she brought out a sense of inner hurt in me, imperceptibly she was becoming the mirror held up to my own failure. I saw her as way ahead of me, from every angle. But I also thought there was something pathetic about her, a lack of warmth. I never could be persuaded by her gift of the gab, but I often caught myself admiring her for it.

Stelios began to hum an old Theodorakis classic. We all joined in. I liked George's voice. We went through the repertory till we got to the recent stuff, songs of the resistance. The waiter came over and asked us to stop, he was on our side, but the taverna could be closed down. Stelios jumped up and began reciting Ritsos. Aspasia, horrified, tugged at him to stop. There was a commotion at the other tables. Somebody applauded. When Stelios had finished we paid the bill and took a taxi to a *boîte*. But they didn't like it there. We drank up our coffee and left, we ended up at Tsitsanis' old-time bouzouki place. Time for you to get to know the songs of the people, little Myrsini, George drew me onto his lap as he intoned *Cloudy Sunday, you are like my heart*. He reminded me of the time we'd quarrelled about the songs of the city poor, the *rebetika*, because he'd preferred Tsitsanis to Solomos. He'd been joking then, of course, but I'd been such a stubborn little thing I'd driven him half insane. I took it as a bad sign that he remembered. And the awkward way he held me in his arms, almost twisting my neck from my body, made me feel as if I was being marched before the firing squads that had once operated on this very spot.

They were well oiled by now, but I found it difficult to join in their euphoria. Their steps in the slow, swaying *zeibekiko* reminded me of a down-and-out staggering in the effort to assert himself. Sometimes it was the musicians, sitting bolt upright as they played, sometimes the writhing movements of the girl singer, and the flower girls going about between the tables with their wilted gardenias, I seemed to study them, all too soberly, as I sat pliantly, an outsider in their midst. George sang love ditties in my ear and I tried to laugh to please him. In the end a lump settled in my throat. Some fat oaf got up and started smashing plates, if I'd had a whip in my hands I'd have marked him for life. Stelios rose with a glass balanced on his head and circled round the dance floor, Aspasia clapped time for him. Then George got up and he and another man danced a fast *hassaposerviko*. They made a fine sight, the two of them. But as I looked at them admiringly, I felt myself stripped bare. No lilies flowering at the cliff's edge for me, no fine erotic fantasies either, there was only naked desire. And I found I could contemplate with sober curiosity the moment when we would at last be alone together. I could see in advance our every movement that lay ahead. George came over to me and tried to pull me to my feet. I held back crossly, he realised I meant it and let go. When the dance was over he wanted to know what the matter was, why was I so glum? I said I couldn't stand these wankers. This wasn't what I'd been looking forward to. He wiped a hand across his brow, and filled up our glasses. He said this wasn't the moment, but yes, he could see what I meant. But what worried him about me was that I couldn't ever let myself go, I was all uptight in here, and he tapped me lightly on the head. But I'd have to get used to the idea, so as to set the record straight because we were bound to come up against this

one again, that his parents had lulled him to sleep with
the old street tunes. And not in the Hatzidakis versions
either. I gulped and simpered inanely, how right he was.
But I felt hurt by his manner, he'd never let slip a
chance to rub my nose in his social origins. And I was
expected to humble myself still further. But I had a
dread of the tarty bohemian ways affected by my Aunt
Victoria: the last thing I wanted was to end up drooling
over the *rebetika*. And, although I could never get
George to admit it, I'd always had a great admiration
for the spirit of the people that had been absent from my
upbringing, while he, who had it anyway, adulterated it
by showing off: *When first we ever met my love, I
thought you sweeter than a dove, But when you kissed
me first of all, Your kiss was bitterer than gall* — no, I
didn't think much of it.

About four in the morning we broke up. As I got into
a taxi I saw in his eyes that he would have liked to come
with me. He kissed me and it felt as if he'd belched into
my mouth. He said no way, it was a shame, but there
were his sisters to think of, it wouldn't do to sleep out
on his first night home. Tomorrow we'd be on our own.
He pronounced the words *on our own* with a smack of
the lips that seemed to imply all the rest. I slammed the
door of the taxi shut, in a foul temper. It's at moments
like this, I muttered furiously to myself, that women get
pregnant with monsters.

14

HE LIT A CIGARETTE, made room for me on the bed beside
him and began to talk. Right from the week of his
release, his mother had been nagging him, what's to
become of you, what are you going to do for a living?
And she'd done the rounds of the churches lighting
candles in his size. He complained that his old friends,
when he'd caught up with them, seemed like fixtures in
their café chairs, going out to the taverna on the corner
every evening and singing Theodorakis songs under
their breath; and the Sunday football match. It wasn't
like old times at all, with poor old Dimitris in Germany
and Fondas in the Navy, we'd lost touch. And then there
was me who'd waited for him, and he didn't know how
he ought to behave with me. The thought of me had kept
him going through all those years in prison. To be frank,
he wasn't sure how to put it, he felt we should be starting to type leaflets, but then he had to admit that he'd
always thought leaflets a waste of time. It all got
jumbled up in his head, somehow we weren't getting
anywhere like this, there was something missing. He
begged me to help, there were a lot of decisions he'd
have to take. And him with a mother who was going to
end by making him feel like a migrant returned pen-
niless to his hearth, a guest in his own home, owing his
keep.

He lay quiet for a while, then drew himself on top of

me, I was still consumed by my anxiety to make these moments last as long as possible. Afterwards our hold on one another began to relax, our breathing slowed, as his body withdrew from mine. When I'd suggested living together he'd liked the idea at first, but then he'd been doubtful how his mother would take it. Anything like that was bound to upset her. He explained what a close family they were, they'd been through such terrible times together and now as a man he felt himself responsible for them.

His father had died of cancer. But before that he'd been an invalid and an alcoholic. Euthymia his mother had had to work to earn the family's bread. Sometimes olive-picking, sometimes working in the soap factory in their town, wherever there was work to be had, with a black scarf tightly bound about her head. Each time she was laid off she would cry hoarsely, with inarticulate sobs, as though even the right to weep had been taken from her. George remembered the flying ants every summer at their basement window. In Mavilis Street, because of the way the ground sloped, the single-storey houses in neoclassical style had each a damp basement with bulging, yellow-green walls. Not surprisingly the silence of the street was regularly broken, particularly in the afternoons, by the children spilling out of the basement flats to play in the road. And a chamber-maid would pop her head out from one or other of the upper houses, why couldn't they move their game to the alley further down, the mistress had her headache again. Above their rented basement lived a retired colonel. He liked to take charge of the housework, with his wife as his batman — Metaxia fetch me the salt, Metaxia where's the big spoon? They had a daughter called

Artemisia who was rumoured to be mad. Whenever she had her fits the whole house would shake. Artemisia's fits took the form of leaping up and down and shouting so fast that no one could follow the words. But at the time they thought it was the language of the devil and were all terrified of her. George told me that Artemisia's screaming had helped him to hold out under torture. The memory of that terror had given him a kind of outlet for the pain he'd experienced at the hands of the Security Police. There had been a son too, called Menelaus, but better known as The Monk because he used to spend all day in his room listening to records of church music. To this day if he happened to hear a piece of classical music it always seemed to him that he'd heard it before, on Menelaus' record player. And every now and then the lady of the house, Metaxia, would make him a present of a fistful of almonds.

Why was he telling me all this? I had been listening patiently, dully, ever since the first afternoon in my bed; he couldn't wait to tell me about the short stories of Vizyenos that the lady Metaxia had given him. Of the days when self-confidence began to grow in him, with Vizyenos tucked under his arm and he'd learned *My Mother's Sin* off by heart, and dreamed of bygone days when with staff and bundle children could create an epic world. Later his heart would miss a beat because he'd heard the carriage bells that brought Mrs Vardoules to her door. Another time he'd tell me about Mrs Vardoules. But for now, he couldn't leave home, when he thought of Aspasia who while still at school had carved the initials of the Greek Communist Party on her shoes so as to tread with a surer step upon the earth. And used to whisper to him of what she'd seen, like a fairy tale before her eyes, '43 or '44 it must have been, men with crossed bandoliers passing in and out of their house at dead of night. And together they'd let their imaginations fly to their father's cousin, Joseph, who had escaped the German firing squad only to be hanged from a royal oak by the monarchists after the liberation. And their father, until he died, had remained secretly a communist. Passionately devoted to the idea of the cause, he'd been a weak-willed man and easily intimidated, outwardly he'd kept his nose clean but the effort had broken him in the end. Even a vote cast for the Left in the secrecy of the ballot-box he had lived to regret. Because there had been a time, George would have been about thirteen, when his father used to receive regular summonses to the local police station, for no other reason than that he'd had the misfortune to have a first cousin who'd fought with the partisans, and to work for a pittance at the soap factory. Hours later his father would hobble home, beaten black and blue. The children had used to console themselves with the thought that the more their father was ill-treated in this world, so much the more happily would *they* be able to live in the next world, the socialist one. Then their father had died. And George went to light the oil-lamp on his grave. More often than not he didn't have the eighty lepta to buy a bunch of myrtle, and he kept a weather eye on the graves round about. Then he'd steal the flowers to strew over the bleached stone that covered his father. He used to look with envy at the graves of the rich and make plans to clothe their own in marble too, one day when he'd grown up. Then one day the verger had caught him red-handed with a flower-holder and thrashed him within an inch of his life. He'd sat and wept by the side

230

of his father's headstone and from that time had never again set foot in the cemetery. So much for his father, whose hair had turned white as his body succumbed in less than three months, at the Cancer Clinic. They'd had the disinterment after the customary interval — his bones now rested in a little box, without a marble cross, or photograph, or oil-lamp.

In those days Aspasia had been a bright young thing rushing off to demonstrations over Cyprus. The following year she'd finished school; and been whisked into a job with the Post Office, she could forget her dreams of going on to study. And when later George's future had been settled, Aspasia had helped him through his Law exams, so that he wouldn't end up like herself, serving behind a counter for the rest of his days. So the years had passed, and since we're conditioned to believe that utopian fantasies belong to the young, while maturity brings us down to earth, just so Aspasia in due course had begun to discover, not so much that communism was unfounded — all her life she would vote for the Party — but that the struggle to bring it about was a futile one. If we only looked about us, she would laugh sadly, we would see the ideologically pure in heart vegetating and maybe that was why, in the final analysis, the Left is always made up of second-class citizens. In this day and age what we needed was top-rate scientists and people of standing, who could corrode the system from within. Hadn't we seen the worldwide sensation caused by the assassination of Lambrakis? If Lambrakis had been a factory hand instead of a hapless wage-slave, who'd have taken any notice?

This was what Aspasia found unforgivable about George. Instead of looking at things rationally, he had to go and get himself locked up and waste three years of his life, when he could have been qualified and practising as a lawyer by now. Couldn't he see that for children of poor families it was an unaffordable luxury to take on the state, because all that happened was they were ruined for life and nobody cared anyway. It's different for rich children, they've always got the chance of returning to the fold. But he'd not thought of any of that, had he, and as if that wasn't enough, now there was Helen following in his footsteps and it had been twice as bad for her, in the hands of the Military Police for three months. If Papadopoulos hadn't gone for a general amnesty, with the reforms he was going to announce, the two of them would still have been rotting in jail. It was all too much, Aspasia wanted one day to be able to sort out her own life. She'd been engaged these last two years, it wasn't fair for her to go on being the mainstay of the family. Time was running out for her, and if George and Helen were determined to spit against the wind, that was their affair but she'd had enough. George had listened as she outlined her plans, to take out a loan and sell the eighth of an acre of barren cliff they owned in Crete, to buy a two-room flat here, but the hire purchase on the fridge and the rest would be the ruin of them. He'd listen and pull a long face, at once Aspasia would round on him: there's more to life than politics and notions. Then George would bow his head and put his arms round her humbly. He was going to work hard to help her to her dowry — however strange that might seem to me.

Of course I'd never be able to understand. The way I looked at him, you'd think I came from another planet. But for him that must come first. He was glad to have had the chance to spell it out. Above and before all else he was going to see his elder sister right, who'd turned thirty-five stuck behind a counter in the Post Office. He loved me more than I could imagine, it was his cherished hope that one day we'd live together. As soon as he qualified we'd get married and have two children, a boy and girl would be nice. He'd been in love with me right from the time when we'd begun working together for the resistance, he hadn't liked to push himself forward though, because he'd taken me for Fondas' girl. By the time he'd realised his mistake, I had seemed to be showing more interest in Dimitris. He'd kept out of my way as much as possible, only he knew at what cost — to be in love, for him, had always been painful. Some day he'd tell me about his first love. But we're talking about us, it's today that matters. When we'd met face to face unexpectedly at Security Headquarters, he'd felt as though his life had changed forever. Then my father had come and whisked me away, and he'd been left in despair, nothing had seemed to matter any more. Later when he saw me waiting outside the court martial his morale had soared, nothing could shake him now. And when his mother had told him I was going to go with her to visit him, and set the machinery in motion for us to be formally engaged, the only question had been what did he think of the idea, was he agreeable, and I'd asked him, too, if he loved me — at that moment, he continued, all the lovers down the ages had passed before his eyes. And when he used to see me there on the other side of the grille I had dazzled him, like the freshness of a new day when it's not the scene itself that moves you so much as your almost unbearable involvement in the spectacle, as it unfolds in pinks and greys before you

233

and the peace and calm of it reach into your very soul.

I glanced up at him, was he being serious? It all sounded somehow false to me — I'd heard it somewhere before, antique sentiments, slightly foxed. At these moments I managed, with an effort, to conceal my distaste, and allowed him to envelope me with the story of his life. Inwardly I resisted as much as I could, but at the same time I felt powerless beside him, passively captivated while he tested out his emotional depths on me, when he touched me I felt myself like a well-tuned, sensitive instrument in his hands, like a set of ivory keys beneath his fingers and gradually I began to tense myself in readiness to break out of this role. Perhaps my depression was to blame too, as the shadows darkened in the room at nightfall. I'd have liked to talk to him about my mother, but what was there to say? The more impassioned his revelations about himself, the less I felt able to talk about my own troubles. In this way the month of September went by, a honeymoon of sorts, though romantic sunsets and purple prose had precious little to do with it. Had it been otherwise I might have gazed in wonder as darkness fell, scattering blown roses that caught on the roof aerials of the apartment blocks. I might even have felt like raving about the honey-gold light and its myriad ravishing tints. It's only a matter of talent. But that wasn't for me. Handsome though George was with his strange olive-green eyes and delicate fingers. But the classical and the eternal had never held any appeal for me. I'd always had difficulty in looking down at the world from a distant plane.

And there it was, we'd been two months together. I learned to relax with him, I made a kind of ritual of the love I'd been deprived of for so long. And there were good times. It made some difference that we were at least sexually compatible, as the gynaecologist might have put it. In any case I was determined to make it work. He wasn't especially ardent about it, but he did try to make things easier for me, he'd had a bad experience once himself, and sharing the same anxiety drew us closer together. But ideological problems were harder to handle. I could see history repeating itself with mathematical precision: George, like Fondas, wouldn't be contradicted; even if he agreed with me, he always had to have the last word. He was cagey about his plans for getting involved in a resistance group again. But I knew he was setting up contacts through old friends of his. On the other hand, I had always to give him a full report of my own doings. Where did I stand on this, what did I think about that, and so on? Not for a moment would he accept that I might wish to keep my own counsel, for the same reasons of prudence that he did. That was different, I might be going off with other men! I put up with this as best I could, I did try to avoid friction. And we confined ourselves to general topics. General topics bored me, I'd got fed up with mulling over Czechoslovakia and the split in the Party, but I came to realise he had hardly moved on since that time. I didn't want to hurt him, I kept on my best behaviour, I even felt sorry for him. I preferred to seem an idiot, rather than aggravate his mood. And I began to feel a little like a nursemaid, as I put up with his petty sniping and demands. And throughout this time his manner was always aggressive, as if the time was approaching for him to settle his accounts with the Left.

Helen on the other hand left him in no doubt that when you've barricaded yourself inside the Law School for two days, and set up your bandit's eyrie on the rooftop overlooking Solonos Street, then nothing exists for you any more but the struggle and do you know something? our struggle goes forward now in the light of the people's candles that one night formed a cordon round the Law School, keeping vigil in case the police tried to rush the building. High up on the roof, we'd watched the cars circling round and round, and found the courage to go on. Like those nights when you feel the old revolutionaries stirring within you and songs and melodies are made.

George would stifle a sigh and remark on her facility for turning real events into battle cries — it was a mentality he knew of old, because he'd been up front in the Youth Movement, chasing wildly after the shadow of socialism and shouting *constitutional rights* as if it was the same thing as class war, yes, he went on, once upon a time he'd been a romantic idealist and taken excitedly to the streets. That was why he couldn't take Helen's strident optimism, it wasn't even optimism quite, more of a party line. He was fed up with the way they watered down reality to protect a party line whose errors had been exposed years ago. To milk the emotions of your supporters like that, he maintained, is to degrade them intellectually. Because you can't change people's experiences with slogans and harangues. Helen retorted, but neither could you advance the struggle by shilly-shallying and complaining, the struggle demands optimism and cast-iron faith. George snapped back that it wasn't something you could argue about, little sister, anyone can take refuge in an argument, what mattered was you yourself at the moment of facing up to the truth staring at you from the shroud of the revolution that's been betrayed. Helen blazed up. She was sick to death of us and our Trotskyist jargon, what she couldn't stand was people mindlessly repeating the same old stuff that was churned out by the anti-communist stable the world over. She turned to me with an unpleasant grin, as if to blame me for all her ideological quarrels with her brother, and went on sarcastically that she'd no time either for all those *stupamaros* (I'd once talked to her enthusiastically about the Tupamaros) who think that all it takes is bombs and incendiaries, for half a dozen nutters of similarly warped mind to make a revolution.

I could hardly take her seriously, nor did I. I coolly allowed her to indulge her passion for making a fool of me — sometimes I even felt sorry for her, though there were other moments when I almost envied her the bliss of her euphoria. And when it came to the bit, even Helen had to find a niche somewhere, so as to live. But I didn't take George's side either. He may have been right about some things, but I didn't like his manner. It disturbed me that he reminded me of Anestis.

15

I FOLDED MY HANDS in resignation and watched the passers-by. I had a headache, I felt lousy, and cross. In the morning I'd been awakened by the sound of furniture being dragged across the floor above. Another day gone wrong, and in the back part of my head was a jumble of wings, children, car horns, women — clashing cymbals. The man sitting next to me at the table was wearing earrings — why not a ring through the nose as well? In my dreams lately I'd been seeing animals that looked like rabbits, perhaps because rabbits breed so easily; I was a rare hybrid, a rabbit on two legs, a tortoise-shell on my back and the neck of a swan.

George reacted to things quite differently — he wasn't one to hang about. But as for you, he used to chafe me, you're all over the place. You've parcelled yourself out, my girl, drifting from one public place to another, from the Park to the Museum, from Exarchia to Solonos Street ... When I first knew you, you were a shy little thing, what's got you into this state, *quo vadis*? he even said, with a stab at humour. You need to watch out, he warned me, you're on a knife-edge between depravity and suicide. Not likely, I assured him. I'd always be saved by the passionate but at the same time disinterested way I had of responding to events — that was what kept me knitted together, and from Solomos' fragmentary *Free Besieged* I'd retained a notion of what a difficult thing is freedom. Words. Myrsini in Wonderland. That was what he wanted me to understand, and the whites of his eyes turned yellow as though I'd been asking him to elope.

In any case it was very naive of me to suppose that George and I would turn into one of those nice little couples you see in the lecture halls or the Museum. As time went by I found it more difficult to adapt myself to his moods. I would let his stifling monologue run on, and listen to the sound of his voice, a fast undertone that reminded me of someone talking in his sleep. I felt numb, as if bitten by insects. Everything seemed so well ordered in his mind, for all his rambling, like stacks of pastry-cases, one on top of the other, one inside the other. And it struck me how much he resembled Elvira's Fotis. Both of them, when they spoke of *life* seemed to understand by it a river emptying into the ocean. But the tributaries that run dry and never reach that great resting place, the brooks that only just make. it, now losing themselves, now barely perceptible as an underground trickle, they'd never thought of, but chose to ignore them instead.

His complaints had developed a characteristic form of their own, if he was annoyed with me he wouldn't come to the point directly, but toyed with it, working round to it through distant parallels and gnawing away at it like a rodent. Why didn't I introduce him to my father? And what *was* the story about my mother? Was it true she had killed herself because my father walked out on her? And what about the rumour that Alexandra was my father's natural child? If I loved him, wouldn't I tell him about myself? Had there been someone before him? If so, who? Had I been faithful to him all that time? What crowd was I in with now?

It wasn't that I minded telling him; but I knew that no amount of self-revelation was going to make me feel any better — I lacked the talent for the kind of talk that would make me feel better by binding my audience hand and foot.

He always turned up late when we'd arranged to meet. I'd no desire to start complaining in my turn, it would only have made matters worse, but it did annoy me that he seemed not to care. He never offered an apology or even so much as mentioned the fact that he was late. He didn't seem to notice that the time we'd fixed was long past, he seemed to take it for granted that I'd still be there waiting for him, I often had the impression it was something he expected of me.

I saw him at last coming up the street, talking to someone. Every now and then they would stop, and then resume their pace, oblivious to the cars that passed them. As they drew near, I recognised his companion as Apostolos, Xenia's brother, whom I knew to be a slob. My father, quite rightly, had diagnosed him as an unreliable type, with an eye to the main chance. He had been the go-between to push Xenia's claims on my father's property and convey her threats. They shook hands and parted. George came up to me with a slight limp. Whenever there was a change in the weather he suffered pains in his left knee, from muscle-bound arthritis that he'd got from being beaten in prison. I stared hard at him, something gave way within me and I felt depressed. He seemed so helpless, almost futile, and I asked myself what does this person live for?

He kissed me as usual. Then asked me how were things. Fine, I said, order something first, and I'll tell you. But before the waiter could reach the table he'd embarked on a tale of his own, tomorrow he was starting work in a law office run by an uncle. I waited to see if he would volunteer anything about Apostolos. The more I thought about it, the more it looked like a conspiracy; how was it possible that George knew Xenia's brother? When it became evident that he wasn't going to say anything, I could contain myself no longer. He seemed taken aback that I should know such a character. He was cross when I told him it was through Xenia. It just goes to show, he said, isn't it a small world, and he fell silent. Only then did it occur to me that it was quite natural for them to know one another, they'd grown up in the same town. He'd often enough mentioned a Mrs Vardoules, the enchantress of his childhood dreams, and although Vardoules was Xenia's surname, it had never crossed my mind to wonder if they might be related. And the connections I hurriedly made in my head set alarm bells ringing, at the same time my curiosity was roused. He looked at me absently, isn't it a small world, he repeated. And how Shakespearean too, I thought. So that was it, Mrs Vardoules was the mother of Xenia and Apostolos, and Nancy's aunt. And George's heart had used to miss a beat, he had said, at the sound of the carriage bells that brought her to her door. On the instant the short stories of Vizyenos would drop from his hand and he'd rush out to the pavement, he'd sell his soul just for a sight of her. Mrs Vardoules always wore matching hat and gloves. Sometimes of purest white, sometimes pink. Majestic, ethereal, she had semed to him like a creature from another world. Their maid, Vangelio, would open the door. He'd manage to catch a glimpse, in the long narrow entry, of potted ferns and creepers before the brown portal was discreetly closed.

The waiter was at his elbow, interrupting. The order given, he asked once more how things were with me. What had the doctor said? I said, finish the story first, I'm enjoying it. He didn't demur and this annoyed me. I could be dead, for all the interest he seemed to take; and for the first time I felt my body with such tenderness, there to be touched and indulged, as I sat enthroned in Exarchia Square listening to him, in the same way that I'd learned to listen endlessly to the tales of others and make my own silent connections with the story of my own life. George took up the narrative again with an urgent air, as if it was all of the greatest importance to him; Mr Vardoules had been a tall good-looking man with grey hair. He hadn't much cared for him. He'd seemed the sort to try and win you over by making a fuss of you, but only because it suited his book to be a popular figure in the neighbourhood. He'd had the biggest textile business in the town. A clothing merchant! people used to say, in tones that suggested something more like a prime minister.

Mrs Vardoules would sit in the afternoons at the window overlooking the garden, making chains of jasmine and jonquil. She threaded them together lovingly, to adorn Xenia's head. Xenia would stand on the balcony facing the street and watch the boys at their games. And the boys would cluster underneath for a glimpse of her lace knickers — what colour would Xenia be wearing today? They'd lay bets. But more often they'd be playing further down the street because Vangelio used to shoo them away, so as not to disturb the mistress. Then Xenia would straighten her petticoat, precocious and alone.

I noticed that he hadn't touched his coffee, and his hands were trembling slightly as he spoke. And across the street was the police spy, stamping his feet outside the pastry shop for all the world like someone treading grapes. For months now they hadn't left me alone; whole surveillance networks with cars, policewomen dressed to look like tarts, the lot. Yesterday I'd had a summons to the police station, they'd treated me with velvet gloves and read me a sermon on patriotism. But when I got home, my room had been turned upside down. They hadn't found anything, but the continuing effort to get rid of pieces of paper and to disguise the character of my room, had become an intolerable burden. Often they drove me to within an ace of shouting the truth in their faces and winding up for good in a prison cell. Like the builder who shouted when he was arrested that he'd a whole arsenal tucked away and he wasn't going to tell them where. And though they tortured him, he never did.

Now and then, the story went on, the Vardoules family had received visitors on the roof-garden. This was a large veranda at the back of the house, all ivy clad with a round stone table in the centre. Until past midnight you could hear the strains of merriment, until silence fell at last. Then George would imagine Mrs Vardoules taking off her clothes, and standing radiant in the darkness.

On another occasion he'd gone with his mother to Mr

Vardoules' warehouse to buy a school dress for Aspasia. George had all but died of shame at the way his mother went on: you'll give us a bit off won't you, it's only neighbourly; she'd kept this up and Mr Vardoules had smiled like an executioner and explained how difficult the market was; when in the end he'd reduced the price fractionally, his mother had been profuse in her thanks. And just to impress on them the favour he'd done them, Mr Vardoules had given an order to an assistant who had brought them Turkish delight on a tray.

This scene had stuck in his memory like an apocalypse, because not three days had passed before the news got out that Mr Vardoules was bankrupt. Many imputations were laid at the door of the Lady with the Jonquil, as she was nicknamed in the neighbourhood: Ride a cock horse, bells on her fingers and bells on her toes, and now there's an end to all that. It used to make George angry to hear the mothers from the other basements. The pair of white horses with their red harness and coloured beads had been, for him, a window into another, and more beautiful, world. And the final catastrophe came like a lightning flash. Day and night while the Battle of Crete was waged all round them, Mr Vardoules had combed and looted the shops of the deserted town. He had hoarded everything, from butter and olive oil to jewellery and fabrics. Even a house that belonged to the godfather of one of his children he hadn't spared, and everything, down to a turnip watch that the godfather had left behind on a dresser, in the commotion of flight, had fallen prey to the ravages of Mr Vardoules. And as long as the Occupation lasted he had kept his head down and waited for the liberation. Everything worked out to a tee for Mr Vardoules. He took his wife away from her job at the Bank, that she'd had before the war, as he believed a woman ought to devote herself to her family. At the same time, too, Vangelio had been brought into the fold.

But call no man happy before his dying day: George's father used to repeat the saying of Solon the Wise and find solace in it, call no man happy ... And in due course Mr Vardoules had come to grief, his business ruined by the off-the-peg trade. Before he knew what was happening, the town was full of ready-made clothes that undercut him. Chain stores started to spring up like mushrooms. And the merchant in textiles was obliged to delve deep into his treasure-trove. In the fullness of time the stolen watch, that had been forgotten for so long, went in its turn to the jeweller's for cash. And this had been his undoing, because the jeweller was a friend of the godfather. This godfather had in his time washed dishes in New York for twenty years and brought back a fistful of dollars to buy up land that had once belonged to the Turks, and at the same time had brought back the turnip watch with its chain of white gold and engraving on the back, and when he caught sight of it there, after close on seventeen years, in the jeweller's window, he'd set the whole place about its ears.

Within a year the story had gone round that Mrs Vardoules had cancer. She'd been away six months, it was said she'd had a breast removed in Athens. Their maid had to go and work for another family. No more carriages or visitors came to the door. But for all these disasters, the humiliation of the Vardoules family that had been so eagerly awaited among their basement neighbours was averted. Mrs Vardoules recovered and took up again with her jasmine and jonquil. Mr Vardoules acquired a suitcase and came and went. He'd become a door-to-door salesman in fabrics, they learned. And one fine morning the neighbours had woken up to see parked outside the Vardoules front door a little open truck. The master of the house, apparently, was off to do the rounds of the villages.

George by this time had outgrown most of his friends in the street. He now preferred to kick a ball around the the football field. Apostolos, sour-faced and unsmiling, wouldn't speak to him when they met at the pinball machines. He wouldn't have spoken to him today, if they hadn't met face to face. He remembered him being prominent in some demonstrations about Cyprus and *enosis*, later he'd turned up wearing the badge of the right-wing Youth Movement. He'd recruited a gang of like-minded heavies and gone about at night mugging known left-wingers.

It had been August when Mrs Vardoules left them for good, and Mr Vardoules had soon got married again — to Vangelio of all people. It was rumoured that they'd been carrying on for years. Some such thing had been the final straw for Mrs Vardoules, and she'd died of a broken heart. The carriage bells echoed sadly in George's ears, as though an era had died within him. Not long after, they'd moved to another basement flat.

And so it came about that Xenia had been his first love. The best part of his school days — six long years — he had spent with Xenia. Sometimes together, sometimes apart. But all the time in love; it was something he couldn't describe to me exactly, it surely had something to do with the age they'd both been then — he hoped I understood. An age when you're defenceless in the grip of love.

Then one night they'd been caught by the beadle in the darkness. In an alleyway behind Mavilis Street. They'd been kissing at that moment and the beadle caught them at it. Xenia he'd allowed to go home, but George had had to go with him to the police station. They'd worked him over, threatening and kicking him, till past midnight. And when he'd got home his mother had set up her wail. His mother had always had a way with her, this George had to acknowledge, of casting a blight on your most secret dreams. She'd light upon a proverbial saying, or recount some story, as a moral example. And that night she'd reduced him to despair.

Xenia had thrown him over at once. Without a word of explanation even. He'd gone almost out of his mind then. He couldn't begin to think of life from then on without Xenia. By degrees he'd come to accept the inevitable, like an incurable disease. That was how he'd seen his life at that time. And for the remainder of his school days, up until the family's move to Athens, he would hear from time to time that Xenia was going out with somebody different. There wasn't an officer on the American base that hadn't been out with Xenia. And he'd lurked in alleys just to catch a glimpse of her. Later they'd got back together once or twice briefly, but she'd never allowed it to last. And the neighbourhood talked of Xenia's sew-up jobs, a whole mythology arose in which Mr Vardoules had sworn eternal virginity for his daughter. And the poor thing, they went on to say, had got the same demon in her as her Aunt Nancy.

One evening, at the pinball machines, Nancy had picked them up, George and two friends of his. She'd bundled them into her large hatchback and taken them off to Akrotiri. There she'd got them to screw her, one after the other. And though the other two had brought it off, George had dug his nails into the sand with humiliation, until she thrust him more dead than alive from on top of her. He'd been scarred by this experience. For some time afterwards he used to go round the red-light district of their town in a manic state, then one night he'd bumped into his father leaving one of the houses, and if he'd had a knife he'd have drawn on him there and then — not because they'd seen one another, but for the fleeting reflection he'd seen in his father's eyes of all the suffering and all the humiliations of the life that lay ahead of him. Not long after that his father had taken to his bed. And when he died, George in contrition had gone to the cemetery to light an oil-lamp for him. He'd been fifteen when the verger had caught him red-handed with the flower-holder and thrashed him within an inch of his life.

If he recounted all this so dispassionately, that was because by now it had ceased to hurt; quite the opposite in fact, he'd been pleased today to meet Apostolos and hear his news and he'd found him changed, funny you know how people change, he wouldn't ever have imagined Apostolos expressing such admiration for the students — the salt of the earth, he'd called them. At last he took a sip of coffee and went on now about Xenia, how well she'd made out, he was glad for her sake. Apostolos had told him she was starting a career in television, great, she deserved to do well, she'd been through a lot, that girl had. He'd met up with her again years ago now, when she'd been doing training at some drama school and she hadn't sounded as though she was enjoying it. But George had given himself body and soul to the Youth Movement in those days, he'd no time to spare, not really much inclination either, he'd had the feeling she still had her eye on him.

Now's my chance, I said to myself; I felt a growing urge to tell him the story of Xenia and my father, to get it out of my system, but I couldn't bring myself to do it. I listened to him in weary silence. All I'd asked was, how come he knew Apostolos, and I'd got an American-style best seller for an answer. The only confession left for him to make was that our first love marks us for all the rest of our lives. And he *had* made that confession too, although not in so many words, in his own devious way. But it was early days yet for him to do me that favour straight out and have done. I felt he was deliberately playing cat and mouse with me.

When at last he paused, he glanced at me and his eyes slid sideways, as if to conceal his anxiety — what had happened, had I gone to the doctor, what had he said? he asked and kissed me impatiently. It's all right, I said, I'm not, and involuntarily I wiped my lips, because his breath upset me. That's a great relief, he said, this was no time to lumber ourselves with brats. He went on talking and breathing heavily while I curdled inwardly and felt myself like a dead weight on the pavement, my head had lost all sensation, like the rabbit's ears the moment before the punch lands.

Then he relaxed as if he'd said his piece for the day, absently he fixed his eyes on the mature woman sitting opposite. Nice legs, I said to myself, and heard a throbbing in my temples. I couldn't have been more than twelve, the first time I'd heard my father regaling

Anestis with the details of an affair with a woman well past her prime. This old lady, you see, had had three daughters. My father had set his sights on the middle one but she was holding out. Boxes of chocolates, *fruits glacés*, no end of social calls, were all unavailing. And one fine evening he'd been seduced by the mother, What fine hair you have, what beautiful eyes! My father had been helpless before such blandishments. And they'd had a merry song and dance together, until henceforth the old lady's tunes became proverbial. And it was my father's habit to recount these escapades among close friends, and mine to eavesdrop.

All the time I stared at him I was trying to comprehend him — I wanted to be relaxed and tolerant towards him. Perhaps we'd manage to pull through. I was determine that the break, if it came, was not going to come from my side. But it seemed it was usually me that reacted thoughtlessly and put a strain on our relationship. But I found his manner tiresome. Always traumatised, but supercilious with it, always confident of his words. And I didn't like to be endlessly consoling him for past misfortunes. I didn't deny, obviously, that he'd had a terrible time; it was vital for him, now, to pick up the threads and go forward. But it didn't look to me as though he was even interested in going forward, or not as I understood it. His revelations about his past, touching though they were, I found suffocating, I felt thrust backwards by them, back to where I'd started. To his friends he would introduce me as his fiancée. And to my ears it sounded like a life sentence, inwardly I was poised for flight. And one of his most persistent complaints was, why wouldn't I let him meet my father? I gave in finally and the meeting took place. My father rose to the occasion with his customary good manners and extravagant phraseology. I sat listening to their florid platitudes about eternal womanhood and more garbage that made me want to vomit. I felt disappointed in George, it was as though he was doing it on purpose to alienate me. I hated to feel ashamed of the man I loved. But the more infuriating I found him, the more I felt sorry for him as well. And it's fatal to feel pity for someone you think you love. In the end it's like something going bad inside you. I tried to make him see this, but I might as well not have bothered. He took offence very easily. Whenever we talked, he'd never let me finish saying what was in my mind but would break in with jokes and teasing. He'd set up a sort of artificial ambience of being in love, and within it would strike various poses. It was all rather macho. And he never could get it into his head that he repelled me when he was like that. With feigned laughter he'd mimic the sound of my voice, as though I were an infant learning to talk. And at the opposite extreme his whining drove me to despair, if he grovelled much lower his nose would hit the ground. There were moments when I'd have liked to shake him to his senses. Urania when I told her this took a dim view. That isn't love, she protested, more like brutality, it's fascist. I did my best to explain what hard going it is to see someone you love through a bad patch. Especially George, with his delusions of grandeur and self-abasement. He kept on so about his blighted life, I even began to dream of him eyeless with opaque dark glasses, his cap held out to beg in the centre of

251

town, then in the middle of the night cheerfully sorting the coins into piles while I looked on in tears and likened his fate to the torments of Tantalos. And I got so angry with myself for behaving badly to him, that I used to drag myself round all day, aching all over with a sick feeling in my stomach.

It was his mother's idea to invite us all to a family meal, they were having Aspasia's fiancé and his parents, why not ask my father along as well? George, though baffled at first to see me so put out by the idea of my father at their table, accepted finally that I was serious. He could see what I meant, he didn't much go for these formal things either, but what could you do about it? They had some meaning after all, his poor mother had to tell people her son was engaged, where's the harm then in getting to know the bride's family? Then, for the first time, I hinted that I'd got engaged to him chiefly so as to be able to visit him in prison. We could still be in love, I continued, without exchanging rings. Did that mean I wanted to break it off then? I replied that he was going too fast, I'd only said we didn't have to behave like *them.* He wanted to know who *they* were, in a tone of affected innocence that was calculated to get on my nerves. But once again I drew back from the brink. And I was hurt and surprised by his harshness, which seemed out of proportion to anything I'd done or said. But this came naturally to him. He could be harsh without realising it. Often he'd wound me deeply and not even notice. Because *he* never did anything wrong, not the slightest thing. He kept making demands of me in the name of love, though whether as a protection or a drug I was never sure, but all he ever did was make demands. And even when I did make concessions to him, in his macho way he never took any account of the effort that they cost me. All his submissiveness that had so moved me when he was in prison, had turned now into a kind of passive despotism, as if he'd found my weak spot and was determined to put me to the test and make me suffer. I'd submit to everything he said, but no flicker of satisfaction ever passed across his face, he never gave the slightest sign that my capitulation even mattered to him.

The day this historic meeting was to take place, his mother phoned me in the morning, all sweetness and light, that was her style, to reduce me with the softly softly touch. Now listen, dear, whatever you do don't turn up with your hair in a mess and those awful baggy clothes, be a good girl and put on a proper dress, make yourself decent so the in-laws don't look at you and think oh, so this is the little rich girl that's the talk of the family, to look at her you'd think she was one of those unwashed foreign girls that sleep rough on the pavement. I didn't say anything back, but I dug my toes in and stayed at home.

My father scowled at me, I'd made him look an idiot, sitting there among knaves and fools. He didn't know what to do with his hands, or how to chew his meat. I was supposed to have had a temperature of a hundred and two, so as to save face with the in-laws. Euthymia had brought the conversation round, how would it be, she supposed he could fix up George with a good job, and that wasn't all, how much was he proposing to give in dowry? My father had replied that that was for the young people to work out between themselves, their elders shouldn't get involved. But, she'd retorted, their elders have the final say-so, they're the ones responsi-

ble. And if he had it in mind to give me a dowry, it would
be as well if he said so in good time, George, you see, has
two sisters of marriageable age on his hands, and he'll
need to know what he will get, so as to know how much
to give them. My father was appalled, but what century
are we living in, the Middle Ages? He'd never known
anything like it. And George just sat there, a grown
man, and never spoke a word. Dammit all, it had been
as much as he could do to get through the rest of the
evening. And now he was letting me have it.

But to *me* George was voluble in his disapproval.
Heaven help me if I took that sort of thing to heart.
Laugh it off as a joke. And anyway I ought to have been
pleased that his mother wanted to see me nicely turned
out, it showed that she cared. But does she care about
me? I broke in, or just about making an impression on
the in-laws? Not even my own parents, who when it
came down to it were my *parents*, had I ever permitted
to prop me up beside them in their image. In fact I felt
I'd achieved something when I realised they were
ashamed of me. At this George called me a head case
my past was my own affair, but don't try to saddle him
with it. And let one thing be absolutely clear between
us, he wasn't going to follow my example, go round the
bend in other words, he'd got quite enough on his plate
as it was. I responded in kind. If he thought I was going
to be his skivvy and his whore he'd better think again
because it had taken me a lot of trouble to get this far
and I wasn't turning back now. He beat his fist against
his forehead with rage, and accused me of wrecking his
life, I'd maimed him and so on. At some point
screamed. Quick as lightning he landed a slap across my
face, then he seemed to freeze in his tracks, and when

254

movement returned he clasped me tenderly in his arms
and said over and over again that he was sorry. We both
began to cry. So we bit back our grievances and tried to
make it up. Then the telephone rang. It was his mother,
for him, and I heard the things she said about me, she
was warning him, she said, I'd wear him out. He cut her
short and put the phone down angrily. But I didn't quite
believe that his anger was genuine. He could hardly
have acted differently, since he could see I'd heard. He'd
no alternative. But I was supposed to show some
understanding. It's natural for a mother, when she feels
another woman stealing her son away from her, to put
up some kind of resistance. I ought to make allowances.
Eventually she'd get used to it, and things would be
easier. He made it all sound most portentous, whether
he really believed in what he was saying or not. It
sounded more like something he'd learnt off pat, common knowledge, the best-tried clichés. But I knew them
too. It had been with some such philosophy that I'd
forced myself to get on with her for so long already. At
first I'd been much moved whenever she spoke of
George. Of how he liked his stuffed tomatoes without
mince. Then it had begun to dawn on me that everything she said to me about him was said out of malice,
to hurt me. As though to make it plain to me from the
beginning that never so long as I lived would I learn to
make him stuffed tomatoes. But that had been en-
durable for as long as I was visiting him in prison, once
he was out I saw no reason why I should still put up with
it. We'd never once been together without him bringing
the conversation round to her, and how sorry he'd felt
for her all those years, from morning till night, knitting
shawls for the tourist shops. That his mother had suf-

fered a great deal in her life I didn't doubt. What hurt me was not the fact that he loved her, but rather the lengths he would go to, to vindicate her and to see things from her point of view, something I had never been able to do with my own mother. And I felt great remorse for the unkindness I had shown my own mother. It was inconceivable to me that, even eventually, I might come to feel love for Euthymia, it wasn't as if I'd any reserves of understanding or compassion left over, now that I was bound, by quiet remorse and a lasting sense of loss, to my mother's memory. It couldn't have been easy for George either, but he didn't even try to understand this.

And so a wilderness began to open out between us. We went for walks together and didn't see the same things, we talked and each of us meant something quite different. It wasn't even, I concluded as best I could, that we were growing apart along parallel paths that would never meet but would at least keep in sight of one another, rather we were growing apart and that was that. I began to despair at the thought that I might never see him again. Then I would take a grip on myself and conclude that it wasn't yet inevitable. But when I told him I was planning to take up dancing again and then that I was going to go to England, he coughed drily and objected. He called me Fifi, I don't know why, but it certainly sounded as if he meant it nastily. You can never be sure with words; perhaps he didn't mean to hurt me as much as he did. There may have been prejudice and ill-feeling on both sides. I, for instance, often had a tart reply ready before he'd even opened his mouth, though I kept it to myself. But I took it for granted that he was going to say something silly. Thinking back now, that was always the way of it. I was in a permanently foul temper. Though in the early days one or other of us would give in gracefully, disarmed by the spell of first acquaintance. And once Lucy, my step-mother as she now was, had spoken sagely of the compromises and mutual concessions that it takes for two people to live in perfect harmony and breathe as one. But I could only be myself. I couldn't bear the constant feeling that George was getting me down.

He seemed almost to be flirting with the mature lady opposite. But I continued to breathe normally. And inwardly I laughed. He remembered my presence and pulled himself together. He took my hand in his and stroked it. Well that was a relief wasn't it, that I wasn't pregnant? He'd been worrying all the time since the day before yesterday. You know, he said, we'd be properly up the creek if we had a baby now. Yes, I agreed, we certainly would. And I imagined the pair of us as fish, two long fish threshing about on a sandy foreshore. I remembered the dream where I'd been a kind of tortoise with tall legs and an upright neck. By my side was a creature that followed me everywhere I went. This creature was my child, it had two eyes bright with intelligence like a seal's. It clung to my skirt and I was teaching it to walk. Then I was feeding it with tender care, I looked down at my breast as it drew the milk and it was as though it was my own mouth that sucked. And in my sleep I thought, wait till morning and I'll go to the doctor first thing. The doctor declared in tones of prophecy that I wasn't destined, for the present at least, to become a mother. And added something about having my tubes sounded, at which my ears buzzed with the blaring of trombones and sackbutts, wind and brass together.

As we sat together it seemed to me we made a sorry sight. I said to him, let's go and see what's happening, the students are having another mass demo today. He looked unenthusiastic and I said I had to meet someone near the Law School, he could come if he liked. He stared at me irritably. Couldn't we sit in peace and finish our coffee? We've finished it, I replied and rose to my feet. All right, he sighed, let's go.

16

AND I who will always stand out against slogans and easy visions of the future, will never let go at them either, with tears in my eyes, as I cannot forget the sight of a boy propped against the classroom bench, his chest a mass of blood. We stared at him, at a loss to help. He laughed and joked to keep our spirits up, and we stared as though hypnotised at the spreading stains. They bandaged him tightly to stop the flow of blood and each time the wounds bubbled up and spurted from somewhere else. The student next to me could put his hands inside them. I was blinded by all the blood. I excused myself, saying I felt faint, and left the lecture hall that contained the makeshift field hospital. I ran to the wrought-iron gates. A police armoured car was firing tear gas from the street outside. Scattered groups beyond the railings, those who were left, were picking up the spent canisters. They'd put out the flames that expelled the gas by peeing on them. Through the railings they handed in cotton wool, vaseline, water. Now and then you heard: bravely done lads, like the heroes of old. Someone beside me was shouting and cheering at those outside, as if it was his sacred duty to acknowledge the solidarity of anyone who stopped for a moment to draw breath before running on through the fires and darkness — it was a sight to make you want to die. *Among the deaths of many, death's not worth a penny* and I was ready to die with the two hundred or so there outside the gates. And thanked my stars that I'd ended up in the Left. In the Left and out on a limb, face to face with all the petty deaths that had lain in wait for me so long, scarecrows that used to terrify me. I had been ten, with my parents in Florence, on New Year's Eve, St Silvester's day. And round the palace on the crenellations were lighted torches. Crowds danced by the loggia and the statues, whooping it up and breaking bottles with the David standing oblivious in their midst. A little later had come my mother's screams and the make-up scoring rivulets down her cheeks, like a madwoman out of a Fellini film, and my father tightly clutching her hands as his desperation overwhelmed us like a flood. That night for the first time I'd wanted to die so as never again to hear my parents tormenting one another.

An ambulance appeared, its siren wailing, and stopped outside the wrought-iron gates. From a side street police marksmen sniped at its tyres, and from the hotel opposite, the crack Security Corps opened up. The wounded were brought out on makeshift stretchers. We made room for them, staring. A girl next to me burst into tears, she couldn't stand the sight of blood, she cried out. A boy pushed her aside but she kept on, she'd no idea how she'd got mixed up in this. She'd come down in the afternoon to see what was happening. All Athens was buzzing with it and she'd wanted to see for herself. She'd caught sight of Pulia, her schoolmate, and come into the forecourt. And while they'd been exchanging news the police were starting to fire tear gas, she couldn't escape. She'd waited to see if things would calm down but they didn't, it had got worse. And now here she was out in the middle of the night. Her parents would die of worry. She'd told them she was going out to buy a record. But what was to become of her now?

Her solemn, frightened face was twisted with anxiety, as I looked at her closely, I began to feel sorry for her. She seemed bemused by the spectacle before her eyes. I put an arm round her and told her not to be afraid, in here you're safe. The boy came over to us. He gave her his assurance that we were guarding the railings with all vigilance — we were an inspired brigade and *they shall not pass.*

Word had got round that there were tanks on the move and heading towards the Polytechnic, but we took it as psychological warfare. The barrage of tear gas had been proof that they'd finally lost their nerve. They wanted to spread panic and disperse the thousands who were standing by us in support, outside the gates. We were cheered by reports that diversionary tactics were being prepared. Given the scale of the occupation, and the extent of its impact outside, they'd be digging their own graves if they moved against us. Our basic duty, that night, was to hope. *Tonight fascism dies*, we chanted, and we believed it.

But the schoolgirl wouldn't be reassured. She was worried sick about her parents. And her father had heart trouble, it was terrible. I thought to myself sarcastically, usually it's the mothers that have the heart trouble, but the girl was crying in real distress and I pulled myself together. How could she have known they'd be barricaded inside? It was all Pulia's fault, her father had been a political prisoner once, she'd been egging on all the girls in her class with her talk of heroism and great deeds, reciting the long-dead poet Kalvos, *except by virtue and by courage may never Liberty be won*, and generally turning their heads, she'd almost been expelled last year, but her literature teacher had stood up for her and threatened to raise a scandal, don't you dare pick on my best pupil, and the headmaster had backed down because, you see, the literature teacher was very highly regarded, otherwise they'd have had to say goodbye to Pulia and her chatter about fair distribution and carving hammers and sickles on her desk.

At that moment someone else was hit and fell, out on the traffic island in the road. The girl saw, and her rush of words was cut short abruptly, she clung to the railings in desperation. I glanced at my watch, eleven thirty, the hour when poets skulk and later, when they crawled out to air their verses, would claim silence for the events of the Polytechnic. But they have no claim at all to the Polytechnic. Nor could I, at that hour of eleven thirty, have imagined how that night would end. They were singing the national anthem now. The Red Cross vehicles were having difficulty, because of the shooting, in stopping at the gate. Up above, on the roof-space of the porter's lodge, there was a group of young people perched.

It occurred to me that if all the apartment blocks in the neighbouring streets were to throw open their doors and windows, if all the rooms and balconies were suddenly to be illuminated, then we could not be massacred this night. And I knew that whatever was to happen here tonight, would happen with the complicity of the apartment blocks — of the silent majority. And what Franz Fanon says about cowards and traitors, could be applied with perfect truth here. I wondered what they could be doing in these flats. Surely not sleeping? I thought of my father — yesterday he'd come to look for me, I'd been much moved when he'd taken me unexpectedly in his arms, quoting in broken tones, *my eyes have beheld no land more glorious than this small battle ground*, and kissed my hair and the realisation came to me once and for all that no matter how much or how wrongly I might judge this man, he was after all my father, and thank you, I said to him softly, for getting me to read Solomos and the *Free Besieged*. He begged me earnestly to take care of myself, the news was not encouraging, but he hadn't the right to hold me back, only he begged me to be careful, and he kissed me. I was his bulwark against mortality, let me not forget it for an instant, I had been his mainstay all those years, everything else, he begged me to believe this, had been nothing but a kind of parenthesis round me. So I'd gone with him as far as Omonia Square, it had the air of a final parting. And now I thought of him with love — I saw him folded on the sofa listening to the appeals of our pirate radio station, hands clutched to his temples, downing one brandy after another. I saw Anestis too, a veteran far from the battle, once again weeping tears at this moment while Zoe tried to comfort him by talking of the vanity of vanities. Out in the courtyard we were asking for petrol from the labs to make Molotov cocktails, we're like sitting ducks here under fire, and we haven't even sticks for kindling. But the committees said no, they wouldn't endorse such tactics, we weren't to start another civil war. So much for the victims of all those historic compromises, in the Lebanon, at Caserta, at Varkiza, that refused to be forgotten, better to tie

263

stones round their necks, and sink all those corpses — get my meaning: no more defeats. The invisible hand of the Coordination Committee was everywhere — come on now, cut out the wartime stuff, come on you anarchist, leftist, provocateur, terrorist, petty bourgeois extremist, and all the rest of the shit. Then Helen appeared, there were a lot of serious casualties, a number of dead. Martial law had been declared, tanks were heading in our direction, but we the inspired brigade with our paper tissues and cigarettes, with chocolate bars and biscuits, would still dictate our terms:

a. The evacuation would take place in daylight, and not earlier than 8 a.m., so that the streets would not be empty.
b. Foreign diplomatic observers were to be present, together with representatives of the Red Cross to receive the wounded.
c. We demanded a guarantee of no lynching as we left.

If they didn't accept these terms, we would refuse to open the wrought-iron gates. Either way it was bound to end in violence. Morale among us was running high, we were on course for eternity — *thy murd'rous hand, oh Pasha, sends me to Heaven straight,* the chorus swelled, *thy murd'rous hand,* like an old *rebetiko* song of the city poor, *Pasha oh Pasha send me to the Pearly Gate,* in full cry, like a dithyramb, *thy murd'rous hand, thy murd'rous hand.*

The tank continued its advance, I was caught up in the backward surge. I was running, hands thrust in the pockets of my overcoat, I could hear myself sobbing —

like the howling of an animal, I tried to take refuge deep in myself. Outside the Engineering Faculty I crumpled to my knees in a corner and wept. Someone turned to me and said, hold up there comrade. I scrambled to my feet and stood up straight. I took my hands out of my pockets and sorted out my hair. I could see the tank, its gun barrels levelled at the Faculty of Architecture. The soldiers were moving into position. One with stripes on his sleeve shouted an order. Just look at these cords under his armpit, I said to myself. I saw the smaller street that ran along the side of the railings, chock-full of police. Apparently the soldiers had opened fire. Get down, we shouted to one another. I remained rooted where I was, waiting. For two, maybe three seconds the silence intensified and became general.

We began to file out, hands held above our heads, in groups. I was caught up in the crowd as it moved forward, with the soldiers' rifle-butts pounding at us from either side, any minute, I thought, they'll shoot me in the back at point-blank range. I could feel the vertebrae all the way down my back, held together by a refined tissue of terror. I lost my footing and stumbled forward, near to collapse. I was through the wrought-iron gates, treading on blood and torn leaflets. The soldiers jeered at us and stamped their boots as though to round up cattle, we went forward with bowed heads and fumbling steps, terrified. At the corner of the block two plainclothes thugs grabbed me by the hair. I tried to fight free of them, a young soldier took me by the arm, I could see tears in his eyes. He whispered something to me, but it was too late. The thugs jostled him aside, I tried to resist and my head spun with the pain. As they dragged me, limp now, towards the police van they kicked me again and again in the stomach. Then they propped me against the door of the van and punched me in the face. They bundled me into a seat and I let myself go with the gulping sound of my sobs. The boy next to me put an arm round me.

I felt I was swallowing back blood. Tasteless blood. My whole face was on fire. The boy took a piece of cloth from his pocket and wiped my face. Then he tilted me backwards to stop my nose from bleeding. I pricked up my ears the way blind people do to get an idea of what was happening. A girl was screaming, she was sorry, she was sorry and would they let her go. The thugs said to her, filthy bitch, so now you've come to your senses, have you? They shouted at us to surrender our weapons and knives, if they found anything on us they'd kill us. The van started off. Passing along a deserted Stadiou Street, it was like the end of the world. Only the shadows of police and plainclothes men lurking at every corner. We heard the co-driver on his walkie-talkie, receiving an order. We began to realise we were being taken to General Police Headquarters. Relief spread through me that I'd got off so lightly. At least I hadn't been killed. I thought of George and Helen. If Helen fell into their hands again that would be the finish of her. Last year at Military Police one of them had broken his truncheon in two on her shin. They'd kept her standing upright in a cell for a week and every time the military guard passed outside she'd made herself spit at him. As my wounds began to cool, my face felt swollen to twice its normal size. The boy at my side held on to me tightly.

He stroked my face and whispered, they can do all they like, but *they shall not pass*. Their days were numbered, of that he was sure. I turned my head a little and looked at him through half-open eyes. I recognised him, he was the tall one I'd seen before. I'd been bumping into him since the first night. I'd been standing at the railings shouting slogans with the others. I'd heard the sound of my own voice and a fragrance came back from the leaves of the orange trees outside. As if a great beneficent eye shone indulgently on us, my spirit had taken wing: *People of Greece unite, now's the time to fight.* That had been the first time I saw him, shouting alongside me, but in a way of his own. He was making himself heard without any sign of effort. He struck me as remarkable and I stopped shouting myself to watch him more closely. He had his own rhythm for every slogan we chanted, but always within the general pattern. It was rather that he kept to the rhythm more strictly than everyone else, never out and never rushed. While I watched him I had felt myself magnetised, with an uneasy feeling. Perturbed, I'd left the railings and avoided him. As the darkness wound itself around me I had felt afraid; but in a different way though, like a still sea. And I'd felt exalted by the voices. I'd immersed myself once more in the crowd and recovered my equilibrium.

The police van stopped outside General Headquarters. What's your name? I asked him. John, he said. Before he could ask I said, Mine's Myrsini. Then we were hauled out of the van, move it scum, at the double lousy bastards. They hit out at us with their truncheons, one by one we ascended the stairs, under a rain of blows. As we went John's eyebrow split open. I watched his blood as it dripped from his forehead, on each step of the stairs, careful not to tread in it. They lined up on either side of the stairway and hit out at us at random. I felt a glancing blow down one side and thought they'd taken my ear off. At last we reached the top. There another lot were waiting for us, in plain clothes. They separated the girls, and took away our handbags. Policewomen body-searched us. One of them I recognised, she'd used to follow me last year. She recognised me too, her eyelids flickered with an old-fashioned look. They threw us in a cell where we had to stand upright to get everyone in. The girl beside me cried unremittingly, Oh my God, what have they done to me? Her arm was broken. The bone was bent double below the elbow. Her face was disfigured with pain. I was overwhelmed·by despair and hammered with my fists against the door of the cell. The others told me to stop, they'd only come and beat us up some more.

Several hours passed in a state of lethargy. Only the girl with the broken arm could be heard moaning, but by now tonelessly, wearily. We heard helicopters passing overhead. Then a guard came, tore into us and beat us at random. The girl with the broken arm screamed shrilly and drowned the swearing of the guard. Whores, he shouted at us, Allende lives does he? Whores, been enjoying yourselves have you, all that time in the whorehouse? He beat us with his truncheon and shouted at us to chant instead, *Down with the people, the army forever, Allende is dead.* Then he left us, to charge on to the next cell.

There was a lot of noise in the corridor, as though a large crowd was going past. We pricked up our ears and waited. The door opened and they lined us up against

the wall outside. The one with the American crew cut
came before us and delivered himself of a speech. I
heard nothing of what he said, only the beating of my
heart and the thrumming in my ears. We were to get the
hell out of it. It was a quarter to four. At four the curfew
would start. Anyone found in the street after four o'
clock would be shot. On your way now, get lost.

We stumbled carefully down the stairs, I thought of
the hands of the cleaning woman that had washed the
early morning bloodstains from those same stairs. No
one took any notice of us, we could have been spirits. I
wondered about John. The girl with the broken arm told
me she lived in New Philadelphia. Another lived at
Kolonos. How could they possibly get home in a quarter
of an hour? Without transport, there wasn't even a taxi
to be seen in the streets, what were they to do? And I
had my flat just around the corner, but no keys. They'd
kept our handbags. We could call and collect them in a
day or two, they'd told us. I said if they wanted they
could come with me to Kolonaki, where my father lived.

The wide avenue stretched endlessly in either direction, not a soul was in sight. As we passed along it all
the windows were shut fast, no sign of life came from the
buildings. Just before the American Embassy I suggested we should take to the side streets, if we ran into
them again they'd make mincemeat of us. The words
were hardly out of my mouth when we saw three men
at a distance running towards us. One of the girls made
as if to run, I called out that that would only make it
worse, and held her back. They caught up with us and
made a show of demanding our identity cards. Then
they backed us against the wall, drew flick knives and
threatened us, shout *Long live Metaxas, the Third*

Greek Civilisation. Or else they'd slit our noses. One of them held me by the hair and slapped me several times. My nose started bleeding again and the sight of the blood seemed to excite him further. The other one brought his blade up close to my nostril, now I'll slit you he snarled and ground his teeth. The sound of a car came in the distance. They dropped us and fled, swallowed up in the side streets. It was an army jeep, it stopped alongside us, and the one with the stripes asked what the hell were we up to, out at such an hour? He shook his head and sent us to the devil.

Calliope opened the door to us and the moment I fell into her arms I fainted. When I opened my eyes an unbearable void seemed to tell me I'd grown old. Others who came after us could weave little myths about us, and facile ones at that. The street sellers would sell badges with pictures of revolutionaries, and the flower-stalls red carnations, popular composers would make songs and the youth movements of the various parties would put out slogans for the future, *Forward on the road, Bloody November shows the way*; all this for three days, and then the anniversary would be over. And since for many months afterwards the Polytechnic would remain a dubious birth, later when Democracy returned its foster parents would turn out to be the political parties, that would in time turn it into a litany. And later still the official line would decree immortality. Once upon a time it had been *Lambrakis lives*, and after that *Petroulas lives*. Tomorrow the Polytechnic would live, the failed uprising.

I felt as though I were very slowly being rehabilitated after long confinement in an asylum with high rusted railings. From one afternoon to the next, I had no sensation of the passage of time. They told me that the next week the tanks had come back into the streets in a counter-coup. And everyone was proud of the gallant lads again. And some even said, good, at least we've seen the end of Papadopoulos. My father passed an arm round my shoulder and Lucy, perched on the edge of the bed, fed me some pap on a spoon. I looked from one to the other and was somehow reminded of Puss in Boots. They could scarcely conceal their happiness, a happiness that seemed to set my paternal home ablaze. They'd changed everything round. My old room was now Alexandra's. I heard her having tantrums and Calliope soothing her, Calliope was now devoted to her, as once she'd been to me. Later they took me away, into safe hiding. The word was that the prison islands were filling up again. So they were keeping me in hiding. I never had time to get used to one room, before it was changed for another. The only thing missing was the blood and the severed hand that drags itself octopus-like across the ceiling in primeval nightmares. But no such thing. I was flat on my back, and thought of George. And as the brightness of his face darkened in my thoughts, I began to look instead for John's. And I felt something taking shape within me; soundlessly, like a flower opening. I allowed my father to make a fuss of me. As he seemed to like me better with my nerves in shreds, I left them like that on purpose to please him. But I knew I was recovered. I asked for news of George, had they heard anything? They promised me I could see him as soon as I was able to stand. They said a lot of things, but their voices faded in my ears, leaving only the fascist's knife. The knife in the fascist's teeth and the grinding noise that came from his mouth. Outside the wrought-iron gates the tank-treads ground the roadway and my nostrils dilated with the threat of the naked steel.

Easter was on the way. The dictatorship was rumoured to be tottering. We moved out to Kifisia, Lucy had long ago changed the house out of all recognition, which meant it was now habitable. And the garden, a cool paradise, was like something out of a novel by Kosmas Politis — only it left me unmoved. Hawthorn or ivy or honeysuckle, a mass of lush things that I never shall know how to call by their names. I kept to one room and at last read Rilke. I wasn't in hiding by this time, but I was in no state, either, to pick up the threads from where I'd left off.

They wouldn't hear of my leaving them, and this was actually rather a relief, although I put a glum face on it; I liked to appear despondent and have them fall over themselves to raise a smile. It began to dawn on me that they were really sorry for me, or even alarmed by my manner, so I made an improvement and found myself suddenly able to bring tears to their eyes and drive them wild with enthusiasm by the simple expedient of leaving open the door to my room or allowing Alexandra to sit beside me at the piano and watch. With her deep blue eyes and Lucy's dimples in her cheeks, she was what you might call a charming and lively child. All at once I felt goaded to tell her all I knew. I was impatient to force her into adulthood, to impose on her with my love, burden her with my failures, systematically to corrupt her with an infinite admiration for me: *to play Lucy to her Myrsini.* Then I felt sorry for her and threw her out.

I was greatly impressed with my father — sleeping the sleep of the just, as if Lucy had released him from a spell. Her austere serenity seemed to have calmed the surface of the waters, like a magical still in a Bergman film. He wandered happy as a sand boy from room to room in his dressing gown, playing with Alexandra, and his laugh echoed with open-hearted innocence, neither Nancy nor Xenia would ever trouble him again. They'd no need to, since Lucy had persuaded him to recognise all his children with due form. As for me, she took care, with her impeccable love for me, to keep me on the outside. I knew she would never allow me the pleasure of a head-on confrontation. And I had no desire, either, to present her with a spectacle of hysterical girlhood. Often, during these heavy days when I would mix up the ticking of the clock with the beating of my heart, and suffocate in the silence they had imposed on me, I would have liked to talk to her about my mother, and how easily we had left her to rot in the First Cemetery. But when I rediscovered the ticking of the clock, I found myself very easy-going and peaceable. I gave myself up to lassitude and watched myself ageing. And on the whole it gave me more pleasure than otherwise to see them happy: in unforgettable, stupefying boredom in front of the TV.

At this time Uncle Joachim, the General, had found himself out in the cold. And when he came back to us, a pathetic convert to the resistance, I'd been reminded

273

of the madman who thinks he's Alexander the Great or some such. He told us how he'd ended up in a cell six feet square. After twenty days they'd let him go of course. But it had been no laughing matter. And he'd lain on his back on his prison palliasse, staring at the stripes on his sleeves, the medals and ribbons on his chest. When the door of his cell had slammed shut he'd felt his cheeks burning for very shame — my country, he'd cried out aloud, how have I failed you? At once a lightning flash had shot through his brain, and he'd seen a vision. He was on Mount Olympos and Zeus no less had called him over: have no fear Joachim, the army is with you: and my uncle had leapt for joy. And so, borne aloft by his vision, he had got through his twenty days. As he told us all this, I was overcome with nausea and despair to think that with old gaffers like that they can frighten us into submission, here at the far end of the Balkans.

I was entirely cut off. The only person who didn't leave me alone was Elvira. Fotis was taking his degree, in any case they were getting married and she wanted me to be a bridesmaid. It always touches me when Elvira insists that I'm her best friend. She makes a point of it, as though our friendship were part of the eternal order of things. All the same, I had nothing to say to her and didn't hide the fact. I didn't even hide my disappointment in her. For three days I'd been expecting her at least to put in an appearance in the forecourt of the Polytechnic, but her precious Fotis had been revising stolidly for an exam he had to take in December, and she'd had to butter biscuits for him.

George had gone into hiding, I didn't know where he was, and I wasn't even all that anxious to find him. My father assured me that he was well, and told me that he got news of him occasionally. But I didn't worry about him. When I thought of him at all, it was chiefly out of habit. I saw him again outside the wrought-iron gates, among the fires. News had just come in of the first deaths. I had felt the damp coolness of the night penetrating through me, I closed my eyes and felt myself whirled aloft with wild music — insistent, metallic thrumming that wound round me like a cocoon. George could have died that night. But the same George, on the Wednesday evening, had taken me to task, it was a sign of my immaturity that I could quote the ready-made sayings of Franz Fanon, so naively and out of context. He had pressed me to tell him what good, in the end, could come of the occupation, what had we gained from occupying the Law School last year? And when I'd replied that at a time like this only cowards and traitors turn their backs, he'd turned on me furiously, can't we cut out the slogans? he could do without the third-world arguments. What were we aiming to achieve by occupying the Polytechnic? I wanted to answer that I didn't expect him to be such an old fogey. If he couldn't work out the answer for himself, that was his problem, not ours. But I let him walk me as far as the bus stop and put up with his talk of responsibilities and massacres. But the moment he left me standing in the queue, I'd bolted straight back.

The street had emptied. Soon there would be nobody about but plainclothes spies and provocateurs. Outside the Supermarket opposite, the 'Electric', they were drifting into groups. And now the siege committees had

275

to make sure that the iron gates opening onto the side streets were secure. The dampness of the night had settled upon our hair; the fear of attack, right from the first evening, had kept us constantly on the move about the forecourt. Further over people were gathering up sticks and bits of wood, breaking up old chairs they happened on — something to defend ourselves with. Yes, morale was high, somewhere up there in the clouds with the long-dead poets of national independence. We were all strengthened by the knowledge that this time the site was ideal for occupation. While I was caught up in all this whirl, I ran into Themis. For some months past Themis and I had been working in the same resistance group. We went apart beneath the orange trees and talked in whispers. Our task was to keep on the crest of the wave, to set an example for the people. Mass meetings were being set up in each Faculty. And in the Engineering Building they were trying, he went on, to get a radio station going. We parted because we didn't want anyone we knew to see us together. This time I had managed to pull it off, none of my friends knew I was actively involved. Not even George. From him especially I had been at pains to keep it dark. I knew that he'd try to stop me. I couldn't be bothered trying to persuade him any more, now that I was fully persuaded myself.

Later I'd been present at the mass meeting in the School of Advanced Business Studies. The slogans from the wrought-iron gates on the main road were wafted to our ears, everywhere there were voices and grinning faces. Someone turned to me and said we were going to propose the motion that would be handed tomorrow to the press. The speaker got up and took his place on the platform. He said this and that and then gave the floor to whoever raised a hand. Until little by little the lecture theatre had divided into small groups putting pressure on the remainder. Everyone had something to say, I couldn't make head or tail of it, but my temples were throbbing. Then before our bleary eyes someone stood up on the platform, next to the speaker. And launched into, see here comrades, I say we got to look to our defences. We're all of us comrades in here, ain't we, comrades? But we got to look to our defences. You're educated kids, you people here, you know how to talk proper better'n I can, but we got to look to our defences, that's right to my way of thinking. I've put some bolts on these doors, see, that ten blokes couldn't get to budge, not if they all pushed together. What I want from you folks is some people to help me guard the outer doors. The time it takes to get a team together, then find a few more, by that time the first lot've disappeared. Today, comrades, I told my boss what I thought of his wages and chucked it in. Thought I'd be more use here. I'm a practical man you see, I work with machinery. And I done karate once, for six months. I'm ready for a fight if need be. I'll help you finish off the colonels all right.

For a moment you could have heard a pin drop. We were seized with embarrassment and regarded him as though he'd escaped from a lunatic asylum. There he stood, a tubby little man in deadly earnest in the middle of the platform. Suddenly the hall was shaken by applause and the old codger was hailed as a comrade in arms. Everyone was touched that he'd given up his job to come and join in our struggle. Our first workingman, and *there* was the proof for the doubters that the student movement was part and parcel of the wider popular movement. Everyone wanted a glimpse of him. From the seats at the back came shouts that they hadn't been able to hear, what had our comrade said? The speaker repeated it. The old codger lowered his head. By this time day had broken, but no decision had been reached. The meeting would resume at seven a.m. We dispersed towards the wrought-iron gates.

For all my efforts to impose some sort of order on these events, they were too much for my brain to cope with. I slid like an eel within myself and slunk in darkness. All the doubts I'd carried with me throughout my life, that I'd cajoled in one way or another, spread about me now unchecked, like a poisonous leaden cloud, enveloping me. Face down, choked with tear gas, the fumes raking my eyeballs and blinding me. The fascist of the Third Greek Civilisation bending over me, his face contorted, the blade of his flick knife glinting, the chill of the metal against my nose. Then *he* took shape vaguely before me, I didn't remember exactly what he had looked like, only his touch as he mopped off the blood and his name, John. I'd wake and feel his presence in the darkness, the quiet whistling of his breath, as though he was there beside me. I tried to imagine him. I knew it was impossible, or at any rate highly unlikely, that I'd ever see him again — and this certainty gave me an involuntary incentive to retain his image so far as I could. I remembered when the wrought-iron gates had opened, this was at the eleventh hour, when one by one they'd come in from setting up the barricades, among them had come John, lifting a wounded man by the armpits, his arms clasped round him, and set him down with great care on a stretcher. Then he'd stood still, poised

278

for action, looking out at the street. I'd watched him and felt for him. But he hadn't seen me. Our eyes had never met. And now in the light of day I lost sight of him more and more, in my waking moments I had only George to remember.

17

AT LUCY'S INVITATION, Anestis and his family were spending Easter Day with us; they now had a little boy. Their cheerful spirits got up my nose. Though Anestis did treat me with a degree of reserve, as if I embarrassed him. And his shoulders had developed a stoop.

Victoria, for her part, had signalled her retirement, no more wild parties and loose living for her. I was struck by how quickly she'd gone downhill, all at once her face had become a mass of wrinkles. There was a change in the way she talked as well, as if at last she'd understood. And she showed her age, too, by living so much in the past. Perhaps she had been more affected than any of us by my mother's suicide. She talked to me about those unforgettable years. The years she'd spent with my mother had been truly unforgettable. When they'd gone to school together and read the same novels. They'd shared a passion for romantic fiction. It had been she who had introduced her to my father. And for all the airs he gave himself, her poor old cousin had been badly smitten, the trouble was that Natalie had been too weak. She could have had him where she wanted him, if she hadn't lost the initiative to the other one. And for that, the blame lay squarely with my mother. When Victoria had warned her to be on her guard against

Lucy's hidden depths, she had only laughed ingenuous-
ly. Right up to her death she'd still been ingenuous. And
paid for it with her life.

My godmother had got it into her head that I was a
willing audience for her embittered reminiscences, and
I observed the pleasure she took in trying to undermine
my father's marriage to Lucy. But apart from the
boredom she inspired in me, I'd nothing to gain from
taking sides against them. Indeed I looked on their marriage as an inevitable necessity. It relieved me to think
that my father had at last found the safe haven that had
eluded him for so many years, now that my mother was
no longer alive to see it and suffer — but had bequeathed
her taste for jasmine to me.

I used to smell its heady scent, my fists full of the little
white flowers, and imagine myself hitch-hiking up the
national road. It had been pouring with rain a couple of
hours before, the smell of damp earth was strong in the
air, it came to me from the fields wafted by the breeze
and deep breaths of it pervaded my lungs. The asphalt
glistened beneath my feet, and beckoned towards dark
distances, infinitely remote, as though I were treading
on the edge of an ebony band that unfurled beyond the
Greek frontier and far away. I was hitch-hiking on the
national road and waiting for the long-distance lorry-
driver who was destined to help me escape. Only a little
while ago, I reminded myself, I'd been running through
the downpour, I'd only just made it out of the low dive
where they'd made me sit bolt upright in a chair and
sing the old *rebetiko* song, *You picked up sticks in both
your hands and beat me just for kicks.* My agent, a
famous pimp, the incarnation of all my own toil and
misery, is sullenly poised behind the curtain that marks

281

off my dressing room, since of course they see me as a
fallen diva, furious to hold me to account and demand
explanations, I'd been showing signs of disobedience
lately, begun to have opinions of my own on the subject
of my prostitution, but that was *his* job, and hadn't I
been concealing things too? — I'd been giving him the
slip and deceiving him with other men whose company
I seemed to find more congenial, the nub of the matter:
I was deviating more and more towards myself. Even
with the beatings and the degrading treatment, I'd sung
to him this evening, *You picked up sticks in both your
hands and beat me just for kicks*, then I'd made myself
scarce through the back door of the low dive and headed
for the national road. I ran for it, and my destiny obliged
with a cloudburst overhead. I was dripping wet and
shivering as I waited for the long-distance lorry-driver
allotted to me from among the billions of mankind.

Already he's loaded up with lemons and lit a cigarette,
I can make out the burning circle of his cigarette end,
I can see his eyes now, he's of medium height, rather
short. With curly hair, like intertwined black and white
cotton threads. A deep furrow lies between his brows,
others less marked are scattered about his forehead. His
upper lip bears a scar — for no other reason than so that
I can imagine him as a little boy, blood pouring down
and though I wasn't there of course, even then I was a
probability in his life, and now here I am beside the national road all set for our fateful encounter. He's wearing a wide shirt with long sleeves, clean white although
he's a workingman, more like a journalist really who's
lived for many years in Paris and shaped his personality
there, with specs, a wife and children. The shirt is belted
above tight-fitting trousers, and falls loosely over his

282

waist, below it his thighs are a bit like a footballer's, with a suppleness born of the hidden lust that informs his whole appearance, he reminds me of a sailor or a wideboy — I'm especially interested in his thighs and calves, it's there, in the paintings of Tsarouchis, that the apotheosis of masculinity is most fully achieved, exactly that swinging step that seems to advance towards me but remains fixed, remote, a movement captured but at the same time elusive, like his expression as well. His eyes have a rather tired look, penetrating and dreamy, they've often a stickiness in the corners from the strain of peering ahead into the darkness of the road. But part of my appointed role, as well as changing the cassettes, is every time we stop for coffee to wipe the stickiness from his eyes. Perhaps even to tuck back the hairs that protrude from the end of his nose. These hairs he doesn't cut as most men do, but from time to time, with a furtive movement taking a hand from the wheel, he'll nudge them upwards, back into his nostrils. But now that he's got me beside him, I can make that movement for him and no one will be any the wiser, we can share the complicity of that most heretical of hand signals.

He's started now, warming up the engine of the lorry, a juggernaut of a Mercedes decked out with fairy lights all round the cab in all the colours of the rainbow, and little icons of Orthodox saints, though I suppose he might be a Catholic from the Aegean islands, Santorini, Tinos, or Syros, birthplace of Vamvakaris king of the old-time *rebetika* songs, his name begins with V as well, or maybe B? Vangelis or Vasilis or Valentino, Bessarion or Bellerophon, Barlaam or Barnabas, Belthandros or Belisarios — and he's hung up little flags with pictures of footballers, and pin-ups of girls with huge boobs and bums, he's particularly into bums, if he'd been a writer he'd always have begun a description of a woman with her bum. But even as a long-distance lorry-driver he'd be likely to size her up from behind and of course what he said would be pretty crude. But his reserve would peep out, like a frozen animal shyly warming up next to his skin, actually he's waiting for the one woman in his life. And here I am waiting for him by the side of the national road, not far beyond the boundary of Attica, let's say somewhere near the turning for Thebes, here I'll be waiting for him and shivering. Where are you George, I said to myself, come and hear my fantasies of the working class and I'll sing you Vamvakaris: *You picked up sticks in both your hands and beat me just for kicks.*

Then Alexandra would come in and try to cheer me up, that was the end of my reveries, I'd turn away from the veranda with the jasmine and tell her to go away and play. I'd shut myself in my room exhausted, as if nothing more could now be expected of the day.

I remember the Easter candles and the traditional kisses. Then in a happy atmosphere they cracked their red Easter eggs. They talked of youth and its sacrifices, that sort of thing. The first creakings in the wings, that would herald the fall of the Ioannidis regime, were becoming audible. And still far off behind the curtain one word was gaining resonance in their ears: Polytechnic.

I found a resonance of my own in Rilke. I knew that I was in no state of mind to curl up in front of the fire and browse; so I made myself read him as though I were studying for an exam, and turn over each page as an act of will. Each time I'd ask myself where I'd started and where I'd got to because, for all my different intentions, I'd always get to the same point of traumatised open-mindedness. Whatever I said at the beginning, by way of a prologue and somewhat defensively, about rhetoric and rambling on, wasn't quite the whole truth. Anyhow, at that time I was in a state of social shock. The condition isn't easily described, in my case it took the form of exaggerated symptoms of pathological complaining and the abiding obsession that I had been taken for a ride. The feeling of having been taken for a ride doesn't have to be a bad thing, of course, but it's unlikely, in the nature of things, to be positive, unless you can control it well: for which you need a certain glibness in redefining your relationships very precisely. I don't know what went wrong in my case, but I was making heavy weather of it. On the one side I'd renounced the background I'd grown up in, but on the other I was continually rebuffed by the world I wanted to adopt. And I wondered why it was I should constantly be making difficulties for myself and binding myself with the grandest resolutions, so grand that cut down to my size they verged on the ridiculous. Why was the road behind me becoming closed, while my forward flight was so beset with pitfalls? I met people I'd once known and it was like looking at the shadows of my past life. I didn't even like to look for long at the mirror, for fear of the doubts that would paralyse me, the mote was lodged in my eye and I could see nothing straight. My father accused me of trying to pull birds out of the air, instead of being content to watch them as they flew. I replied that that's what it means to grow old: he was content to

285

watch the birds as they flew, I had to pull them out of the air. But I knew that I was deceiving myself, my blithe self-confidence was replaced by agonising anxiety that all I did was to chase after the birds without ever catching them, swept up by their flight into a kind of flight myself, in which some grabbed at my tail while others observed me through binoculars — I constructed fantasies to try to escape from an overwhelming sense of impotence. At times like these I would come close to despair, how was it that the least jolt could change my mood so drastically? The years might pass, but the vanguard of the Left stood firm, unflinching despite defeats, proudly bearing their scars. But I couldn't easily reconcile the practicalities of ordinary living, and its ineluctable difficulties, with the socialist ideals that kept buzzing in my head. Perhaps I believed less than others did, so that my courage would evaporate at the very point where the real fighter fixes his gaze unswervingly on the future. But I had somehow inserted myself into a present moment that stifled me. And at this present moment Heidegger was much in fashion, now that the memory of Nazism was largely confined to the Jewish-American film industry. And the focus of the absurd came to be systematically transferred from the gas chambers to the silent infernos of Kierkegaard — and all this was the benign legacy of world peace: the poorer peoples of the world could starve so that people in Europe could admire themselves making war on obesity.

Things have changed since then; much has happened to make that kind of introspection an inadequate defence of my case. A few days after Easter George rang and we fixed to meet in town, on Patission Avenue. He needed to talk to me urgently, he said. Lucy snapped that if he was in such a hurry why couldn't he come out here? How was I going to get myself into town? I felt like telling her I hadn't asked her to protect me, but actually her anxiety for me gave a fillip to my self-esteem. And suddenly I was excited at the prospect of seeing him again, after all those months. All the way into town I kept thinking that I still loved him just the same, though some things *had* left a bitter taste, and I pretended to have stopped caring. The important thing was that I'd been in love with George all along. I affected not to care, because the last thing I could bear was the idea of having been cast off by George.

At the first sight of him I realised that something was wrong. He was gentle with me, but I could see he was hiding something, he avoided my eyes. And he had the air of someone who has rehearsed his behaviour carefully many times. He was asking me questions, but I could feel his thoughts elsewhere. He told me what had happened to him that night, how he had run desperately up Patission Avenue, dived into an apartment block and mercifully, by good luck, someone had given him refuge. He'd been on the move since then, in constant hiding. They'd gone to his house, he said, looking for him. If they caught him, it would be one of the prison islands for him. He told me that he'd heard what had happened to me. I said, was there anything I could do? No, he said, but it was good to see me. He touched me hesitantly, but as we talked his manner cooled. I broke out earnestly, if there was anything the matter, he mustn't hesitate, if anything was worrying him, he could tell me. He didn't answer. I asked for news of Helen. She was in hiding too.

We'd sat down on a bench in the park. I huddled closer to him, his embrace was without warmth, but it gave us the appearance of a courting couple. Then he asked me about my father. With curiosity, and also a touch of sarcasm: how many brothers and sisters had I? Without thinking, I told him. He showed signs of astonishment, but I plunged straight on. I said, is that the only reason you wanted to see me? There's Catherine by Xenia, Agis by Nancy, Alexandra by Lucy. One big happy family, is that why you wanted to see me? He seemed unprepared for this and began to mutter, it was just that he'd begun hearing certain things and frankly it had come as a great shock to him. Why had I kept all this from him? I tried to imagine who could have told him. With the thought that during his months of hiding he'd met up with Apostolos again, and one thing had led to another until they'd ended up dissecting me and my family, I was suddenly furious.

His expression hardened into a look that could have been hatred. I was shaken and opposite us on the bench an old man was making eyes at me. Then half opened his legs. I turned my face away, look at the old man, I said to George. He took my arm and we got up, he said, Greece is a country of spies and exhibitionists. Look, I said, I don't understand this at all; we haven't seen each other for five months, and now you want to see me to talk about *that*? He made no reply, but I could see that he was working himself up. I felt him coiling inwardly like a spring, poised to repel me as far from him as he could, and in the process hating me. We'd come out into Patission Avenue again. We didn't speak, I was thinking that I'd take the underground from Victoria Square.

Then he asked, what would I say to our splitting up? I said, what was there to say? He asked me again, mollified a little, did I love him? I said I did. But I wished it hadn't come so easily. I'd have liked to ask him if he loved me, but there seemed no point, I could see the two of us and didn't much like what I saw. I realised that this was it, the break, but I still couldn't imagine what it was that he was hiding from me. I found myself almost hating him in my turn. When we came to the square, and before I could go down the stairs to the train, he caught me suddenly, put his hands on my shoulders and looked into my eyes: anyway, whatever happens, we'll stay good friends. He tried to make me promise, it sounded like an order. I laughed to think how painlessly the novelistic clichés came out. Because the one thing I had never felt for him was friendship. Friends don't need to promise, I told him, there's no place for friendship when people fall out of love. He said I'd got it wrong there, but for now that wasn't our problem. My stomach was on fire and my knees were sagging, it was hard for me to stand and I gripped the railing of the stairway. He saw, and held me firm. Come on, let's think no more about it, his nerves were bad from being shut up in hiding, he hardly knew what he was saying. He was sorry. Then we parted. He made as if to kiss me, but I pulled back crossly.

On the train I found a window seat and gazed out. When I got back, I must have looked a wreck because Lucy took me in charge and wouldn't let go. I was to tell her everything that had happened. Had the young man

289

forgotten that I still had to be handled with care? But what could you expect? She spoke with animation, almost angrily, about George and this surprised me, since they had never met. But little by little it emerged that she knew a good deal about him, quite enough to form an opinion. How one time, could I imagine it? who should phone up and ask after me, but Xenia? She'd been phoning on George's behalf. This had been while I was ill. You'd have had to be there on the end of the phone to feel what a lot of spite lay concealed beneath her words. The point was that all this time Xenia had been hiding George at her place. I was surprised, but no more. I explained to her that Xenia and George had grown up together in the same town and the same neighbourhood. It was the most natural thing in the world for them to know one another and for her to give him refuge. You don't say! she gaped at me. That's all, I said. And put a brave face on it. Lucy's surprise had helped me to regain my balance because, try as I might to conceal it, I was in a state of shock, I felt like foaming with rage and pain, I was ready to howl, could I but spew up all the bitter gall George had fed me with for so many years.

A day or two later he phoned again. I was frosty and embarrassed. He said could we meet? What did he want to ask me this time? I said. The past few days had been almost unbearable, and I'd begun to think it was all over with him. But he pleaded earnestly and I relented. I found him with Xenia, waiting for me. From the moment I saw them in the distance it was as though a cloud had descended and enveloped me. But I had a precise sensation of the picture I made as I walked up the street, as I sadly observed my own footsteps and beating heart.

By the time I reached them I'd persuaded myself it was quite natural for them to be waiting for me together. Anyhow, in trying to come to terms with the break, it had always been with Xenia that I had imagined him; I knew quite well that she couldn't merely give him refuge. Xenia, as always, was laughing, probably to hide her embarrassment. But George looked troubled, there was a glint in his eyes, as though he'd been crying. I shook hands, and was immediately depressed to be greeting George in this way. I remembered the first time we'd slept together, when he'd held me tight in his arms with tears in his eyes, and said it was the best moment of his life. And what a fantastic privilege to be with me.

Then they told me the whole story, or rather Xenia did. The night of the massacre, she said, George had been running for his life and they'd stumbled into one another. They'd stared at each other, it had been like a miracle. Ever since, throughout the months that followed, she'd been keeping him in her flat, and had taken care of him. And gradually their old love had flared up again. Perhaps, even, they'd never quite stopped being in love. But George had still felt very close to me. He couldn't bear the thought of not seeing me again. So now she was asking me as a favour, would I please stay friends with George and behave as if nothing had happened? George listened to her with head bowed, and all at once I felt sorry for him. He kept moistening dry lips. I could guess at the bitterness of the saliva on his tongue, and my eyes filled with tears. All right then, I stammered, friends it is. My whole life had silted up with good friends that were no good to me, but there they were all around, superfluous on every side —

the one problem I didn't have was finding friends. I could still have died of boredom all alone, with perfect ease, or even more easily have suffocated from happiness without witnesses. But I felt sorry for them, I may even have felt flattered that they seemed to care. They appeared to need me and I found a crumb of comfort in this, at least for that moment, sitting between them; and they did make some effort too not to let me feel a gooseberry. I knew that before long George would no longer need the prop of seeing me, and this was clearly what Xenia hoped, since a thing like that can't end all at once, can it, like turning off a tap? I felt as though I were conspiring with Xenia to fix him up with a future that he lacked the will or the power to achieve for himself, and felt tender towards him. Xenia was very pleased with me for showing such understanding. She'd have expected no less, mind you, she'd always told him that. George on the other hand shot me a quick look that seemed to say I'd hurt him dreadfully, his hands were shaking. He might have been praying inwardly that I'd react in some other way, so that he could still cling to me. He looked ill. All this time he hadn't spoken a word. What pained me was just the fact that he could get on with her. The whole responsibility seemed to have fallen onto my shoulders, I had been powerless to exert the kind of influence over him that Xenia had with such obvious success. But I could never bring myself wilfully to hurt those nearest me; I either took them on their own terms or ignored them altogether. And I felt quite safe as I watched the smoke spiralling from his cigarette. Xenia, though she seemed to prattle, kept a tight rein on what she said, not a word about my father, for instance. And so we parted: good friends.

But two days later George rang again. In a changed voice, as though calamity had struck. He said he was coming out to Kifisia, he didn't know exactly ... could I meet him at the station so he didn't get lost? He was quite transformed. Like the time at the Polytechnic. He'd appeared on the Thursday, during the day, and looked about him with an afflicted air. I'd run towards him and he'd flung his arms around me, it was as if our earlier coldness had never been. He flung his arms around me now. He loved me, he said, we couldn't possibly break off and he was bitterly sorry for his mistake. It was the fault of all that had happened, he didn't know what he was doing. Well, I must know what it was like, to be shut up in a single room for months on end; you end by seeing ghosts. But we couldn't break it off, no way. I listened deeply moved. But at the same time he no longer mattered to me at all, I felt finally and cleanly separated from the past and breathed with relief, as though I'd escaped from the shadow of a spell. I said, let's give it time, and see. Everything sorts itself out in time. Perhaps you *are* in love with Xenia. It obviously wasn't what he wanted to hear. Perhaps he'd imagined I would hang round his neck and dance for joy. He looked glum and miserable. We stayed together a little while longer, then we ran out of things to say and parted, both of us feeling wretched.

It went on like that all summer — and even after the fall of the dictatorship. It was a stifling separation, the kind you could spend a lifetime planning, but never quite put into practice. I had left home once again. Slowly everyone was drifting back. I didn't take them altogether seriously; because suddenly I felt myself exposed on all sides. They nitpicked over their differences with impunity behind the mask of high seriousness, questions of ideology and expediency burst out on every side and I couldn't see the sense. Fondas said to me, what sort of a part did I think I was playing? And bitterly analysed the inevitable process of wear and tear, we all of us, in one way or another, got hooked on something. It didn't matter whether it was the Party, or marriage, or books and all that, or even football or cards, we all got hooked. I listened to him sadly and noticed the scar on his brow; my good friend Fondas looked at his watch, mustn't be late, his fiancée wasn't supposed to know we'd been together. We got up and said our farewells. I wondered what there could be for *me* to hang on to, but I didn't really feel the need. I had a touch, too, of Fondas' compulsion for explaining himself. And for inventing alibis. My own alibi was that it wasn't precisely a part I was playing. The alibi of telling myself that every day is unique and may be my last. Only yesterday afternoon I'd been walking down University Street. When I raised my eyes, who should I see but him: John. He was forging along on the other side, his long hair streaming behind him in the breeze. I'd made a move to run and catch him up. But the urge had died within me. I'd stared after him with wonder but quite without passion, the way you can stare in wonder at a painting without having the slightest desire to own it. Because it belongs to a different world. Until I lost sight of him at the traffic lights by the university. And felt only relief that I'd lost him.

At about the same time I learned that Themis had been one of the dead. And couldn't believe it. My brain refused to function when I tried to think of it. I'd always got on well with Themis, he hadn't been like the others, all my so-called political friends. And because he belonged to no party, of course no slogan now proclaims that he *lives.* That afternoon when I'd heard the news, the world had suddenly turned white before me. The streets became stretched out to eternity and emptied of people, no workingman would ever again take a leaflet from his hand. We'd used to get up at dawn and rush out to the underground stations, to catch the morning shift as they went to work, and hand out leaflets, because the most important thing was to make the workers aware, and realise their position in the slave market, and I was amazed by Themis' gift of the gab as he canvassed them, I always had my heart in my mouth, the harassed worker just out of bed I was sure was going to shout at us to get lost but no, with Themis they always listened to what he had to say and talked back with easy familiarity — later on the way back his eyes would be shining and I used to feel a warmth go through me to hear him speak. So Themis will remain my secret, the first death and the first unburied comrade on a road that disappears like an arrow into the future.

And Democracy returned on golden wing to the tune of our slogans. *The people don't forget, they unite and win. We fight to honour our dead comrades* and so on. And others would say, steady on, couldn't we show a bit of respect? At least keep our voices down: with all that had just been happening in Cyprus, with the junta making such a tragic cock-up and then the Turks invading, and let none of us forget, the Turks invaded *afterwards,* so much for national unity — and where for Chrissake would we be now if it hadn't been for the Turks? a frenzied anarchist wanted to know. It was all very well, *France-Greece, Allies for Peace*, but where would that get us? I'll tell you where it'll get us: our bourgeoisie that has sold out already to foreign interests would go full steam ahead for the Indies to lay claim to plots of land once conquered by Alexander the Great. Or maybe you've forgotten that Christopher Columbus, who laid waste the West Indies, was also distantly a Greek?

18

AND SO THE VOTERS took to the streets once more in droves. Aris Velouchiotis and his wartime partisans became all the rage, and the same groups that had once denounced him as a traitor and a homosexual, were now the ones to bring out posters and hawk him at anniversary celebrations, their stalls set up outside stadiums at nightfall, with red carnations and the whiff of sausages on charcoal and old partisan songs in the air. When that time came I would remember the leaflets, in a poem by Ritsos, that had been used as firelighters in the Occupation, to boil up weeds, while the room was flooded with sunlight. In due course the streets would be strewn with unburnt, trampled leaflets that you couldn't even be bothered to read, you could guess what they said and walk on. It was to be every man for himself in the scramble to net supporters on his own account, and class consciousness would be demoted to a party or perhaps a partisan proselytism. Either you were proselytised all your life, or you proselytised others. Instructor or instructed. Never *conscious*.

When I saw George entwined with Xenia at Elvira's wedding, I thought of the little ship that used to take me to Aegina and my heart pounded as though a gun had been trained on the small of my back, and I had to smile sweetly with my hands aloft, beneath the vain idea of my image that I still struggled to hold on to. I ached inwardly as I exchanged the marriage crowns on the heads of Fotis and Elvira, but I followed them down the aisle under a hail of rice grains and I laughed, and later with a smile on my face stood patiently accepting the good wishes of the guests with all the seriousness the occasion demanded, and the cloying handshakes.

Afterwards we went to a workingman's taverna in Kesariani and pinned red carnations on our lapels. Every now and then George would nuzzle with his lips against Xenia's ear, and Xenia would respond with a droop of her eyelids, until she got drunk and started to sing. First she sang communist songs, her whole attention fixed on George as though mouthing love ditties at him. George was proud of her; and she certainly had a fine voice. Then he asked her to tell us the joke about the Party instructor, that was a good one.

Once upon a time, the story went, there was an instructor in the Party. And when I say an instructor, I mean a communist of the old school. Well then, this instructor goes to a village to check up on the Party faithful. He's met by the local commissar. He asks what's what, everything shipshape comrade. The instructor takes a look round and satisfies himself it really is all shipshape. The comrades are hard-working, on their mettle. The instructor's very pleased, but of course he doesn't show it. Because instructors have a duty to the Party to be sparing in their praise, it's not often you see a Party instructor smile. He lays down the Party line, and lists the achievements of the USSR. On this point comrades, be on your guard, on that, strict obedience to the order of the day, and so forth. And when they've had something to eat and drink, they have to sort out where the instructor's going to sleep. They're very sorry but they're poor folks, no one's got a room to spare. They're all houseful with kids, they sleep on top of one another as it is. So the commissar has to take him to his own house, he hasn't got children. They spread out rugs, and make themselves comfortable as best they can on the floor, the three of them — the commissar hasn't even a bed in his hut, he's a poor man, remember. And so they pass the night. In the morning, at the moment of leavetaking at the end of the village, he takes the commissar aside and whispers a comradely admonition: comrade, a cardinal Party virtue is morality. I urge you to keep a watch on your wife. The weaker vessel. Do you know what she did right through the night? Right through the night she held on to my penis. Then the commissar laughs and answers: Comrade instructor, even higher than morality, a cardinal Party virtue is vigilance. It was me, mate, kept a hand all night on your prick.

When the punch line came I joined in the laughter, even though I'd heard it so many times before. I wasn't going to do Xenia the favour of not laughing, because all the time she was speaking she looked ready to pounce on any reaction I gave. We all laughed, we each had our reasons. The ghost of the instructor swept them into noisy hilarity, though it sounded a bit forced. Because all those Party activists had been tripping over one another in the scramble to take up their positions. And vied with one another to laugh the loudest, it wouldn't do to be taken for a Stalinist. George was staring dewy-eyed at Xenia. For the first time since I'd known him he seemed happy and relaxed, with Xenia he seemed to

299

have come into his own. And as I watched her I observed — at least, this seemed to help me come to terms with it — that Xenia had just that quality in a woman that elevates a man with her stupidity and enhances him with her beauty. Even when he was cross with her — for instance, when she launched upon the tale of how their love had blossomed once more, interrupting herself every so often to impress on us how terribly jealous he is, he'd be the death of her, she'd never known anyone so possessive. Even in this frame of mind, she roused no more than a grimace of feigned distaste from George, who seemed if anything rather flattered and shot me provocative glances as if to ram home some major deficiency on my part. In the meantime, as I listened to her I was laughing sardonically to myself, and began to cheer up. I could doubtless have analysed his behaviour and applied as much as I wanted of Freud and Dostoyevsky, but I wasn't in the mood. It pleased me only that I saw nothing to regret. And concluded inwardly that George, in his own true colours, could never have won me over. Even in his moments of frankness he had had the air of someone devising a special kind of frankness just to impress me.

Shortly before Elvira's wedding he had sent me a long letter, he wanted to set it down in black and white that everything was finished between us. He asked me melodramatically if I was going to listen to him. Are you going to listen to me? Because he was convinced that I'd never in my life listened to the voice of another person. I'd never listened to another's heart. He'd watched me passively taking imprints, like a record, dispassionately, mechanically, and making a little collection of the sufferings of others — but I'd never shared in those sufferings, only transcribed them and appropriated them and found cerebral explanations every time and seemed to enjoy talking affectedly about the tribulations of other people. Ever since he'd first been in love with me from behind the prison grille, I'd held him immobilised in a freezing corridor, he'd looked forward without any hope to the time of his release, he hadn't ever been able to count on me. This was why he had talked to me so much about himself after he got out, he'd kept nothing from me, from the serious to the trivial; all the time he'd been watching me and waiting. And for what indeed? For the moment when I would unbutton and be myself with him. But instead of that I had done the very opposite, I'd plotted evilly to break it off. Who but I had driven him into the arms of Xenia? How did I look on him? Like an alien phenomenon in my utterly phlegmatic world. I had listened to the story of his life as though he'd been reciting from the *Odyssey*. Not that I'd been indifferent, oh no. He could see from the way my eyes were shining how avidly I was following his revelations, as though I'd got such a kick out of it all there was no place left for *him*. He'd often come close to giving me the hiding of my life, just to reassure himself that I was real and tender, and above all *there*.

As I read this letter I felt the colour draining from my face. But he was very doubtful if anything he said could ever touch me, and so every ten lines or so he kept repeating that he saw me as a porcupine with my bristles up to protect me in advance from any real feelings. But how long could I go on like this? The day would come when I would have to face up to my true self. And on that day no amount of deluded soul-searching would help me. He had met Paul, he continued, the two of them had discussed me. Not long before, I too had met Paul again, we'd chatted about nothing special, almost like friends you might say. He was thin and pale, handsome as a lover. He'd got himself an important position in the same party as George. Once when I'd caught sight of him outside the Polytechnic, I seemed to see, in the wide-eyed faces of the girls clustered round him, myself as I had been years before when first Paul and then Fondas had taken me along to keep them company as they went about their ideological tasks. And the wide-eyed little things had gazed up at him in rapture, thrilled by his eloquence and the ideological scars he bore.

So Paul had compared notes about me with George. Had sat down and told him the story of our time together. How all those years ago, constantly on the move and in terror of the Security Police, he had managed to shake me off. And when his mother had told him of my visits to the house, he'd given her instructions to be distant with me, and on no account to let me wheedle from her the secret of where he was hiding. Because Paul had been afraid of me. I'd had the habit of fixing him, George's letter went on, with a glassy stare, I'd no sooner left off being intimate than I seemed to take it all back, he'd never heard a true sigh of love from me. In the act of love he'd seemed to lose me, as though he was being lured ever further into a void, that left the taste of ashes in his mouth.

George repeated all this obsessively more than once, as though he was trying to convince himself that he was well out of it, he'd had a lucky escape. He went on to ask if I remembered the morning at Kifisia when he'd pleaded with me earnestly not to end it. A nod of my head would have been enough. But what had I done? I'd stared at him out of empty eyes, like a witch at the burning. I hadn't seemed to care, only looked at him reproachfully as though I'd caught him out and I was God Almighty sitting in judgement on him. I read and reread this letter, what was it that he still wanted of me? How much more did he need to hurt me? But by now I no longer needed anyone from those days. With every day that passed I became more confident I could walk without the crutches that each one lent me towards his own apotheosis.

It was now that I set to work to spit out every shred of fascism and conformity in my nature, and felt the better for it as far as I was able — once, I'd been summoned to General Police Headquarters, and while I was waiting in the corridor for my name to be called, I'd been watching an elderly man standing there with all the humility and simplicity of a woodcut, and wondered what he was doing there. Then suddenly an office door had flown open and a girl was dragged out, white as chalk and dishevelled, between two policemen. The moment she saw the man she had revived and cried out, father, father. On the instant the two thugs had hurled themselves at him and began to beat up the father: who told you to come poking your nose in here, you bastard? It was over in less than five minutes. Then the silence of the tomb had descended on the corridor once more.

But I had never before seen an old man punched and kicked and for a long time afterwards had been haunted by his eyes. After the return to civilian rule, in the first months when we were all at fever pitch, the time of celebrations and slogans, one afternoon I'd attached myself to a group that had gathered outside the Polytechnic, and was listening to their talk. There amid the group my eye fell on the elderly man from General Police Headquarters. I was quite moved to see him there, as though he'd been a dear friend. I went closer and watched him. His face was red with anger and among other things that he said over and over, was the rant: extremist provocateurs, enemies of Party unity. Some young men were listening and cracking jokes. He kept up the arid chant and his eyes shrank to fierce points. At one point he collared one of the youths and before we realised what was happening had slapped him across the face, beside himself with rage. He screamed that we were all layabouts and corrupt, lackeys of the CIA, and began to make obscene gestures at us as we stared in disbelief. Then he turned his back on us and tucked himself into the bus queue. One of the youths was quick enough to shout: that's right, into the queue, you old git, know your place. I stared at the back of the old man's neck as he pretended not to hear, and said to myself how different he had been when the police thugs had laid into him — that was when I set to work to spit out every shred of the petty fascism that makes people hard and arid, and all the simple conformities that lock up ideologies within iron bands.

Such as the instinctive fascism of Fotis as, with one arm curled round Elvira's waist, he raised the other in a toast as though holding up the globe, and not out of any kind of romantic inspiration, but rather because he had made his bed and was now preparing to lie on it; he'd made his bed, mentally, with painstaking organisation, down to the minutest detail. He would earn his living working for the firm of solicitors run by Elvira's father, they would live together in the house at Kifisia that was Elvira's dowry, they'd spend their summers on the island of Spetses, in Elvira's ancestral home, and for recreation he'd fish in its waters, with the veteran fishermen of the island to show him the ropes and lend a bit of local colour. And at the same time would have gilt bindings made for the classic Marxist tomes that safely reposed on his study shelves, against the witching hour for wisdom as twilight falls and the night draws on, when with a drink at his elbow, before or after dinner, if there should ever come evenings of doubt or uncertainty, as assuredly sooner or later there would, he would take the book from the shelf and open it at such and such a page, where by recourse to the following extract he would expatiate upon the current crisis of capitalism.

But through us capitalism would come through its crises unscathed. Because obviously we had to live — we talked plenty about the better society of the future, but for the time being we had to earn our bread, for Fotis had grown up barefoot in a provincial town, only eating meat at Christmas and Easter and gazing into shop windows like the Little Match Girl in the fairy tale. There was material for a novel there, starting from the evening of doubt and uncertainty on the veranda of Elvira's ancestral home, with the glass of whisky and *Das Kapital*. And in the effort to comprehend what made Fotis tick and the process that had clothed him in silk socks and bow tie — this on their wedding day at the Church of the Areopagite — you could create a rare human drama, provided of course you had the talent and the patience.

And in my case, too, capitalism would come through its crises unscathed, because I, right from the time the smells of cotton wool and incubator first penetrated my senses and started me on the road to knowledge of the world, had found things difficult to take. I had been mesmerized by the nightmares and the sufferings of others, I'd fallen in love with their misery and their bandoliers but who wants to nurture that sort of incubus? And how much more lightly does Anestis trip from salon to taverna and back again, Anestis the idol of my childhood fantasies? He has given up now dwelling on his lost youth, instead the weightiest part of his conversation is taken up with cries of admiration, as his political judgements get to resemble more and more the health and vigour of a dogmatism based on the sun and sea of the Aegean. To me on the outside, they seem enveloped in a boring and rather vulgar rosy haze — of happiness certainly — but very boring, as they conspire fearfully to skirt round anything unpleasant. It's enough in their eyes to have the freedom to read your daily newspaper and if there comes a knock on the door at daybreak it will only be the milkman, or at worst a summons to a civil court. In this way my father· and Anestis have returned to their old verbal sparring about the chances of life after death, but their differences are always amicable. On one thing only are they agreed, and on this they feel passionately. What you've got to crack down on most of all is every sort of terrorism, so-called urban guerrillas and the rest of them. Because these are the people that prevent the normal evolution of capitalism into socialism. And while we're all waiting for capitalism to draw breath, put on humanitarian guise and the helmet of Pericles, while we're waiting for capitalism to belch and smack its lips, all right you masses, you can take your pick of the leavings now, in the meantime these paranoid creatures of terrorists bob up and hold back liberalisation and strike at the very existence of a left-wing opposition. Anestis and my dad might differ in some quaint ways, but fundamentally they're at one even in the way they button their trousers. They're easily panicked by world events, as though the fate of eternally fascist Germany depended on their good opinion — but enough.

And now the penny dropped with the bourgeoisie that they didn't need a king. For the occasion my stepmother Lucy spent a week hunting out old newsreels of Queen Frederica. She also came across the *Battle hymn of the dictatorship* with the wooden voice of Bithikotsis. And some photos of Despina, the dictator's wife, in calf-length boots. This was how they would celebrate the fall of the Monarchy, joining in the general enthusiasm. These were the enterprising classes, fluent in foreign languages and faithful to the ideal of law and order — they made Greece sound like a land flowing with freshly-pressed fruit juice. And meanwhile we, the extremist provocateurs, dared in our slogans to link the Polytechnic with the Liberation Front and the Popular Army in the Occupation and the civil war. And carried the battles of Grammos and Vitsi like a burden on our shoulders. I don't know why, but I was profoundly happy. I felt somehow gorged and ravenous at once, a curious mixture of sadness and calm that wasn't resignation, rather I was at peace with myself, content to follow the course of brightly coloured tropical streams and celebrate an inner exultation. Because the classic authors of the past are right about one thing. Life moves on. Not that I could define precisely what I meant by life, in the sense of identifying it with this or that tendency or with something different again — but whatever it is, it never stays still. Apostolos got a job as a news reader on TV. George was marrying Xenia, with Catherine and Nancy as bridesmaids. A gentle, velvet darkness hypnotizes you and robs you of all movement — and that darkness is the destined goal of all their efforts and all their struggles. Where everything's fine now with all those phonies who aren't altogether phonies either, and that's the saddest thing about it: to hear them going on in just the same old way, like the old hits and immortal melodies that were now back in fashion, and from the balconies and loudspeakers came the same old lyrics with the same old tunes. And I was unchanged too, in these same streets — as I listened to all this quietly winding a cocoon to envelop me. I said to myself, I'm getting old, but not in the usual way, not with wrinkles and white hair, more by metamorphosis. That's why I've taken up ballet again, to rediscover my body, I hope, or at least to prepare it for whatever the future holds. That some sort of trials are in store for me I've not the slightest doubt.

Fondas once told me to let my spirit discover goodness. But that, if it were ever to be, would have to come of itself.

Until it occurred to me in my newfound tranquillity that without realising it I'd been identifying other people with all that I loathed. As though I'd been putting them into masks to exorcise my own fears. And it came to me with clarity that all my life I had never been able to accept people for what they were, to respect their equilibrium and their choices; whatever didn't fit with my own psychological make-up I'd refuse to accept, which is not to say that I did so easily.

A good deal of time, of course, has gone by. I've rummaged through my past enough. It's been a long time. It takes an effort now to recollect the impulse behind each sentence. But behind every sentence is something else that still smoulders. I don't know how writers manage, what satisfaction they can feel, if indeed they do get satisfaction from writing. I've had the impression throughout of constantly leaving things half said, whatever I've wanted to say would involuntarily take off into vagueness, I can't help it, I suppose I was afraid to go the whole way, this is the best I could do. And so I've been left throughout with the bitter feeling that was all hot air. But at least I've been talking about real and immediate things. I've strayed a lot certainly, but never quite lost the thread. And it was nothing like Ariadne's thread either — all I tried to do, quite simply, was to answer some specific questions.

Christmases have come and gone since Maro, the girl I used to know, came up to me; as I remember, it was at a demonstration over Cyprus. Today who gives a fig for Cyprus, to hell with Cyprus, why don't they carve it up and leave us all in peace (and give a sop to public opinion while they're at it!) but never mind, in those days we still cared about Cyprus, I'd arranged to meet Maro, and we'd have coffee somewhere and a quiet chat. We never had the chat. She was in a tearing hurry. She was always in a tearing hurry, rushing about all over the place, there was always something or other she mustn't be late for, and for years I'd marvelled and wondered how she managed it. Lately she's had to slow down, the word is she's pregnant again, her first is walking already, and already her husband has a girlfriend on the side. In any case, she was in a tearing hurry that day, we hadn't that much to say anyway, she regarded me, she said, as very much one of her own, ideologically she meant, all those years we'd been in the same racket. I nodded agreement, it had been a racket all right. But she went on to say, all that notwithstanding, that I'd never ceased to be bourgeois at heart. Deep down I'd never ceased to be a class enemy, because of all my father's shares in the Mineral Mines, one day all that wealth would be mine. I tried to imagine it all piled up at my feet: anazonite onyx, calamine, lemonite, bronze pyrites phosphate, aragonite, azurite and fool's gold that looks like real gold, what underground riches, blessed be the land of Greece! I remembered the cripple who had lost a leg down in the galleries, and had once come to ask my father for assistance, and my father had come close to weeping tears, but hadn't lifted a finger to help him. I stared at Maro, lost in thought, and imagined him descending into the bowels of the earth, among unworked minerals, then the charge blew up and they brought him to the surface maimed for life. Maro, I said to her, have you ever heard of fool's gold? Fool's *what*? oh do stop fooling, Myrsini, and be serious! The exclamation mark she spat from between her teeth, only action and unswerving dedication to the cause would redeem me one day from the bonds of my class. Then she took the questionnaire from her shoulder bag and handed it to me. There you are, fill that out carefully, answer the questions as honestly as you can, give up fooling for once and look at the truth that's staring you in the face, dedicate yourself to the people's struggle, to the future of this country, the common good. As I listened to her I thought, she's off her trolley. I went on nodding agreement, yes, I kept saying, yes, as if I was afraid of exacerbating her condition and making her foam at the mouth. Anyhow I held the questionnaire open in front of me, staring at it surreptitiously as though trying to memorise it. I wanted to tell her it wasn't like that, in as gentle and friendly a way as I could, to explain to her that it had been some time now since my father's shares had ceased to be any business of mine, but neither on the other hand did I intend to spend the years of life still remaining to me in repudiating what was supposed to be my class, all that seemed to me like so much claptrap.

It's enough for me to be myself, I wanted to say to her, and that's the way I mean to live. But it's always the same with people when I let them do the talking, she ended up by giving my answer for me. She took exception to my manner, it had been a mistake to take me into her confidence. She said she couldn't understand it. Huffily she demanded the questionnaire back. I gave it to her. She folded it twice and thrust it into her shoulder bag. Then we parted, and I haven't seen her since. But the encounter had done me good. The questionnaire most of all. It had given me a real shock, as though suddenly I'd seen my whole life simplified, implacably and absurdly, into a handful of questions. And allotted numbers, one, two, three, up to fourteen. There was even a fifteenth question, but that one didn't concern me, about whether I'd done my military service.

So, finally, I fitted onto a single sheet of paper:

OK, MY NAME IS Myrsini Panayotou. I was born in Paris on the 25th of July, 1949. I live at 10 Sinopis Street, by myself. My father doesn't do anything, my mother is dead. During the dictatorship I took part in the resistance, first of all in the Rigas Pherraios group. Leaflets and other printed matter. Later on I was in various covert groups, whose names I may not reveal. At present no, I am not a member of any group. My family, my father that is, is a socialist, or so he says. I have no idea how I first came to join the Left. I suppose because of my first boyfriend, Paul. I have been harassed by the Security Police and continue to be harassed to this day. Intended profession I have none, I may give more time to dancing, though the years have passed me by. I have read a great many books, but very few specifically related to Marxism. Only the *Eighteenth Brumaire of Louis Bonaparte, the Communist Manifesto, State and Revolution* and five or six shorter books. As for my strengths and weaknesses I can make no comment. So when all's said and done, sometimes I feel like a god, and sometimes the merest creature.

HISTORICAL NOTE*

The novel is set against the background of the period of military rule in Greece from 1967 to 1974. The day-to-day events of that traumatic period are naturally more familiar to Greek readers than they are in the English-speaking world. The novel also assumes greater familiarity with the historical events leading up to the dictatorship than English-speaking readers might be expected to possess. The following is a brief chronological summary of the most important events of Greek history alluded to in the novel. For a full account of the history of the period, the reader is advised to consult *A Short History of Modern Greece* by Richard Clogg (2nd edition, Cambridge University Press, 1986).

1821: Greeks in the Peloponnese revolt against Turkish rule which has lasted since the fall of Constantinople in 1453. The heroic struggles of the Greeks to gain their independence are celebrated soon after by the "national poet" Dionysios Solomos (1798-1857).

1920-22: Following World War I the combined governments of the Entente, in an attempt to exploit the oil sources of the Middle East, took advantage of the propagandist inclinations of the Greek ruling class for the extraordinary realisation of Greek nationalist aspirations. This was the so-called *Great Idea*, in which Greece aspired to Constantinople in the North and the site of Ancient Ionia in the East. The Entente convinced the then Greek government of Eleftherios Venizelos to take a stand at Smyrna and promised them military aid.

However, due to their subsequent financial conflicts which resulted in the essential dissolution of the Entente, they terminated all aid to Greece.

* The following note has been compiled by the publisher.

Meanwhile, the governmer.   ding that of Venizelos in
Nov. 1920 promoted its business   terests in Turkey. Kemal
Ataturk's revolutionary forces were able to push back the
Greek army and completely overcome them. The Greek forces
ended in complete dissolution and expulsion from Asia Minor.

The result of the Greek defeat was the relentless persecution
and expulsion of the Greeks of Asia Minor – the bondage of
the Greek population, the seizure of their property and the
creation of more than a million and a half refugees.

1924: The Communist Party of Greece (KKE) is formed
(originally founded in 1918 as the Socialist Labour Party).

1936: On 4 August a fascist dictatorship is imposed by General
John Metaxas whose repressive measures are modelled to
some extent on those of Mussolini and Hitler.

1939: World War II breaks out in Europe.

1940: On 28 October, Metaxas rejects an ultimatum from the
Italians, and Greece enters the war on the side of Britain and
France.

1940-41: During the winter, Greek forces successfully beat
back the Italian invaders through the mountains of Albania.

April 1941: Hitler attacks Greece and occupies the country,
capturing the island of Crete with parachute landings in May.

1941-44: Nazi occupation of Greece, during which tens of
thousands of Greeks, particularly in Athens, die of starvation.
Profiteering is rife, and civilians are executed by firing squads
in reprisal for even minor acts of resistance. From September
1941 a Resistance Movement expanded to cover the whole ter-
ritory of Greece, predominantly under the political control of
the Communist Party.

1944: On 3 December, just over a month after the liberation
of Athens, armed conflict breaks out between communist guerrillas and British forces.

1945: On 12 February, the leadership of the Communist Party agree to disarm, as demanded by the British (the Varkiza Agreement).

March 1946: Parliamentary elections take place, boycotted by the leftist parties. A conservative-anticommunist government is formed.

1946: A plebiscite on 1st September produces a majority in favour of the return of King George (exiled since the German invasion). The validity of the result is disputed by the Left.

1947: Continued polarisation of political forces in Greece and the worsening climate of the cold war. Greece's northern neighbours have become communist and allies of the USSR. The continued repression of left-wing sympathisers by government paramilitary forces contributes to the outbreak of civil war. The war is fought between communist guerrillas and government forces in the mountains of central and northern Greece. For the first time, American military and economic aid, intended under the "Truman Doctrine" to combat the spread of communism, plays a significant role in Greek political life. The conflict lasts until 1949, when American aid finally ensures the victory of the Right.

1950-63: Parliamentary government is restored. Successive right-wing governments are slow to release large numbers of political prisoners held since the civil war.

1960: Cyprus becomes an independent state, after the failure of a long campaign by Greek-Cypriots, backed by public opinion in Greece, for union with Greece.

1961: The centre-left party of George Papandreou is narrowly defeated amid allegations of ballot-rigging. Papandreou launches his supporters upon a "relentless struggle" for electoral success.

May 1963: Murder of a left-wing member of Parliament, Grigoris Lambrakis, in Thessaloniki. Evidence is found to suggest complicity in high places.

November 1963: Papandreou's centre-left party wins elections but falls short of an overall majority.

February 1964: Decisive electoral victory by George Papandreou.

1965: With trouble in Cyprus and amid allegations of sabotage, Papandreou clashes with King Constantine, who demands personal control of the army, and is forced to resign. Violent demonstrations take place in Athens in July. The political crisis lasts until 1967.

1967: On 21 April, only a week before new elections are due to take place, in which Papandreou is once again expected to win, a group of senior army officers seize power. Parliament and the Constitution are suspended, with the consent of the King, and people of known or suspected left-wing sympathies are arrested. Many are held in prison camps on islands in the Aegean.

1967: On 13 December, King Constantine, in an attempt to seize power, stages an abortive counter-coup against the Colonels and is obliged to flee the country.

August 1968: Alexander Panagoulis attempts to assassinate the leader of the regime, George Papadopoulos, by blowing up his car. The attempt fails and Panagoulis is imprisoned and tortured.

1968: The Greek Communist Party, banned since 1947, splits amidst much acrimony following the Soviet invasion of Czechoslovakia.

March 1973: Occupation of the Athens Law School by students leads to violent clashes and arrests of students.

Summer 1973: King Constantine is formally deposed by the regime, which announces a referendum and some limited reforms (never to be realised).

1973: On 17 November, tanks and troops are used to crush a revolt by students who have been occupying the Athens Polytechnic for three days. More than thirty students are killed and hundreds injured.

1973: On 25 November, Papadopoulos, out of favour with the USA, is ousted from power by several of his ex-supporters. Brigadier Ioannidis, supported by the Americans, is the strong man of the new regime.

1974: On 15 July, under the leadership of Brigadier Ioannides, the new regime organises the attempted assassination of Archbishop Makarios of Cyprus in order to install a puppet government. The attempt fails. Turkey, taking advantage of the ensuing instability, threatens retaliation on behalf of the Turkish-Cypriot minority.

1974: On 20 July, Turkish troops invade northern Cyprus.

1974: On 23 July, largely due to its failed coup in Cyprus, the military regime collapses and civilian government is re-established.

1974: On 17 November, free elections are won by the newly formed New Democracy party, headed by veteran right-wing Prime Minister Constantine Karamanlis.

1974: On 8 December, a free referendum abolishes the monarchy in Greece.

MARO DOUKA

Maro Douka was born and brought up in Hania on the island of Crete. In 1966 she entered the University of Athens as an archaeology student and after the coup d'état of 21st April 1967 became actively involved in the student movement. She was imprisoned for a time by the military authorities for harbouring a member of the resistance but escaped with a suspended sentence.

First published in 1979, *Fool's Gold* is Maro Douka's first novel, which became an instant bestseller and was made into an acclaimed TV serial. Before that she had already published three volumes of short stories. More recently she has followed up the success of *Fool's Gold* with three more novels, *The Floating City* (1983), *The Still Poplars* (1987), and most recently *At the Bottom of the Picture* (1990), all published by Kedros.

In 1982 Maro Douka was awarded the Nikos Kazantzakis Prize, and in 1984 the National Book Award for *The Floating City.*

RODERICK BEATON

Roderick Beaton lived for three years in Greece during the 1970s and has since published books and articles on modern Greek literature. He is now Koraes Professor of Modern Greek and Byzantine History, Language and Literature at the University of London.